EATING YELLOW PAINT

To John
Happiness Blooms Within!
Susie Newman

SUSIE NEWMAN

D1520211

outskirts
press

Outskirts Press, Inc.
http://www.outskirtspress.com

ISBN: 978-1-4787-4476-4

Outskirts Press and the "OP" logo are trademarks belonging to Outskirts Press, Inc.

PRINTED IN THE UNITED STATES OF AMERICA

This book is dedicated to my mom and dad, Barbara and Ray, who taught me that lessons live in painful moments and beauty can be found around every corner.

Chapter One

I'm lying on my back, knees pulled up, feet firmly planted on the scorched pavement. The black asphalt gives blistery kisses to the soles of my dirty, bare feet. My skinny white arms lie at my sides, palms facing up, catching the hot sun. A small pool of sweat glistens in my hand. I have puffed and bunched my hair into a yellow pillow, my roots wet from the sweltering heat. A thin trickle of sweat flows like a stream along my hairline, down the side of my face, and drips slowly, like a pulse, into my ears. Red and orange globes dance just underneath the lids of my closed eyes. I am on fire, nothing but light and heat, heading for spontaneous combustion.

"Girl, get the hell out of the road!" Granny Crackers says, kicking my shoulder with her crusty foot. "What ya trying to do? Cook yourself or get run over?"

"I'm not on the road," I respond, eyes still closed, although I kind of am. I'm lying in Granny Crackers's driveway, a short roadway constantly used to reach Granny's store, which is not exactly a store, but rather a garage full of junk with price tags.

"Get your ass up and get a drink of water. We ain't got time to mess with no heat stroke. I'm expecting a busy day at the store tomorrow, and I need your help with the organizing."

I pull myself off the hot tar and head through the front door. I enter our overly furnished and cluttered living room, cold from a window air conditioner on full blast. Granny's three neurotic chihuahuas bark at me aggressively from the back of the couch and then go back to humping each other, a doggy threesome. I walk from our overstuffed living room into a crowded kitchen in less than ten steps. I guzzle cold tap water from a jug out of the fridge, grab a blue popsicle from the freezer, and walk out the back door, down two cracked steps, and across the drive, toward the garage.

Granny Crackers is sitting on a lawn chair folding a basket of linens. In front of her, on a TV tray, sits a small old box television, and she is watching a sitcom from the past. The canned laughter competes with the whirl of two large fans circulating hot air. "Price these." She hands me a stack of folded fabric. "Napkins, fifty cents apiece; placemats, a dollar; tablecloths, two dollars."

Unlike what Pottery Barn does, I low-price our vintage linens using masking tape and a black Sharpie. Granny Crackers is next to me, babbling on about her TV show.

"You know, Mayberry is not so damn great," she says. "Ya hear people all the time saying they wished life was like Mayberry. Wouldn't it be nice to live in Mayberry, they say, as if it's perfect."

Honestly, I've never heard anyone say either of those things, but I didn't argue.

"I'm gonna tell you the truth, Savannah Jo," Granny Crackers continues. "There ain't no perfect place. Even Mayberry has its problems. They got Otis, the town drunk, an irritating fool who should just keep his ass at home when he's on a binge. And that Barney Fife is a damn moron. Imagine a sheriff deputy that doesn't know how to safely operate a firearm. The only mechanic and barber the town has are idiots, both of them, dumb as a box of rocks. I wouldn't let either one of them simpletons touch my car or my hair. Then there's Aunt Bea, Helen Crump, and the rest of them ladies, running around, gossiping and judging one another. They ain't nothing but a bunch of busybodies with their noses in everybody's business. Hell no, I wouldn't be any happier in Mayberry than I am sitting right here in my very own garage, selling shit. Do you understand what I'm trying to tell you, Savannah Jo?"

"I guess."

"Child, you gotta do better than guess. You gotta know. I'll tell you what the problem is. People go around confusing happiness with a place. They go off looking for it in oceans or in the mountains, spending life on some desperate search party to nowhere. Truth is, the only state where happiness lives is your state of mind. You have to find happiness where you are."

"Perhaps," I respond, "but I think I would be happier living in Paris, France, instead of Paris Village."

"Shit happens in Paris, France, too, Savannah Jo." Granny Crackers lifts herself from her chair, clicks off the TV, and heads toward the back door.

Maybe so, I think, but at least it happens in a pretty place. I'm sure Paris, France, doesn't look a thing like Paris Village.

My neighborhood, Paris Village, is a shithole, and the only way to leave is by clawing your way out. Twenty-two blocks of narrow one-way streets filled with parked cars. Tall, slender houses line up like dominoes, straight rows of siding and brick, misfortune and circumstance, threatening to tumble. Attached to the front of each home is a porch the size of a small room. The front porch is truly an extension of our living quarters, usually filled with shaky relatives sitting on rickety chairs. In Paris Village every home has a small dandelion front lawn. The back alleys are lined with skinny Whoville trees and trash cans. Neighboring backyards are divided by chain-link fences. Within the confines live barking dogs and feral cats, resembling a cellblock for pit bulls. And if you were to mention curb appeal in Paris Village, then you're probably referring to the crack whore or candy man, as that's the only allure on any curb.

Those of us who have found ourselves stuck here in Paris Village are part of a tribe, a cluster of people made of plaster and mud, an intermixing of races bound by common troubles. We make up a color wheel of faces, from alabaster, ivory, beige, and khaki to russet, cinnamon, mahogany, and coffee. Yes, we are an assorted box of chocolates, white to dark, fruits and nuts included.

I haven't always lived with Granny Crackers. Six months ago my sister, my brother, and I were living with our Mimi. Mimi is our grandma (our mom's mom), and Granny Crackers is Mimi's mom, which makes her our great grandma, but doesn't make her great. With Mimi we lived eight blocks away from Paris Village in a small, neat, gray-and-brick house at the end of a dead-end street. I know eight blocks doesn't sound like a large distance, but when you're talking about an inner-city "hood," eight blocks in any direction is a huge difference.

I am the cursed middle child, sandwiched between two siblings. My sister, Montana, is two years older than me, and my brother, Phoenix, is two years younger. My name is Savannah Jorja, immediately shortened to Savannah Jo, by Mimi. Our mother, Ava, named her children after the places she dreamed about, the towns she longed to see: romantic states with mountains, deserts, and oceans. Ohio has none of that. No breathtaking natural beauty to seek out, no godly wonders to ponder. Being poor in Ohio sucks.

I heard that Granny Crackers laughed her head off when my mother named me Savannah Jorja. Granny Crackers says Ava is the only mother who could take two beautiful names like Georgia and Savannah, screw with the spelling, and then smash them up against one another to create a stupid name.

It seems my whole life has been a series of misfortunate happenings, starting with my stupid name. Savannah Jorja, fifteen years old, a vanilla ghetto girl named by a drug-addicted mother, raised by a young Mimi who got sick and then died, stuck in a junkyard in Paris Village with a granny that's crackers (truly bat shit crazy).

Chapter Two

*T*hings just haven't been the same since Mimi died. It's more than our shitty environment, and besides the fact that we moved from a cute remodeled ranch-style house in a blue-collar neighborhood, where I had friends, into a slum-hood pick and pull, where I have nobody. It's heavier than going from a fun, understanding, pretty, and cool Mimi, who spoiled us, to Granny Crackers, who makes us pick trash to sell. It's sadder than having to give your yellow lab, Honey, to neighbors and live with three humping chihuahuas. It's more depressing than watching a drug-addicted mother live and a vibrant Mimi die. It's harder than switching schools, finding friends, or running a never-ending garage sale. It's a pain that is so immense, intense, sharp, real, and raw that we have been altered. Montana, Phoenix, and I have literally changed, morphed into new beings.

Our Mimi had swooped in and saved us from Hurricane Ava. She swam us away from destruction and dysfunction to the quiet ocean floor where life was serene and blue. She carefully unwrapped us from tattered blankets of distress and placed us in happy little shells that were hard and protective, colored in shades of bone-white innocence and pale pink laughter. We were happy as clams, toes in the sand, as Sea Queen Mimi, with sterling-silver rings and a crown of ash-blond hair danced around us. Mimi swirled up bubbles of fun and pointed out ordinary wonders. Life on the ocean floor was so much safer than the riptide named Ava, until the day that the turquoise sea turned to black and gentle ripples became violent crashing waves and in crept Cancer, the sea monster.

We watched in horror as Cancer ruthlessly devoured our queen. The three of us frantically scurried from our shells. Without our protective coverings we witnessed Cancer gobble up our Mimi. The sea monster took vicious, giant bites, starting with her cervix, gnawing at her from the inside out.

As Mimi lay there dying, we clung to her, three sad ocean children named after land. We pressed our soft bodies into the black cave that Cancer had created. We hid in her crevices and tried to heal her with our tears. We begged Mimi not to go. We asked God not to take her. Neither one of them listened.

After Mimi died we needed new shells to wear to Paris Village. Montana traded in her pale pink shell for a dark blue one. She shaved her head, pierced her nose, changed her name from Montana to Mo, and changed her pronouns on all social media from *she* to *he*. He now dresses like Eminem. He packed away all of his jockey girl clothes bought by Mimi and invested in a drawer full of white men's T-shirts and baggy faded Levi's. Mo wears a collection of leather straps around his left wrist and a tattooed bracelet around his right wrist that reads MiMi.

Montana's jump from tomboy to transgender after Mimi died was almost immediate, as if he was leaping out of one skin and landing in another. Quietly and selfishly I cried. I had not only lost my Mimi, but I also lost my big sister.

Phoenix's transformation came about a bit slower, but it's just as dramatic. Phoenix replaced his shell of ivory and innocence with a covering of slate, dark gray and rock hard. Slate is created from volcanic ash, but in Phoenix's case, anger did the same thing.

After Mimi died, my baby brother changed from a sweet, young, innocent, ornery little boy into a thirteen-year-old delinquent, who now smokes cigarettes like a grown-ass man and pot like a throwback hippie. Phoenix hangs with older kids and tries to run the streets. Mo tries to watch after him the best she/he can, pulling him away from gangbangers and thugs, but it's hard for a girl/boy to advocate for a misguided baby brother and not get her/his ass beat.

My shell changed too, an exchange from peaches and cream to the color of dark plums that I wear like a bruise. I went from a happy blond and popular cheerleader to a sad and lonely poet and artist. I have no friends in Paris Village, just pen and paper.

I spend my days taking cell phone photos, snapping pictures of things that stir my emotions. My phone holds edited and filtered images of Granny Crackers's junk, abandoned houses, cluttered porches, broken-down cars, broken-down people, alley cats eating from overflowing trash cans, the sun setting over tattered roofs, and dandelions growing in asphalt. For each ghetto photo I write a heartfelt poem and post it on Instagram. I have more than a thousand followers. They mean nothing to me.

Mo says I have gone emo, but I disagree. Emos are emotional teens looking for reasons to be sad. I'm a non-emotional teen searching for a reason to be happy.

A poem written by Savannah Jorja:

MIMI

Mimi
My grandma-mama
My lovely G,
I close my eyes,
And there you be.

Light green eyes
The color of pears,
Smooth, olive skin,
Ash-blond hair
Pulled up in a messy bun,
Stray strands frame your sharp face.

Mimi,
Your skinny waist,
Your faded Lee's,
Your small breasts
And tight Tees,
You're such a throwback.

God molded you strong,
One of your charms
Wrapped in your arms
Of bones and muscles,
Even though you never worked out.

Mimi,
Your touch lingers,
The feel of slender fingers
Dressed in rings
Of sterling silver and turquoise,

Hands smoothed by lotion,
Your scent survives,
Living upon my emotions,
The smell of skinny cigarettes, and Red Door.

Mimi,
Shhh, I keep you secret.
I never boast,
And when I'm lonely,
I hang with a ghost.

Chapter Three

J woke to the familiar noises of a Saturday morning and the scent of salted pork, grease, and fresh-brewed coffee. I lay still, eyes closed, and listened. The air filled with the sizzle of bacon, the static of the old kitchen radio, and the cackle in Granny Crackers's voice as she shamelessly sang off-key. I heard the scampering of Granny's chihuahuas, their long nails tapping the kitchen floor as they scurried around her feet. From these sounds I knew that I was waking with the sun and Granny Crackers was cooking up her usual Saturday spread, food meant to fuel us for a busy day.

"Are you up?" I asked Mo, my sister/brother in the bed next to me.

"Yeah, I'm up," Mo groaned, rolled out of bed, and stumbled out of our room. As Mo headed toward the bathroom, I wiped a tear from my eye. I hated that my feelings were so easily hurt. What I really wanted when I called out to my sister/brother in the morning light was for her/him to talk with me.

I miss our bedroom talks. I miss the nights when we'd stay awake for hours being silly. I miss Saturday mornings when I crawled into her bed, the two of us side by side, whispering dreams and secrets, our bare mosquito-bitten legs tangled in bedsheets, knobby knees pressed together as we curled around each other in laughter.

I don't care that Montana wants to be called Mo. It doesn't bother me that she binds her breasts and hides her figure or that she threw out her silk panties for boxer shorts. None of it matters. What hurts is we don't talk about it.

Montana and I have always been different. When we were little, my side of our room was littered with Barbie dolls and pink nail polish, while her side was strewn with athletic equipment and sporting gear. But those things didn't stop us from playing, strapping Ski Barbie and Snowboarding Ken to her skateboard and sending them flying down the driveway. So it's not that I don't like Mo. On the contrary, I love him. I just miss Montana; it's a shame she had to die with Mimi.

Mo returned to our room polished and dressed, carrying with him the scent of Axe body spray and men's deodorant. He's such a pretty boy in his crisp white V-neck and high-top Converse shoes. I quickly shoved my hurt feelings to the pit of my stomach, as I always do, trying to make every moment with Mo good.

"Savannah Jo, you'd better get out of that bed before Granny Crackers comes up here and pulls you out."

"I know, I know," I said. "Wait for me."

I stood in front of my sister (now my brother), pulled off my T-shirt, and comically searched our room, looking for my abandoned bra. Finding it under the bed, I waved it in the air like a Victoria Secret flag before putting it on. I then dressed in the same T-shirt I'd just taken off. Grabbing an elastic band from the dresser, I finger combed my hair into a ponytail. With my hands still on my head, arms extended, I sniffed my pits and then sprayed myself down with Secret.

"Okay, ready."

"You're so gross." Mo laughed. "Aren't you even gonna brush your teeth?"

"After my orange juice, not before."

Mo and I giggled through the hall and into the kitchen. Surprisingly, Phoenix was already there, dressed and at the table devouring a plate of bacon.

Granny Crackers fills our stomachs best on the mornings she predicts will turn into long days. She knows that the remaining hours of sunlight will be hot and busy, with no lunch, just quick popsicles and apple slices. Tonight for dinner we will have pizza delivered to our door. We four will sit, worn out, on a crowded couch in front of a window air conditioner with the TV blaring. Lo and behold, that's my summertime Saturdays in Paris Village.

Granny Crackers says summer days and garage sales go together like movie theaters and popcorn; where you find one, you will find the other. There are people who spend weekends scoping out garage sales. They come with written itineraries of each noteworthy sale, directions and a timeline, an expecting mom hunting down a crib, a first-time renter looking for a kitchen table. Garage salers have an agenda, and they are in and out of your yard quickly. There are the thrifty women who come in pairs, talk too loud, and sneer at your stuff; middle-aged women with brightly polished toes, wearing ugly, fancy flip flops, searching for treasures. These girls get on my nerves.

However, the men shopping for tools and toys can be just as annoying. Know-it-alls who give little to no regard to an old woman and three teens. Granny Crackers accepts the men as a personal challenge, because quite frankly, they spend more money. Granny Crackers likes to show off her knowledge of tools and play things. She finds enjoyment in negotiating a fair price. She relishes the act of gradually earning respect by crushing arrogant presumptions. It doesn't take long for these grown boys to learn that this old woman is no dummy, and she enjoys playing hard ball.

Personally I like the lonely people who ponder for hours, walk circles around your table picking up items and telling you their life story, or the silent introvert who overloads a backpack buying hardcover books.

Granny Crackers says garage selling has changed with Craigslist, Facebook, and eBay. Nowadays people go online to find used items. There's no need to spend days running from garage sale to yard sale, when you can just as easily go to a community Facebook page and find everything you need and a thousand things you don't.

Since moving to Paris Village, Mo has become Granny Crackers's marketing assistant, and sales have increased. Mo created a business Facebook page, naming Granny's store "The Barrel." Granny Crackers's page shows her seated inside the garage, surrounded by junk, a big floppy flower hat resting crookedly on her head. Mo convinced her that the hat gave her a gimmick and made her look more approachable. It really just makes her look crazy.

We would have named the store Granny's Cracker Barrel (which is what we all call it), but Mo was unsure of copyright infringements, and God knows we don't need any more problems. I painted THE BARREL on a big barrel drum that sits just outside of the garage door. The bottom reads Granny Crackers – owner.

The Barrel is fully stocked with merchandise that we have either acquired, found, trash picked, made, or bought. Mo makes weekly posts on Craigslist and several neighboring community pages. With advertising, word of mouth, and just common knowledge, Granny Crackers pulls in a pretty good income.

The truth is, in Paris Village (unlike anywhere else in the world), Granny Crackers is considered a success, and that is why she will never move. Granny Crackers was born in the house that we live in, and regardless of the fact that Paris Village has changed quite a bit since 1940, this is where Granny remains and this is where she will die (at least that's what she says).

Besides our residence, Granny Crackers owns two other properties in Paris Village and rents them both out. Owning three houses makes her a rich woman. In addition to being a landlord, she's also a notary, as evident by the sign in our front window. Notaries are important and popular. Seems somebody is always in need of a signature on the title of some junk car.

Yes, outsiders may assume Granny Crackers is some old, crazy, white trash, urban hick, but the people of Paris Village know she's a lifetime resident and entrepreneur with legal and legit businesses. These facts alone give her the respect of the cops and the thugs.

I don't know if Granny Crackers is actually rich. I do know that she has more money than Mimi ever did, and Mo believes she is secretly loaded. It seems crazy to think we have more money in Paris Village than we've ever had before, and the only way you can tell is by cell phones. All three of us kids have phones, something Mimi could never afford. But that didn't matter. With Mimi we had each other, and there was no need for cell phones.

The surprising thing about having a cell phone is that Granny Crackers hates them. She doesn't have one. She's had the same house phone and number forever. However, when it comes to us three, she is paying for cell phones. She justifies the cost by saying it's important that we stay connected. Granny Crackers would never admit that Paris Village is a dangerous place to live, yet we are armed with phones. Even though she's strict and we have limited data, we're grateful.

Having cell phones gives us some freedom from the house and each other. Monday through Friday, Granny Crackers can handle The Barrel all by herself while we roam. However, on weekends she needs our help. Since Granny Crackers's garage sales are legendary, The Barrel gets real busy on Saturdays and Sundays.

It's not so bad in the winter when half our customers call and schedule a time to come by. Fifty percent of our sales this year were from Mo's online advertising, and the other half were folks familiar with Granny Crackers who stop by looking for a second-hand snowblower, car seat, artificial Christmas tree, and so forth.

In the summer, however, it's old-school garage sale all the way. We stick a sign in our front yard, tie a sign onto the street post, and hang one inside the corner store. We then sit all day as folks come and go.

This weekend was as busy as the rest. Phoenix, Mo, and I spent our time moving large, eye-catching items out of the garage and into the yard to attract customers, while Granny Crackers counted money and scanned the growing crowd. Granny Crackers is really good at profiling people. She knows who's there to buy and who's just loitering. Her senses become keener the busier we get. When her back lot and garage are a forest of people, Granny Crackers has the eyes of a hawk and can spot a rat.

This time it was a kid that Phoenix knows. Granny Crackers watched him fill his pockets as he rounded her table of trinkets. He couldn't have seriously wanted the stupid stuff he was taking. Maybe he just likes the thrill of stealing, or it could have been his mother's birthday. Whatever the reason, he had a glass bluebird in one pocket and a beaded purse in the other. As he began walking toward the front of our yard, Granny Crackers called after him.

"Son, you're gonna need to take that stuff out of your pockets before you reach the sidewalk."

"I don't know what you're talking about, lady."

"Sure you do. You must have forgotten you picked them up. But now that you remember, you can put 'em back on the table."

Everyone stopped and looked at the boy, who must have felt awkward as hell, trying to lift fifty-cent items from a garage-sale table. The kid skimmed across the staring faces: a large black man looking at bikes, a shirtless white dude with tattooed arms buying a power saw, a young bohemian couple with matching dreads, and a Somalian woman, six kids in tow, the youngest strapped into a dirty stroller, holding and eating a raw cucumber as if it were an ice cream cone. These are the faces of Paris Village, faces that keep a man honest.

"I was going to buy these," the boy said, pulling the proof from his pockets and dropping them on the ground, "but why would I do that, when it's nothing but crap? I don't want your damn junk, lady, so you can quit worrying."

"Child, it's not my junk I'm worried about. It's your soul. You see something you like, you come to me like a man, and we'll work out a deal. But don't you dare step foot in my yard thinkin' you're gonna steal from me."

"Like I said, there ain't nothing here I want. It's all shit."

Granny Crackers ignored his last comment and returned to the man with the power saw. The others went back to minding their own business. Without the stolen items or any more atten- tion, the delinquent walked out of our yard and down the street, cussing as he went.

Afterwards, it was Phoenix who had an attitude. I'm sure he felt anxious, knowing he'd be the one to suffer retaliation. Why is it Granny Crackers feels she has to be a moral compass for every misguided soul? It would have been easier on Phoenix if Granny Crackers had let the kid take the stupid dollar stuff that she would never miss. Instead she shamed him in front of a crowd of on- lookers. The emotional anger and embarrassment he felt would be taken out on Phoenix later, and all for a measly glass bluebird and beaded purse. Phoenix slumped down in a chair, a scowl on his face. Now it was his turn to act out. He would ruin Granny Crackers's day. Why not? She had just ruined his.

Phoenix grabbed a spooky rubber clown mask from a box of Halloween decorations and went to the back of the garage. He sat on a lawn chair, a silent, stoic boy wearing a terrifying mask. At first nobody noticed. People absorbed in their treasure hunt went about shopping, and then slowly, as if by turn, someone would look over, see a creepy clown, jump three feet back, and just about piss their pants. Some recovered with a shake and chuckle, while others bolted. Both Mo and I watched the exchange with amusement. If Granny Crackers noticed, which she probably did, she said nothing.

After fifteen minutes of sitting as a creepy clown with a continual cycle of people coming and going, I watched as one guy eased his way to the back of the garage and nearly shit himself when he saw Phoenix (the frightening clown) sitting still, staring at him.

After coming to his senses, the man laughed. "Hey, kid," he said, "I like your mask."

Phoenix responded like a deranged golden retriever, cocking his head to one side.

This made the man laugh harder. "There's a pretty girl over there. Dark hair, red top," he said, pointing. "That's my girlfriend. She's terrified of clowns. I'll give you five bucks to sneak up and stand beside her."

The guy must have thought that scaring the hell out of his girlfriend would be a riot; so did Phoenix, who did exactly what he was paid to do, stand next to some poor, unsuspecting soul.

The girl was standing in the front yard where we had wheeled the racks of clothing. Phoenix's approach was both horrifying and classic. As the pretty brunette stood on one side of the garment rack flipping through T-shirts, he stood on the other side, silent and gazing. The girl focused on the clothes before her as she slid the hangers down the bar. She must have felt his presence, because she slowly looked up and into the insane face of a terrorizing clown. Instead of running, the beauty's instinct was fight over flight. She lunged forward with a bloodcurdling scream, fists flying, knocking Phoenix hard onto the ground.

The boyfriend, in hysterics, videotaped his feisty girlfriend as she straddled my baby brother, pinning his arms to his sides with her muscular thighs. A rack of clothes laid across Phoenix's chest, and small, strong hands wrapped around his throat as the terrified woman choked him.

At first everyone stood stunned, watching a screaming woman strangle a boy in a clown mask. Phoenix's legs frantically kicked through strewn clothes. The girl violently shook his upper body as she pressed her thumbs into his larynx. It was Mo who leaped to his rescue. He dived onto the woman's back and rolled her off Phoenix, who scurried backwards and ripped the mask from his face.

"He paid me to do it! He paid me to do it!" Phoenix shouted, pointing to the man who was doubled over in laughter. The pretty brunette, knocked to her senses by Mo, looked at Phoenix to see a thirteen-year-old boy with tears in his eyes and red, angry claw marks on his neck.

"Scott, you ass!" she said, jumping to her feet and punching her boyfriend in the chest.

"Jesus, Ashley," he said, still laughing, "I didn't know you were going to go ape shit on the kid."

"You're an asshole!" she repeated as she stomped out of the yard and toward their car.

Watching the two have a lover's spat in front of their vehicle, I noticed a U-Haul truck had pulled up to the neighboring house. On the sidewalk, mouths gaping, stood two well-dressed, equally beautiful men. An extremely handsome white guy held a cardboard box with the word *Kitchen* written on its side, while next to him, a beautiful brown man carried a massive mauve vase.

"Welcome to Paris Village!" Granny Crackers waved, coming

off the porch. The men smiled nervously, gave a slight wave, and quickly scurried into their house.

"How much did he pay you?" Granny Crackers asked Phoenix, turning away from our new neighbors.

"Five dollars."

"Is that worth an ass whooping to you?"

"She didn't hurt me." Phoenix sneered.

"I'm glad you don't think so," Granny Crackers said. "Now, hand over the five dollars."

"What? I made that money fair and square."

"You made that money by scaring away half of my customers, so I figure it's really owed to me."

Phoenix had been beaten down enough that day, so instead of arguing, he placed the crumpled bill in Granny Crackers's hand and crossed the yard to walk into the house.

Granny Crackers, Mo, and I stood together in the front yard, watching things return to normal and our new neighbors move in.

"Queers," Granny Crackers flatly stated as the men made a second trip from the truck into the house.

"What?" Mo and I said in unison, surprised by her nerve.

"Thank God," Granny Crackers praised. "We finally got some faggots moving into Paris Village. It will do the neighborhood good. Gay men really know how to fancy up a place. Just look what they've accomplished on the east side."

Now it was Mo and I who stood with our mouths gaping. Granny Crackers never fails to shock and enlighten, usually in the same sentence.

"Nope, I don't mind living next door to some queers," she said. "I just hope they don't mind living next to a cracka."

Chapter Four

Summer is the best season for trash picking, and the college campus is our favorite place to go. We've been driving to the university every night, alternating dumpsters to dive in. Timing is everything. Within a week the garbage will be emptied, and we will have to wait until the next big move-out to dive again.

It seems college kids leaving dorms dump anything and everything. I'm not sure if the trash comes from graduates who, after four years, throw away their rooms or rich, lazy students who leave it all behind and replenish every year rather than pack up. Regardless of the reason, the picking is great. Besides books, wall hangings, desk lamps, and mini fridges, we've pulled out shoes, purses, backpacks, dishes, oval rugs, duffle bags full of clothes, and even potted plants.

It saddens me that those who have so much care so little. I guess the situation is balanced by the fact that what's sinful for a spoiled person to throw away is absolutely delightful for an unspoiled person to find. As cliché as it is, truly one man's trash is another man's treasure.

As gross as dumpster diving sounds, we've been having a blast, especially Phoenix, who has turned out to be a champion trash picker, a title he wears with pride.

During life with Mimi, Phoenix spent his summers on a swim

team. With the zodiac sign of Pisces, Phoenix was born a fish and could freestyle the length of a pool by age six. This summer he's a gold medalist dumpster diver, swimming in trash.

It's Phoenix who consistently uncovers the greatest finds. With the intuition of an archaeologist, he's able to dig out and brush off the valuable junk so thoughtlessly tossed aside. We all love what Phoenix collects, and our congratulatory pats on his back and high fives bring him tremendous joy. When my sad little brother beams, it's so nice to see him feel successful.

Before we came to live with Granny Crackers, it was Uncle Ross who helped her pick trash and stock The Barrel, but as I've learned, life changes. After years spent saving, Uncle Ross finally bought his own semi and hit the road. He fulfilled his dream, buying a brand-new, bright blue Peterbilt, the same month Mimi died. A day after the funeral of his only sibling, he was gone. He left behind a white Ford pick-up that had been used for trash picking. He also left behind a wife who cheated on him with his best friend (who now lives in his house) and two grown sons who have lives of their own.

The trash-picking truck is large with a small backseat. Uncle Ross built up the bed with a frame and wooden sides. Mo is now its driver. Even though Mo has just a temporary permit, he can maneuver this beast down alleyways and narrow streets. Granny Crackers says Mo is a natural, and as soon as his driver's education classes are finished, Granny Crackers will take him to get a license. I'm hoping I don't have to learn how to drive in that big old truck loaded with trash. I think it would be terrifying as well as embarrassing. Mo delights in it. He drives with the same enthusiasm that Phoenix picks trash. It seems I'm the only one who hasn't found a comfortable niche in the family business.

Yesterday, after two successful dumpster dives, Granny Crackers told Mo to go to Taco Bell for some Icees and beef burritos. Our bodies needed fuel and our dry mouths longed for a drink. We bounced down the road in the top-heavy truck. Granny Crackers rode shotgun, her head hanging out the open window like a pet dog. Phoenix and I sat cramped in the back seat. As Mo made the swift turn into the fast-food restaurant, I caught a glimpse of our mother. She was hardly recognizable, standing across the street, her hair long and stringy, her body so skinny. Maybe she's melting away. She wore a thin, dingy wife-beater T-shirt that clung to her bony frame. Loose dirty jeans hung from her hips. A large dog lay at her feet while she stood at the busy intersection holding a cardboard sign.

While we waited in the line of cars, Mo also noticed our mother. "Jesus Christ," he whispered, causing Phoenix to look up and around.

"She got a dog."

"She must be living on the street," Granny Crackers informed us.

"Well, then, why would she get a dog? Her sign says she can't feed herself! How's she gonna feed a dog? She's so stupid."

"Your mother may be broken, Savannah Jo, but she ain't stupid. A homeless woman's dog is no different from a rescue dog and is needed every bit as much. Sure, a canine has to be fed and might keep you out of shelters, but it will also keep you from getting robbed or raped."

Phoenix turned in his seat and looked away. I believe he was crying. However, I'm not sure if his tears were for the dog or our mother. Mo looked away too and turned his nose in the air as if our mother weren't panhandling right in front of our faces. I refused to look away. My dry eyes, stone cold, didn't leave her for a moment.

I've seen my mother high and low; I've seen her wasted, unafraid, and scared shitless. I've seen her glass-breaking mad and tap-dancing happy. I've seen her sick, healthy, strong, and weak, but I had never seen her look so pathetic as at that moment, so I stared unflinching, an exercise in resilience.

I often force myself to do uncomfortable things, testing my tolerance level. I'm trying desperately to strengthen myself. It's the reason I photograph ugly things, take cold showers, lie on hot tar, walk barefoot on rocks, and watch the news. All these things are resistance builders. They appeal to my curiosity about pain. I wonder why some are given so much and some so little. And I wonder how much pain one human can take.

I watched pain, an evil monster, push Mimi up a mountain of torment. Pain snatched her by the shirt collar and dragged her to the brink of anguish, the highest point of tolerance, before it slowly and reluctantly relinquished her over the edge, free falling into the arms of Jesus.

It's not that I like pain. I don't; I hate it, but pain is inevitable. There's no way around it. Although I believe that pain is passed out unfairly, I know it will affect every living soul in some way. By forcing myself to do painful things, I'm building my strength, which is good, because I think I was born way too sensitive for this cruel world.

I snapped a couple pictures before we took off. In one photo I angled my phone in a crooked manner, so she and her dog were in the left side of the frame. To the right, behind her, I captured the urban background, buildings, and traffic. When I edited it, I covered the image with a bluish filter, blurred the background, and sharpened the image of my mother. The second photo I set in black and white. This time I enhanced the background and blurred my mother, as if viewing her through tears. For both pictures I wrote a poem.

Grandmothers by nature are creatures that feed people, so as Mo drove by Ava without slowing, Granny Crackers leaned out

her window and tossed a bag of tacos at her feet.
  A poem written by Savannah Jorja:

LOST

Lost Patience, Lost Control, Lost Weight,
Lost Ground, Lost Touch, Lost Sleep,
Lost Site, Lost Out, Lost it.
Lost Soul.

Chapter Five

There are moments in life so awkward they're painful, situations without a shred of grace or harmony, embarrassment you feel for another with enough intensity that the ground beneath them shakes. With mercy you pray the earth will open up and swallow them whole, releasing you both. That's basically how it goes every time my mom shows up.

Ava was sitting on our front porch when we returned home from dumpster diving, a large German shepherd seated between her legs. As Mo turned into the driveway, the dog howled a series of welcoming barks, and Ava gave an uneasy smile and waved. In that instant, out of the Ford windows flew the air of normalcy, taking with it giggles, silliness, wisecracks, and sarcasm. They were immediately replaced with a deafening buzz of anxiety and the fluttering of nerves.

It was Granny Crackers who reacted first, moving her hands back and forth, swatting at our worries.

"Shoo, shoo, go on, now. Y'all get outta the truck and go greet your mother."

The three of us hesitantly opened our heavy doors and ambled out. While we walked toward our mother, Granny Crackers jumped into the driver's seat and drove the truck to the back of the house. I could tell Ava shared our nervous energy, and within her skinny, empty stomach sat a small ball of nerves, wound like frayed yarn.

Ava stood up on shaky legs and dismissed her jitters by acting happy and excited. "Montana!" she squealed. "I thought that was you driving. Oh my god! You're driving now. And Granny Crackers got you driving that big ol' truck. Pretty damn impressive."

"It's not so hard."

"Hell, no, not for you, girl. You've always had a way of making hard things look easy."   I looked over at Mo, anticipating his response to being called a girl, but Mo just gave a cocky nod.

Apparently somewhere along the walk from the truck to the porch, Mo had found an invisible shield and held it in front of himself. I could not see his armor, but I knew he was guarded, so did Ava. Phoenix and I forgot to take precautionary steps. We stood before our mother, vulnerable and weak.

"Damn, son, you getting so tall," Ava said, setting her gaze on my brother, "and so handsome."

Phoenix smiled proudly.

Ava reached out and brushed her shaky hand down his pretty face. "My little boy is growing up. Kinda makes me sad." Ava touched her baby tenderly. With Phoenix's permission she rubbed his shoulder and his neck and then buried her fingers into his soft brown curls.

"You're gonna be a lady killer for sure, cuz you're killing me right now."

"Thanks, Mom." Phoenix blushed.

Like a good middle child I waited patiently for our mother to notice me, which she did, after a long moment of gazing at my brother.

"Savannah Jorja, sweet girl," Ava said, wrapping me in a tight squeeze.

Without meaning to, I fell into my mother's sweaty hug and

inhaled the strong scent of body odor, unsure if it was hers or mine. I hated myself for hugging my mother, especially when Mo was so strong and stoic, but it had been such a long time since I was held. Mimi was tender and affectionate, Granny Crackers is not. Ava has the same gentle touch as Mimi, and I've missed it.

Granny Crackers came around the front of the house just as our embrace ended and began barking orders. "Y'all head on out back," she directed. "Mo and Savannah Jo, start unloading the truck. Phoenix, light up the grill. Ava, turn on the hose and give your dog a drink." For once it felt helpful that Granny Crackers is so damn bossy. Specific instructions and jobs to do moved us forward and away from tricky hugs.

Phoenix loves building pyramids from charcoal. He delights in lighter fluid, often using it to write on the driveway. When he strikes a match at one end, a blazing trail of cursive letters quickly scripts his name. As Phoenix played with fire, Mo and I unloaded a truck full of trash, and Ava and her dog took turns drinking out of the hose. All of this was witnessed by our new neighbors, Jason and Kaleem, or as Granny Crackers calls them, "the Fruit Loops next door."

The two gay hotties have been working nonstop on their yard. While we spent the last couple weeks diving in dumpsters, Jason and Kaleem have been transforming their yard into a garden oasis. We hoard trash, and they beautify their surroundings, reconstructing a barren back lot into a Japanese garden with a winding bed of rocks and plants, a koi pond, and the cutest little bridge I've ever seen. The privacy fence will be finished by the day's end, blocking our view of tranquility. In our yard, the wind blows black smoke, and in theirs the breeze carries the song of wind chimes and bluebirds.

Ava, not knowing what to do, walked in circles, helped Phoenix with the grill, unloaded some treasures from the truck, carried them into the garage, sleuthed around inside The Barrel, sniffed over tables, poked inside boxes, and then retreated back outside.

I felt sorry for my mother, uncomfortable in her own skin, distracted and irritated. It's as if God placed her in an invisible wool sweater and sentenced her to walk the earth itchy and miserable, scratching at her arms and rolling her neck.

Granny Crackers called me away from the tense backyard into the kitchen for help. While I stirred potato salad she went into the bathroom with a plastic bag and cleaned out the medicine cabinet. I could hear the collective sounds of pill bottles hitting the sack, and I knew she was working fast, quickly swiping the shelves to leave the cupboard empty. She hid the plastic bag in the crockpot and hid the crockpot in the back of the pantry. Acting as if nothing was out of the ordinary, she then stirred up a large pitcher of Kool-Aid. We carried out plates, cups, food, and fixings and placed them on our large, trash-picked patio table.

There is something about a cookout that brings a semblance of normalcy. A barbecue is good for any occasion; doesn't matter if it's a wake or wedding, graduation party, birthday, or a simple family get-together with a prodigal mom.

Our scorched anger slowly swirled into the charcoal breeze and drifted toward downy clouds. With hostility melting like cheese, we happily filled our plates with burgers and grilled onions. Each scrumptious bite replaced tension with food. It was not just protein and calories that gave Ava energy to talk, but also the normalcy of it all, the nostalgic feeling of her grandmother's backyard, the presence of her children, and the pink and purple hue of a sunset sky. It's small wonders that call a lost person home.

Ava's dog is named Sarge. She recently rescued him from a thick chain connected to a dog house that sat in the hot sun, next to an empty water dish. In other words, she stole him. Ava told us she left town six months ago with a friend. They went to Florida to see the ocean and feel the sun. When she returned home, her roommate had moved someone else in. (Translation: After Mimi died, Ava self-destructed once again, left the boyfriend she was with, and took off with another dude to Florida, and when that fell apart, she came back to find her boyfriend had replaced her). Now she floats from house to house and couch to couch, in and out of hotels with extended stays just until she finds another place to live (another place means new boyfriend).

We listened to our mother's adventures under an airbrushed urban sky, the sun setting at one end and the moon rising at the other, a magical Instagram moment. As she spoke, I felt saddened by her abandonment, irritated by her recklessness, and awed by her grit. Ava's stories faded with the last bit of daylight, interrupted by silence, an eerie quiet filled the space. I looked away and stared at our neighbors' newly constructed cedar fence, a row of flat, reddish boards obstructing my view of beauty.

"Goodbye, koi pond," I loudly whispered, which caused everyone to stare at the fence with pained eyes until Granny Crackers shouted.

"I love it."

"You do?"

"Hell, yes! It's great! Now we have somewhere to hang all the hubcaps."

Her statement caused me to suck in my breath and my mother to burst out with laughter. Ava doubled over in hysterics and laughed for a good two minutes, and when somebody laughs like that, you can't help but laugh with them.

We continued to laugh and talk as we cleaned up dinner, feelings of awkwardness replaced by an acceptable dysfunction. This ended when Granny Crackers told Ava to go into The Barrel and find something to wear, promising to wash the clothes in her backpack. Next she gave Ava a bath towel and a new toothbrush.

When our mother went to shower, Granny Crackers instructed the three of us to carry a pillow, sheets, and a box fan out to the front porch and set them on the chaise lounge.

"You makin' my mom sleep outside tonight?" Phoenix asked in disbelief.

"Child, I am too tired to lay awake all night listening to your mama prowl around my house. Me, worrying about my purse and things. Besides, Ava doesn't like being cooped up. She's happier outside with the stars and the breeze; it's where she breathes best. Trust me, that cushioned chaise lounge is gonna feel like a damn vacation."

When Ava got out of the shower, I expected there to be a fight. Seems like an insult, putting your houseguest outside, but Ava acted like the front porch was the best idea she'd heard, which pissed me off.

If my mother's life were baked into a cake, the recipe would call for two cups of regret, two cups of pity, and a teeny-tiny pinch of self-esteem (which could probably be left out). And if worthiness was icing, my mother's cake would not be frosted.

Life has shamed and humbled Ava to a mere existence. She's fine sleeping on a front porch with the dog or panhandling for food. It doesn't occur to her that she's better than that. And that's why I sometimes hate her.

A poem written by Savannah Jorja:

FEELING LIKE WHITE TRASH

Sometimes the grass
Really is greener
On the other side of the fence.
Beside our backyard's junkyard
Is a serenity garden.

Chapter Six

Sometimes we know the people missing from our lives best; although they are absent, their presence overwhelms our space. Their stories get handed down to us like heirlooms. Memories and images are pressed into our mind frame, and hang crookedly on our heart. So even though my mother has lived in and out of my life for the past twelve years, I know her as well as anyone knows their mother, maybe better.

Mimi talked of Ava excessively to anyone with a compassionate ear. Her audience was made up of family, friends, counselors, social workers, and doctors. I've heard Ava's story a thousand times, a song sung by a concerned mother.

The good mom of a bad child is like a musician without an instrument. My Mimi was like a pianist, up nights, mindlessly tapping her fingers on an invisible keyboard, desperately trying to save a lost melody. Mimi's life was orchestrated by worry. The tune of Ava constantly played in her head, a symphony of sorrow. Even so, Mimi stayed attentive to Mo, Phoenix, and me. Thoughts of Ava were never a distraction. On the contrary, I believe they caused her affection and led to our spoiling. Thoughts of Ava triggered soft touches to our hair, sudden hugs, and random kisses. Ava was her reason for overcompensation and why we stuck to each other like glue.

Mimi always described Ava as a happy baby, smart toddler, sweet child. She was perfect—up until high school. At age fifteen Ava mutated from a shy, angelic girl into a sneaky, devilish bitch. She broke rules, sassed teachers, and cursed her mother. Mimi believed it was the influence of Ava's new friends, Heather in particular. Heather was a spirited girl who took Ava under her wing, taught her how to dress and smoke and took her to parties. She introduced her to boys, alcohol, and weed.

These days Heather is a pretty nurse married to a doctor. She works in hospice and took care of Mimi at the end of her life. It's a small world, and ironically, Heather provided the weed that began Ava's journey and the drugs that ended Mimi's life. I suppose I'm just bitter, and I shouldn't blame a high school pothead for my mother's issues or Mimi's death, but it feels pretty freakin' unfair how life worked out so nicely for Heather, but not so much for my family.

Addiction is an evil thing. It picks its victims with care. Heather managed to escape devious addiction. She ran far away to a life of houses with backyard pools and fat paychecks. Ava was not as lucky. The sad and harsh reality of addiction is that wild child Heather grew up to be respectable, and Ava became a broken, dip-and-dab, ack-ack, poor white girl, chasing the dragon.

By seventeen Ava was flunking out of high school, chronically cutting classes to get high. She spent her days at her boyfriend's house. He had parents who didn't care if they laid around all day together in the same bed, smoking blunts and listening to music. No surprise, Ava was pregnant with Montana before her eighteenth birthday.

Montana's daddy is Billy, once a punk-ass kid, now a broke-ass man who has five more kids and changes oil for a living. I'm not sure what happened to Billy and Ava except that it was a teenage romance that didn't last. They split up before Montana was born.

Opposite of what one might think, Mimi saw Ava's teenage pregnancy as a good thing, a reason for Ava to settle down and stop partying. Ava was forced to think of someone other than herself; a baby was coming, and Mimi would help. Life would get better, not worse. For a minute it did, and then came the baby.

Like a fool's child, Montana entered the world on April first. Her birth was traumatic for both baby and mother. Ava labored for twenty-six hours as Montana punched and kicked her way into existence. Montana beat the hell out of our mother. Ava left the hospital with stitches, an ice pack, Tylenol #3, and the pink bundle that had caused her so much pain. Once home, she sat stunned, while Mimi fussed over the baby.

It rained every day the month Montana was born. The low-hanging, flat gray sky of Ohio matched Ava's overcast mood, and with each dreary April shower, Ava wept. In May the rain stopped, the trees blossomed, white and pink petals glided on gentle winds, birds sang, wildflowers sprang up, the sun shone down on the newly watered earth. Still, a dark cloud hovered over Ava. She floated from room to room in a smoke-filled bubble of gloom. Mimi hadn't predicted the postpartum depression that would consume Ava and therefore was not prepared. Instead of treating Ava, a scared, sad teenage mom, she soothed an infant.

In Mimi's defense, she believed a baby's coo, lullabies, *Good Night Moon*, and sunbeams would lead Ava out of the fog and into "Hey, diddle diddle, a song, a fiddle," and happy honey-colored days. That's not what happened.

After four months of lying on the couch, Ava decided that all she needed to feel better was a little weed, and that's how she hooked up with my father, Lance Romance (that's what I call him).

Lance is fourteen years older than my mother. My dad was a hottie playboy who made his money selling marijuana and pills. Every pothead knew my dad as the weed man. Lance provided Ava with the pot that calmed her rainy-day moods and restless nights. She gave him an undying devotion, money, and sex. Ava fell head over heels in love with her dealer, and he must have loved her back, at least enough to allow her to move in and play house.

Shortly after Montana's first birthday, Ava took the baby, moved out of Mimi's, and moved in with Lance Romance. Mimi tried to stop her, but she'd lost control a long time before, and Ava was an adult. Besides, Mimi had no idea that Lance Romance was a drug dealer. Yes, he was too old for Ava, but he was also a nice guy, established, clean, kind, and handsome. And Ava was not yet an addict.

I was born a year after Ava left Mimi's and a month after Montana turned two. Lance, Ava, Montana, and I lived like a happy little family for the first six months of my life. Lance then got popped with drug charges. Some dope boy thug had rolled on him. Turns out my daddy was a big-time weed man. Even though he mostly dealt in pot, he had lots of it, and the police had an informant who knew all about Daddy's secret stash. Ava was out of the loop, oblivious and completely naive to Lance's large operation. Her ignorance was a good thing; it kept her innocent. Ava was never sure how much marijuana and pills the Feds confiscated from a storage unit three blocks from our house; however, she was certain about the 146 thousand dollars they pried out of the floorboards of Montana's and my bedroom-nursery. I think what pissed her off most is that she never even knew the money was there.

After Lance Romance went to prison, Ava tried really hard to get her life back on track. Instead of going home to Mimi's, which she should have done, she applied for government assistance, moving us to a trailer park. Ava got her GED and took a three-month certification course to be a nail technician.

My mother was the only white woman working in an Asian nail salon, and she was the head airbrush artist. Ava can draw. She's creative and meticulous. Mimi was happy that Ava was using her talents. I think Ava was happy too and felt good about herself. She had her babies, a home, a career, and several boyfriends.

Ava is a boy magnet. She's simply stunning, much like her mother. Even now, hardened from drug use, Ava is still beautiful. There is a striking look and eye-popping quality that strings through the generations of the women in my family. Believe it or not, Granny Crackers has it. She passed it on to Mimi, who passed it to Ava, who gave it to Mo. It skipped me. Their beauty lives in their olive skin, almond-shaped eyes, and high cheekbones. Everybody thinks Granny Crackers is Native American, but that's mostly because she wears her long silver hair in a braid. Their looks attract men like moths to a porch light. Granny Crackers has been married four times (buried them all) and Mimi only twice (she threw hers out).

As much as men like Ava, Ava likes men, and one-night stands can happen frequently. Ava has never said who Phoenix's dad is; we know only that he's black, as is evident in my tall, handsome, curly haired, caramel-colored brother.

Life in Wood-Springs Gardens Trailer Park was good until Ava met Devious Addiction. He circulated throughout the subdivision and befriended most of the community. Devious Addiction began to court my mother. He wooed her with opioids, which banished her feelings of stress, helped her sleep at night, eased her inner pain, and made her feel euphoric.

My mother's obsession with drugs is intense, making her a pothead at age fifteen and a heroin addict by twenty-three. Ava took to opioids like a hummingbird to nectar. She must have been born with a sweet tooth, because one snort of brown sugar produced a craving so strong that no matter how hard she tries (and she has tried) she just can't keep her hands off the jolly pop.

My mother fell in love with Devious Addiction. The problem is that it never loved her back and made her feel like shit in the morning, waking up to scattered powder dreams and bottled hearts. Devious Addiction stalked Ava, becoming her abuser. She lost her job, her home, and her kids, in that order. It turned her into a thief, a slut, and a liar. Devious Addiction wrecked Ava's life, thinned her narrow body, dulled her shiny hair, rotted her pretty smile, and turned her olive skin gray.

Chapter Seven

I wake every morning before dawn. My internal clock is still on school-bus time. I don't mind; sunrise is the only quiet time in Paris Village. Nights are not silent, not in the summertime. Summer nights in Paris Village are electric, the high-kilowatt hours, when everything is pulsating with energy. Nights are filled with the sounds of loud voices, laughter and fun, fist fights, arguments, gunshots, traffic, sirens, and music. You get used to it. In the early morning, just after this town has gone to bed, I go outside and take cell-phone photos and write poems in my journal. After an hour on the front porch, I go back to bed and lie down until noon like a normal fifteen-year-old.

I love watching darkness fade to light. The sun, a yellow-orange globe, breaks the horizon and rises into a sea of black sky. Slowly the light steals the night. It creeps, changing colors as it comes. In the west a transparent moon sits in a van Gogh sky with altering hues of indigo. In the east, gold, red, and orange light sets the rooftops ablaze. Sunsets are magnificent too, when the sky resembles an airbrushed painting of heaven. Both sunrise and sunsets are proof that ugly places have beautiful moments.

I sat in the corner of the porch on a hard plastic chair, writing celestial poems and taking sunburst photos, while my mother slept. Ava and Sarge have been living on the front porch for more than a week. She was sleeping hard, without concern, sprawled out half nude. She must have gotten hot last night, or maybe high, because she'd taken off her shirt. Lying on her back, arms stretched over her head, she exposed newly shaven pits and two pierced nipples standing at attention. Ava's left leg hung off the chaise lounge and rested on the back of her large, sleeping dog. A white sheet had been tossed to the floorboards.

My mother's thin, white body is a canvas, decorated in ghetto tattoos. Ava must have a dozen tats; some of them have meaning. On her left shoulder blade is a pair of angel wings. Written below is Mommy August 1,1961–September 19, 2017. On her right thigh is a mountain, and in small lettering, the name Montana is printed up one side. Phoenix is represented by a colorful, mythical bird rising from fire, inked on her left calf. And on her upper arm, I am tatted as a tree, a southern live oak dripping in Spanish moss. On the trunk of the tree is a carved heart, and within the heart are my initials, S. J. D. I suppose we're to know she loves us, because of her tattoos. Don't ask me how my mother can afford ink and not food; I guess the same way other poor people have piercings and tats.

Lost in my thoughts, I was startled by men's voices. I looked over my shoulder to see Jason and Kaleem on their porch, sitting in classy wrought-iron chairs, sipping from the smallest coffee cups I've ever seen. I smiled with a wave, mindless of my half-dressed mother.

"Good morning," they said in unison. The deep resonance of their manly greeting woke Ava. She sat up, making herself visible to our neighbors. Oblivious, Ava rubbed her sleepy eyes, yawned dramatically, and pushed forth her chest, stretching her arms out wide. Her nipples, like the pink nose of a bird dog, pointed directly at Jason and Kaleem.

"Geez, Mom!" I said, grabbing the sheet and throwing it in her face.

"What?" Ava said, looking at me and then eyeing Jason and Kaleem before realizing she was nude.

"Sorry!" Ava giggled, tucking the sheet around herself. "My bad."

Our shocked neighbors looked like they'd just swallowed live fish, which made my mother laugh harder.

"Good morning," Jason called over, causing Ava to have another fit of senseless giggles.

I sneered at my mother. She laid down flat and pulled the sheet over her head, which was good, because her T-shirt was tangled in its folds.

"I'm going back to bed," I said.

"Oh, Savannah, baby, don't go. I'm sorry."

I ignored her apology and turned toward the front door just as Phoenix was coming out.

"Morning guys," Phoenix said.

"Goodnight," I said, quickly brushing passed him.

"What's wrong with her?" he asked.

"Get some sleep, sweetie," my mother called to me. "I guess she's just tired," I heard her tell Phoenix.

I was angry. I know I'm not the only teen mortified by her parents. The difference is that other adolescents are embarrassed by their mom, because she kisses them in front of the carpool, not because she's sleeping topless on the front porch. Rationalizing, I know her flashing the neighbors is as much my fault as it is hers. I should have covered her while she was sleeping, but honestly, I didn't see the abnormality of the situation until it was viewed by others. That's what makes me so angry. Society has a painful way of reminding you that your family's dysfunctional.

"I hate Ava," I said to Mo, plopping down on my bed.

"I bet not as much as she hates herself," Mo quipped before leaving the room, a comment that made me cry myself to sleep.

When I woke two hours later to a quiet house, I went searching for my family. I found them in the backyard. Granny Crackers had put everyone to work, but for some reason hadn't awakened me.

"Look who's up," Granny Crackers said as I approached the garage. "Today, Savannah Jo, is inventory day. We're gonna clean The Barrel, organize our belongings, and make a list of all our valuable items. By evening everything will have a place. It's gonna make business easier, if we know exactly what we have and where it is." Granny Crackers handed me a broom and told me my job was to sweep and throw away trash.

"Why do she and Mo get the easy jobs?" Phoenix whined.

"Hush, child, I'm gonna compensate y'all accordingly."

This comment shut my brother up, and Granny Crackers went along, working him and Ava like slaves. They emptied boxes, dug through plastic tubs, moved large pieces of furniture, and rearranged the stuff on metal shelves and long tables. Granny Crackers worked alongside them, directing every move and helping organize our overwhelming amount of loot. On a clipboard she wrote down nearly every item they touched, including descriptions and serial numbers on tools.

Mo stood in the driveway messing with the bikes. Phoenix was right; he and Ava got the short stick. Mo loves working on bikes. In fact, it's his favorite pastime. He can switch out tires, seats, handlebars, and chains. Give Mo a frame, and he can build you a bike.

Montana has always loved anything with a set of wheels—bikes, scooters, rollerblades, skateboards, unicycles, you name it. When we were young Mimi had a boyfriend who bought us one of those big Barbie jeeps to impress her. I'm not sure if he succeeded in impressing Mimi, but he sure did Montana. She drove that jeep into the ground, and I was her constant passenger, content to just sit by her side.

I worked behind Ava and Phoenix, sweeping up dirt and mice droppings and throwing away the junk that was tossed in a pile. Mo ended up helping me. Although we all worked hard, it was obvious that the day's chores were a message to my mother and younger brother. It's clear Granny Crackers doesn't trust either one. To Ava she announced, "I know what you're capable of, so don't even think about it." For Phoenix it was a warning before the incident, like a No Trespassing sign at the beginning of your path that veers you in a different direction.

It took all afternoon to clean the garage. We were hot, sweaty, and filthy at the end of it. The entire experience would have been miserable if not for Ava, who made it fun. Ava kept the radio turned up and sang and danced the entire day. She twirled around piles of junk and serenaded clutter. Her mood was contagious. Even while being worked and humbled, Ava chose to be upbeat and carefree, I think more for us than herself. It was a generous attempt at being our mother. When we were finished, The Barrel looked a hundred times better, and Granny Crackers had a detailed inventory of items and prices, which she handed off to Mo, asking him to create her a spreadsheet on the computer.

Granny Crackers ordered takeout for dinner and then compensated us, like she promised. She paid Ava in a sack of clothes picked from The Barrel and a bus pass. "This might help finding a job a bit easier."

"They're great!" Ava replied with genuine pleasure. "Thank you."

Granny Crackers gave Mo and me cinema gift cards and permission to go to the movies. Mo looked puzzled. We all know the reason Granny Crackers doesn't give Ava money, but why us?

"Why not cash?" Mo shamelessly said under his breath.

"Because giving you cash doesn't give me fuel perks." Granny Crackers smiled and handed Phoenix a stretchy swimsuit, goggles, and cap.

"What's this for?" my confused brother asked.

"Seems our neighbor, Jason, coaches a swim team, and you, young man, are swimming butterfly in tonight's meet. Tomorrow morning you'll begin practicing with the team. You'll ride with Jason, so be up and out the door by seven, because he can't be late."

"I don't even know Jason," Phoenix growled. "I'm not gonna join some team I don't even know."

"The hell you ain't."

Granny Crackers held Phoenix prisoner until Jason knocked on our door an hour later.

"Hi-lo," he said, sticking his hand out to Phoenix. "Your grand-mother has told me so much about you. I'm excited to have you join the team. I coach the Northside Sharks. We could really use someone who swims butterfly."

"That's not even my stroke," grumbled Phoenix.

"It is tonight." Jason smiled.

After they left, Mo retreated to the backyard to mess with bikes, and Granny Crackers went for an evening walk. She walks every day, has for years. The time varies, but the route is always the same. She loops around a set of four blocks, passing both of her rental properties, and then up the street to the corner store, sometimes stopping to buy a scratch-off ticket, and then back down the road toward home. It's a good mile. She stops and talks to neighbors along the way. Since Ava's been at the house, she's been taking Sarge along. He loves the walk, and Granny Crackers likes the company.

There are times when the stars above you align in a random pattern of misfortune, jinx touches coincidence, and the perfect conditions are created for something terrible to happen.

Mo had put on his headphones and was spray painting the rusty frame of a classic Schwinn. Ava and I were alone on the front porch when the black truck pulled up to the house. Out jumped a shaven-headed bearded dude.

"Ava!" he shouted, "Where's my money?"

My mother shot up from her chair, looking confused and shaken. "What are you talking about?"

"Don't play stupid with me. You know damn well you took the cash."

Out of the passenger seat stepped a mean-ass white girl with stringy long hair. "Bitch, I know you stole my child support," she said, shaking her head and pointing a finger.

"What?"

"The three hundred dollars I put in an envelope for my baby mama," the man shouted.

"I didn't take your three hundred," Ava yelled back.

"You a liar," the woman calmly stated as she walked straight up our grass toward my mother. Before Ava could act, the woman snatched her by the hair and pulled her off the front porch. She balled her free hand into a fist and beat my mother in the face. Ava tried to fight back, but she had been blindsided, and the other woman was stronger. The man egged her on, laughing and cheering as she hit Ava about her head and tossed her like a rag doll. When Ava fell to the ground, the woman pounced, straddled Ava, grabbed her by the hair, and pounded her head into the cement steps.

I stood frozen on the front porch, crying, no help at all. I heard Sarge bark and registered his low growl seconds before I saw him. Granny Crackers released his leash. He tore into the front yard, leaped on the stringy-haired girl, and bit her face and neck. She rolled off my mom and curled into a fetal position, covering her head. Sarge circled, snarling and biting her sides, hands, scalp, and pulling at her shirt with his sharp fangs.

"Help!" she cried, marred in bite marks, bloody tears streaming down her face.

I looked up at the bald guy and saw the gun he'd pulled from the waistband of his faded jeans. "No! Don't!" A primal scream ached from my lungs.

The gunshot vibrated our front yard, and Sarge's howl pierced the sky. The big shepherd fell to his side. The wounded girl scrambled to her feet and limped toward the truck. Within seconds they were gone.

Mo ran around the front of the house, passed Ava, and went straight to Sarge. Kaleem, our neighbor, appeared with a towel. He pressed it to the dog's bloody side. Sarge lay panting. Ava sat dazed. Granny Crackers went into the house and came out with her purse and keys.

"Help me put him in the car," she told Kaleem. Granny Crackers grabbed the sheet off Ava's front-porch bed and spread it on the ground next to the dog. Mo and Kaleem rolled Sarge onto the sheet. When they each picked up an end, it created a hammock to carry him to the car. Mo and Granny Crackers raced off to the emergency vet. I stayed home and sat with my broken mother.

Chapter Eight

My mother sat stunned on her front-porch bed, her dry eyes staring, her body bruised, and the taste of blood on her lips. I sat adjacent to her, close enough to feel near, yet far enough to remain distant, both of us mute, two stone statues dropped on a ghetto porch.

Kaleem approached from next door, carrying a thermal lunch bag. "Hey," he said tenderly, sitting down on the stoop. He reached into his sack and handed my mother an ice pack. "Here. Put this on your head."

"Umm, thanks," she said, finding her voice.

"You feelin' okay?"

"What do you think? I feel like shit."

Kaleem ignored her sarcasm and pulled out a tiny flashlight. Leaning toward my mother, he pointed the penlight and looked directly into her eyes. "Follow the light," he said, zigzagging a small ball of light across her face.

"So are you a doctor or something?"

"ER nurse." He smiled, clicking off the light and reaching into his sack again. Next he handed my mother a bottle of water and two tiny pills. "Tylenol," he said. "I bet you have a headache."

"Hell yeah."

"I think you have a concussion."

"I think you're right," she said, rubbing her temples.

"I can take you to the hospital."

"That's all right. I'm fine. I'm just gonna sit here."

"Mind if I sit with you for a bit?"

"Be my guest," my mother said, opening up her arms like she was an elegant host and not a beaten woman.

Kaleem reached into his bag. This time he pulled out three Icee sleeves. "What color?" he asked, a large white smile stretching across his brown face.

"Blue." Ava smiled back. He snipped the plastic with scissors and then turned toward me.

"No thanks."

"Aww, come on. Everybody loves popsicles."

"Then green, I guess"

"Awesome! That leaves red for me, my favorite."

It occurred to me that our new neighbors were a couple of heroes. While Jason was busy saving Phoenix's summer with scheduled play and competition, Kaleem had come to our rescue as first responder and charming paramedic.

Ava tenderly rubbed the frozen ice to her bloody mouth. "Is your boyfriend a nurse too?" she asked, using her come-hither voice. One would think that Ava would be too worried, hurt, or shamed to sound flirtatious, but it comes naturally. It's an innate quality. At times she's not even aware of her sultriness.

Sex permeates Ava in the same manner a skunk reeks, unaware and unapologetic. Her ability to disconnect emotionally and move forward, fancy free, is a striking quality, and by far her most profound survivor skill.

"Jason's my husband," Kaleem said, flashing a charismatic smile. "He's a high school history teacher and swim coach."

"Newlyweds?" she asked, flicking her tongue over her pouty blue lips.

"Committed to each other for ten years, legally married for one."

"So I guess it's true what they say."

"And what's that?"

"The good ones are always married or gay. In your case, it's a double whammy." She batted her long lashes and winked her bruised eye.

Kaleem let out a thunderous laugh.

"Thanks for the popsicle," I said, rolling my eyes at my mother and walking into the house. I did not inherit Ava's elusive personality. I'm a sensitive mess. I was still reeling from the fight and gunshot. I could not erase the image of the wounded, beautiful dog lying in the front yard. I could hear the echo of his crippling howl. I sat on the couch, staring at a crack in the wall. The conversation outside floated through the open window. Ava's voice had changed, no longer saucy, just sad.

"I didn't steal any money," she said.

"What makes him think you did?"

"I'm just someone to blame," she answered. "If money was even stolen. Maybe he misplaced it. I don't know. I suppose it could be true. His house has a revolving door with constant incoming chaos. Somebody could have stolen his cash, but it wasn't me. Perhaps there never was three hundred dollars set aside for child support. He probably snorted it, spent it on drugs or booze, and needed someone to accuse. When she wanted to confront me, and beat my ass, he had to come along to save face."

"That's unfortunate," Kaleem expressed.

"Nah, that's life. What's unfortunate is that my dog was shot."

Her heartbroken confession brought to my eyes tears so thick they flowed like honey from a comb. I got up from the couch and retreated to the bathroom. I filled the tub halfway and tossed in a bath bomb. Slowly the smell of lavender filled the room as the purple chalky ball bobbed, fizzed, and dissolved into a violet bath. I was hoping aromatherapy would be enough to calm my nerves and stop my crying.

Fully submerged, head lying on white porcelain, I closed my eyes and breathed deeply. My brain would not shut off. It replayed the evening. I could see the flash of metal as he drew the gun. I visualized Sarge lying on his side, panting. That image skipped my mind ten months back to Mimi on a ventilator, the exaggerated rise and fall of her chest with each long and gurgling breath. I hate death, but what's worse is pain and suffering. I thought of the strength and courage in Mimi, the fight in Sarge. I'm such a chickenshit.

I did nothing while my mother was beaten. I should have at least called 911. If only I had helped. I could have jumped off the porch and joined the fight. The two of us together could have taken that bitch, and then maybe Sarge wouldn't have been shot.

I took my head all the way under the water. A low hum rattled my ears. I was lying on the bottom of the tub, knees bent, my yellow hair floated on lavender. I felt my chest tighten, trapped air fluttering, like a butterfly caught in a net. Water filled my nostrils, bringing a sharp pain to my head. I held my breath as long as I could. I fought the urge to rise from the tub. I broke the surface with one large gasp of air, eyes wide open. Hovering over me stood Mo, feet firmly planted, hands on hips, red-rimmed eyes, staring down at me.

"Sarge is dead," Mo softly said. "And your little tolerance tests are gonna hurt you one day." Mo left the room crying. I lay in the tub until the water turned cold and I was waterlogged. And then I stayed there for ten more minutes.

When I entered my room, Phoenix was sitting on Mo's bed, getting an earful. I climbed up and filled in the blanks. Our conversation waltzed across the ceiling, as the three of us lay horizontally, whispering to each other.

"Do you think Ava stole the money?" Phoenix asked.

"I don't know." I shook my head.

"I do," Mo said confidently. "Yes, that thieving bitch took the money. Now the dog she stole is dead." Mo's rationality made sense, and I pushed aside Ava's denial to Kaleem.

Granny Crackers stepped in the room as we lay commiserating. "I want you children to know, your mama didn't take that money."

"Is that what she told you?" asked Mo, sitting up.

"No, Montana, she didn't have to." Granny Crackers used common sense to set us straight and relieve us from the burden of mistrust. "Yes, your mama can be some dumb, but she ain't plumb dumb. And she isn't stupid enough to steal an envelope of cash. Sure, Ava may have stolen hundreds of dollars off that guy at some point, but she didn't do it all at once. Nah, Ava would take it twenty at a time. So it's not her fault they showed up here or that Sarge is dead. It's nobody's fault. That was all a tragedy of errors."

After Granny Crackers left, silence crept in under the door like a thick fog invading the room and kept us still. Slowly we drifted off, lulled to sleep by an inaudible lullaby. The three of us slept like a litter of puppies, in the same bed. The ghost of Mimi drifted between us, and Sarge lay at our feet.

Chapter Nine

As far as days are measured, today was a good one, and my Instagram and poetry reflected my mood. I couldn't help but be happy. Jason and Kaleem took us swimming. Phoenix and Jason go to the pool daily for swim practice or meets. Today when Jason brought Phoenix home, he invited all of us to go back. He told us Kaleem had packed snacks and dinner and we could spend our evening swimming.

At first his lovely invite created some tension. Mo declined the offer in accordance with our unspoken family rule that every opportunity in this house, good or bad, is met with some sort of resistance. "I can't go."

"Why?" I asked, confused.

"I don't have a suit," Mo flatly stated.

These teeny tiny bits of reality sting when they smack your face, even if they shouldn't. I sighed and looked at the floor, focusing on the invisible can of worms Jason had just opened. Mo could tell I was disappointed. As badly as I wanted to go, I wanted him along.

"It's okay, Savannah, you go. You'll have fun. I'm just going to stay here with Granny Crackers."

Granny Crackers stood in the doorway. "First off, Montana Rose . . ."

Mo's head snapped up at the sound of his full name.

"What makes you think I'm gonna sit here while y'all go swimming?" Looking at Jason, Granny Crackers added, "I do hope that invite included me."

"Oh yes, Rosie, of course." He nodded, calling her by her given name.

"Good, because I could use a refresher. And Montana, you have a perfectly good swimsuit in the top drawer of your dresser."

"I can't wear that," Mo snapped back.

I know Montana actually has two swimsuits, a cute black-and-white tankini and a one-piece, navy blue Speedo, both bought when he was a she.

"Then borrow something from Savannah," she said with nonchalance, as if a missing suit was the real issue.

Granny Crackers just doesn't get it. Every time I think she understands her granddaughter is now her grandson, she reminds me she doesn't quite grasp the concept of transgender. Sure, she calls Montana Mo, but nicknames are commonplace around here, and Mo is an appropriate alias for Montana. She also lets Mo dress the way he wants and shave his head. Granny Crackers doesn't feel the need to tell people how to look. She's not judgmental in that way. Besides, Montana's still pretty, which makes it even harder for Granny Crackers to realize Mo identifies as male. Someone needs to sit down and explain it all to her; however, it's not going to be Mo.

Montana has never been a person who explains her/himself. She/he just is. You either get it or you don't. You can't really blame Granny Crackers for her disregard. She's eighty years old and set in her ways. Realistically you can't go around changing your gender and expect a person like Granny Crackers to comprehend, especially when it's been kind of confusing.

When we were little, Montana was a butterfly, happy and free-spirited, with a flight pattern all her own. Then Mimi got sick. Montana formed a chrysalis to protect herself. When Mimi died, Mo emerged, an earthbound caterpillar. We all watched the metamorphosis, but nobody said anything. We were too busy dealing with our own sense of loss. To make it worse, Mimi's illness coincided with Montana's puberty, making it easy to blame Montana's gender transition on grief. In actuality Montana has always been on the nonconformist road, heading straight toward an identity crisis. Truth is, if Mimi hadn't died, she would be here, dealing with the same thing.

Maybe I should be the one to talk to Granny Crackers. After all, she refers to me as the informer child, a name given because I was a little tattletale. Honestly, I think all middle children are snitches; however, it makes sense "the informer child" should be the one to educate Granny Crackers on the paradox of modern-day sexuality and the gender spectrum. Somebody needs to do it.

I visualize it happening, the two of us sitting at the kitchen table, talking over tea. Taking her arthritic hand into my smooth palm and choosing my words gently, I tell her, "Our Montana Rose was born with a birth defect. It seems God and science rallied together to pull off some cruel and vicious prank, and we've all been fooled. Mo is actually a boy living in a girl's body."

It happens all the time, doesn't it? People living without sound, sight, or limbs. In Montana's case, she was born without a penis, and with the sultry beautiful face and body of our mother, making her deformity not grotesque, but still cruel. Mo looks like a strikingly beautiful woman with, a shaved head, men's clothing, and no makeup.

Mo stood seething at the suggestion that he wear a girl's suit.

I was pouting, and Granny Crackers stood her ground. Jason watched our exchange with nervous tension. From the look on his face, he was either holding his breath or biting his tongue. A pool invite should not cause all this drama.

"I'll take Mo to buy a suit," a long silent Ava piped up.

Granny Crackers's mouth puckered and her eyebrows raised as she glanced at Ava sideways.

"I have my own money," Mo was quick to state.

After a moment of hesitation, Granny Crackers's face softened. "Well, if you have your own money and your mother wants to take you, who am I to stand in the way?"

Finally, an agreement was made. Granny Crackers, Phoenix, and I headed to the pool with Jason and Kaleem. Mo and Ava took the car to the mall and planned to join us afterwards.

When they arrived, Montana was wearing a blue-and-neon green surf shirt and trunks from the boy's department. Mo is more petite than a small man, so he has limited choices. Phoenix was just as happy as I was to see Mo. The three of us jumped one by one into the cool, blue water.

It felt nice to swim again. Mimi had been a sun worshipper, and she raised us with water play, backyard pools and hoses, and trips to beaches and creeks. She loved to be by the water. She said it was her happy place. We went to lakes or dams all four seasons, fishing and exploring. We played beside bright blue lakes, shimmering like silvery diamonds, until the sun set on surface ripples like gold. "Water is a healer," Mimi told us as we sat on the grass, watching the colors change.

Mo, Phoenix, and I raced across the pool, went up and down the slide, had a diving-board challenge, and then volleyed a ball back and forth. We swam until we were hungry and then went in search of food.

We spread our blanket and set chairs on the lawn where the

sun meets shade. Kaleem had packed a banquet, and Granny Crackers added to it. There was enough food for four families.

"Swimming makes me hungry," Kaleem explained when he saw my eyes widen at the contents of his cooler. Honestly, I had never seen, smelled, or tasted a picnic like the one Kaleem had packed. It was exotic.

Granny Crackers brought ham and Swiss cheese sandwiches on rye, a large bowl of cut watermelon, and two bags of Doritos. I had been excited about our contribution until I saw Kaleem's. He presented large foil pans of extravagant recipes. There were chicken kabobs and lemon rice, vegetable pan rolls, and fritters made from onions, potatoes, and cauliflower. He listed the fragrant dishes as he spread them out. With each delicious bite their names slipped my mind, but their taste lingered. My favorites were the hummus and grilled halloumi. I could only imagine that we were eating like kings from some foreign land.

As we ate, Jason gave us the lowdown on the pool. He knew everybody. As he talked, children ran by our blanket screaming, "Hey, Mr. J."

Jason smiled, nodded, and called them by name. I remember thinking he must be a good teacher.

Jason pointed out the old women to Granny Crackers. A small circle of white-haired senior citizens floated on pool noodles in four feet of water. He said the women came to the pool every day to socialize and exercise. " A few of them bring their husbands along." Jason chuckled. "The men play cards, spades or poker, betting with change. They carry fistfuls of dimes."

On the other side of the grass, at a picnic table under a large oak, sat several old men.

Jason must have thought Granny Crackers would wander over to the old ladies, make some new friends. He must have been surprised when she got up and walked out to the tree. Obviously

Jason was just getting to know Rosie. Granny Crackers is a ball-buster and a flirt. Mimi always referred to her as a man's woman. She'd much rather play cards with the husbands than gossip with the wives.

To say Ava didn't fall far from the tree would be an understatement. Perhaps she didn't fall at all. We are a family dominated by women over the generations. Granny Crackers, Mimi, Ava, (and yes, even Mo) and I are branches of the same tree, our roots twisted together under earth and soil. We are leaf and limbs connected by stem and twig, an oxymoron of strength and flowers, rough bark and luscious fruit.

Granny Crackers sat at the table, and I knew she had sweet-talked the old geezers into dealing her in. Granny Crackers loves games. She's smart, cunningly so, and competitive. Playing has always been serious business. She has no qualms about beating you. I learned early about ruthlessness. Unlike other grandmothers, Granny Crackers would never throw a game, not even to a child. She always gives it her all, and she expects the same from her opponent.

Within an hour Granny Crackers found satisfaction in her earnings. Collecting her dimes, she rose from the table and passed by our blanket, smiling. Without offering to buy for anyone else, she took her coins to the concession stand and came back with an ice cream, which she ate in front of us. Honestly, she couldn't have been hungry. She just likes the taste of winning.

The bell rang for a rest period just as Granny Crackers finished her treat. Teens, tweens and toddlers left the pool, splashing out with halted play, a perfect time for adults to swim. Ava dove in headfirst. Swimming underwater, she didn't rise until she was halfway across the pool. She has excellent lung capacity for a smoker.

"No diving!" Kaleem yelled. "She really shouldn't do that with a concussion."

"Yeah, well, she does a lot of things she shouldn't," Granny Crackers answered, ruffling through her canvas tote. She pulled out a swim cap covered with rubbery purple flowers. Twisting her long silver braid into a bun, she hid her hair underneath the tight cap. She walked cautiously down the steps into the shallows and kept walking. When the water was chest high, she began swimming with sluggish breaststrokes, as if she were in a pool of syrup. I could tell Granny Crackers was happy in the water, and she who once was a shark was now a manatee, content and pleased to be lazily bobbing along.

"That cap is ridiculous," Mo remarked.

"She looks like she's on a 1950s synchronized team." Phoenix laughed.

"I think she looks fabulous," said Jason.

"So do I." Kaleem beamed. "Where do you suppose she found a retro petal swim cap?"

"Are you kidding?" Mo asked. "Granny Crackers has an entire garage and house full of crazy shit like that."

"Well, I'm in love." Jason grinned.

For a brief few minutes Granny Crackers and Ava were the only two people to occupy the vast swimming pool. They swam together, lost in their own worlds. When the rest period ended, they got out and retreated to chairs to dry in the sun. Granny Crackers pulled two books from her bag. She handed Ava *Fifty Shades of Grey* and she opened *Fifty Shades Darker.*

As my family read and swam, I scrolled social media, looking through Snapchat and Instagram. I snapped several selfies in a bathing suit, lounging in a chair, pouty duck lips, eyes hidden behind sunglasses. It was nice to have something fun and positive to post. My mood is often pulled down by looking at pics of old friends at play. They used to invite me along; they no longer do. I switched over to Facebook, and a video nearly jumped off my screen. It was Phoenix in the clown mask, hiding behind a rack of clothes. Oh my god, Scott had posted the video and it had gone viral, more than 250,000 views already.

"Phoenix!" I shouted across the pool. "You're famous!"

Ava and Granny Crackers put down their books and watched the video over my shoulder. Mo and Phoenix quickly abandoned the diving boards. Soon everybody had their phones out. The video shows a creepy clown looking through clothes at a pretty brunette. She sees him, screams, and reacts, flying through the garment rack, pinning him to the ground, choking him. It ends when Mo dives onto the girl's back. You can't tell who Phoenix is because of his mask, and you see only the back of Mo's shaved head. Thank God, they're anonymous.

"Holy shit!" said Phoenix. "Look at how many times it's been shared."

I couldn't tell how Phoenix felt; he only registered shock.

"Look at all the comments," Mo said, laughing. We watched the video in awe, over and over again, captured footage of my brother being strangled. Eventually we grew desensitized. I still couldn't tell if Phoenix was happy or angry. Maybe he didn't know either. Kaleem and Jason took turns reading the best comments out loud. Most of them were about Ashley. We were careful to treat Phoenix like a star and not like a boy who got his ass kicked in a clown mask by a pretty girl and was saved by his sister/brother.

"Wow, son, you really made her lose her shit," said Ava.

"Yes, indeed," Granny Crackers agreed. "She lost her mind."

Slowly Phoenix's embarrassment evaporated, and he laughed with us.

Viral videos are a walk on a tightrope. On one side is glory, a brilliant and radiant light, and on the other side is hell's fire, and either way you're bound to fall. I wondered if Ashley and Scott were still together.

When viewing the video started to feel unhealthy, Mo and I grabbed Phoenix by his hands and led him back to the pool. The three of us splashed until twilight. Mimi appeared in the sky as a single star and blinked at us while we played.

We closed out the pool on the summer solstice, the longest day of the year. The seven of us walked out with lifeguards and pool staff. Granny Crackers opened the trunk of her old Oldsmobile, and we threw our stuff in. Mo, Phoenix, and I climbed into the back seat, Ava rode shotgun, and Granny was at the wheel. Kicking up stones, we peeled past Jason and Kaleem, who stood loading their Toyota Rav4 with neatly stacked coolers and chairs.

"Thanks for the swim." Granny Crackers waved as she pulled out of the gravel parking lot.

We drove toward the rising moon with the windows down, radio up, all of us singing at the top of our lungs. "Here comes the sun (doo doo doo doo). Here comes the sun, and I say. It's all right."

A poem written by Savannah Jorja:

THE POOL

Behind the school, beyond the fence
A swimming pool is gleaming.
The happiness of present tense
Leads my soul to beaming.

There is a fountain beside the pool
Where chubby babies are playing,
Splashing, running, breaking rules.
The water just keeps spraying.

A bright blue sky of sun and breeze
That lifts my yellow hair;
Underneath a shady tree
We lounge upon the chairs.

Gold-framed glasses shade my eyes.
My turquoise bikini is stylin'.
Feeling pretty—glamorized
Without the pain of tryin'.

The solstice day, a summer banquet
We ate like queens and kings,
A fancy picnic placed on a blanket,
Sweet and savory things.

We swam, we laughed, we played and danced
In sunshine's beams of glee
And fooled them all, if someone glanced
At the grieving siblings three.

Chapter Ten

*A*va has been sleeping on the living room couch. Granny Crackers says that without Sarge, it's not safe for her to be snoozing on the front porch. Her words are a painful reminder of the fist fight and fatal shooting. None of us have recovered. Sarge was replaced by empty space, a teardrop ache at its center.

Reality dictates it's safer for my mother to be inside. First off, we have no idea how many enemies she has made. Second, there are crazy people everywhere. It's possible somebody could pluck her thin, sleeping body right off the premises and throw her into their abduction van, a scary thought. Regardless of the new sleeping arrangement, Ava doesn't come inside until long after the sun is swallowed by a black sky and she's counted all the stars. Granny Crackers was right; Ava loves being outside.

There are people who'd rather be outdoors than in. My mom is one of them. Inside, the plaster walls, excessive clutter, and low-hanging ceiling are much harsher on her than the natural elements. I like to say Ava lives alfresco. It sounds romantic, with open air, songbirds and having no walls or roof to obstruct your view.

On the porch my mom seems relaxed. She lounges in a chair, looks across the lawn, watches children play, pets stray cats, smokes cigarettes, and drinks Nestea. In the house, she feels confined. It shows in one thousand tiny steps paced back and forth across the floor or clicking through a hundred TV stations to watch nothing. My mom is clinging to normality.

At the end of every day she sits outside waiting patiently for the night to wind down. When voices lessen to sporadic, unpredictable shouts from strangers and traffic slows to the squeal of a random tire, Ava comes inside and tries to get comfortable. Last night she succeeded splendidly. This morning she has taken off.

I'm not sure my mother has any goals except to survive. I don't detect ambition, dreams, or a sense of urgency to get her life back together. Ava meanders through her days as if she doesn't have three children to raise. Her lack of motivation is getting on Granny Crackers's nerves, and the tension is thick whenever they are together.

Granny Crackers, not one to play it subtle, went to the beauty supply store yesterday and came home with a full set of acrylic nails fastened to a plastic strip. She also bought polish and nail pens. She threw her purchase into Ava's lap. "I want you to paint designs on those and take 'em around to all the nail salons. Show them your work. See if they're hiring," she said.

Today the nails sit on the coffee table untouched and Ava is missing. She did break out the polish and nail pens last night, though. The two of us had so much fun. We rubbed lotion on each other's feet and did nail art. My toes look adorable, as if I'm taking ten little ladybugs on a walk. I painted her toes yellow with black stripes. After spa play, I scrolled social media, Snapchatting photos of my pretty feet, while Ava, Mo, and Phoenix rolled out plates of dough and made personal pizzas. Phoenix fixed a barbecue chicken pizza, and Mo made tomato and pesto, since he's a vegetarian this week. Ava baked me my very own pineapple pizza and herself a classic pepperoni. We ate in the living room while watching *Jaws* on Netflix. Ava said it was Mimi's favorite movie.

Granny Crackers was pissed off, waking up to a huge mess. "Where's your mother?" she asked, eyeing my feet.

"How should I know?" It was strange that my mom was already awake and out of the house. I had fallen asleep before she did. Perhaps she hadn't gone to bed at all.

"Did she say anything during your pedicure?"

"Not really," I admitted. "But she's probably gone out looking for a job."

"Sure she has."

I don't know why I feel the need to protect or defend Ava. She certainly doesn't deserve it, yet we are all guilty of looking the other way and giving her the benefit of the doubt. I suppose that's what you do when your loved one is an irresponsible, whimsical mess. Living with my mother is like having a pet bird, beautiful and cool; however, you know it will fly away, if given half a chance.

Pent-up emotions buzzed around Granny Crackers like flies that needed to be swatted. She shook her head, grabbed her gardening gloves, and headed out the front door. Since I didn't want to clean the kitchen, I followed her.

Two blocks from the house is a community garden. Granny Crackers digs in the dirt nearly every day for about an hour, sometimes longer. Whoever's at home watches The Barrel. It's not so bad. She usually goes mid-morning, after we've slept in and before we've had a chance to take off for the day. Today I went with Granny Crackers and left Mo on his own, which is just as well, since he would rather be alone. Mo likes to chill and vape while Granny Crackers is gardening. I believe vaping is his form of meditation, so I don't say anything. However, I don't partake. Actually I'm a teenage oddball. Everybody Juules or vapes. E-cigs are hip, and I hear the flavors are delicious. I guess I'm a wimp, but truth is I'm afraid of addiction, and I have no desire to smoke an apple pie.

Actually I would rather be in the community garden than anywhere else in Paris Village. It's a beautiful piece of nature sitting inside a split-rail fence, and it looks completely out of place. The garden is verdant rows of raised beds and green tufts lined up neatly in the soil. There are wildflowers, butterflies, climbing vines, and wooden stakes standing at attention. Once a barren lot, the garden sits between a Drugmart and a vacant house on a busy four-lane street. It stretches as far back as the railroad tracks, and it's the one piece of property in Paris Village respected by everybody.

Rakes and hoes, accidentally forgotten, lean against the fence, waiting for the return of their owners. A long black hose snakes through the garden, and there are several rain barrels, all left alone to do their job. Someone even hung wind chimes on a shepherd's hook, and neither chimes nor hook have been stolen.

The garden is maintained by a collection of souls, old and young, brown and white, a family with young children, a lonely widow, hippies, rednecks, and urbanites. It's where all sorts coexist, working together without arguments or drama.

It makes me believe that a garden is a place of peace and if man were to create a garden that stretched from ocean to ocean and around the world and everybody was invited to help, we could stop not only hunger but also war. Makes sense to me; after all, Eden was the first place God created. But then again, why should anyone listen to me? I'm just a fifteen-year-old who doesn't always believe in God.

An elderly black man named Ambrose Livingston started the community garden in Paris Village. Everybody knows and loves Ambrose. He's a tree of a man with silver hair and deep mahogany skin stretched over bones withered by age. Although he's an old man, he works like he's young. Ambrose is at the garden every day, weeding and digging, tending to the endless number of chores.

Some people with the very best intentions show up to the garden in the spring and claim their little beds. They plant tomatoes, peppers, or green beans and then don't return until they think they're grown. I'm not sure if people are too busy to garden or they forget, or maybe they just assume that nature does all the work. Regardless, it's Ambrose who makes sure that beds are tended. He weeds the forgotten fruit and waters all the plants. He's the one who gives other gardeners advice, telling them what to plant and where and how. I don't know when Ambrose leaves the garden, but I'm sure he does. However, he's there whenever we go, socializing or tending to the soil, always humming a little tune while he works. When I go to the garden, I like to talk to Ambrose. He's interesting and kind.

Just like Granny Crackers, Ambrose gives advice; however, he does it in a much softer way. Granny Crackers uses brute bluntness. Ambrose speaks with kind words picked lovingly, his guidance gifted like a bouquet of wildflowers. Granny Crackers blurts opinions with sassy sarcasm and quick wit. Ambrose talks slowly, his thoughts wandering through his brain before exiting his mouth. The biggest difference is the sound of their voices. Granny Crackers speaks in one key, flat. Ambrose's voice is majestic, low and resonant. If an old Hindu elephant were ever to speak, it would have the same baritone whisper and thoughts as Ambrose Livingston. Despite their differences, both Granny Crackers and Ambrose are wise.

There are smart people and wise people. Smart people can tutor you in English or help you with math. Wise people teach you about life. It's best if you have both smart and wise people in your circle. That's not the case for me. That's why I flunked algebra, but I know it's possible and sane to love a broken mother.

Granny Crackers and Ambrose are best friends; sometimes

I think there's more to it. She gives him our leftovers and bakes him cookies.

"My Rosie," he says in soft words, flashing a sweet smile as she hands over a container of pulled pork. "I just love your barbecue sauce."

Granny Crackers smiles back, and I can see a small hint of bubbly floating to the surface of her personality. Suddenly, in her ugly bib overalls and urban environment, she is a glass of champagne.

I mentioned to Mo just yesterday that I thought Granny Crackers has a crush on Ambrose.

"Those two? Please, girl, they've been friends with benefits for years," responded Ava, who was eavesdropping. Her remark caught both Mo and me off guard.

"Benefits!" I screeched, the taste of bile rose in the back of my throat. I didn't want to think about old people having intercourse. And certainly not Ambrose. I want to imagine his home as a sanctuary, where he meditates around candles and is spoken to by God. "That's crazy," I argued, "and gross! Even if they did do it before, they're not doing it now. They're too old for sex."

Mo nodded his head in agreement, his eyes wide with horror.

Ava laughed at us both. "Oh really?" she asked, "Tell me, why would a person give something like that up?"

It was an unfair question for a virgin and a person grappling with sexuality. Since I've never had sex, I stayed silent, and Mo walked away.

Today as Granny Crackers and Ambrose talked while weeding the forgotten beds, I stayed close, listening. Ava had piqued my curiosity, and as shameless as it sounds, I was looking for proof that old people still do it. They talked back and forth in low voices, and I pretended to be hard at work, too busy to be listening.

"I saw your granddaughter coming out of Paula the Percolator's."

"Maybe she was just visiting. Paula's nice enough."

"Rosie, they don't call her The Percolator cuz she has good coffee."

"So you think Ava was there buying Percocets?"

"What do you think?"

Instead of answering, Granny Crackers stuck her trowel into the ground and began turning the dirt and pulling up weeds. "You really want to know what I think?" she finally said. "I think loving that child is like gardening . . . strenuous. And I wish to heaven my daughter was alive to help me with her offspring."

Her sentence caused me to snap my head and look over, her sorrow alarming. Granny Crackers never shows emotions, just strength. Mo always says, "Her leaves don't shake."

Granny Crackers went back to pounding dirt. Ambrose placed his hand on her back, stroked her spine, and I moved two garden beds over so they couldn't see my tears. I filled a watering can and sprinkled green growth and dark soil. In many ways my mother was like a garden. Words and prose flowed through my head as they do when I'm troubled. It's hard to stay on task when your brain is turning sadness into poetry.

I abandoned the watering can and sat off in a corner of the garden and worked on my poem, texting it on my phone. I was fully submerged in thoughts, swimming in my cell phone, when I was brought to the surface by Granny Crackers's laughter. I felt relief in hearing her mood change. I looked at Ambrose and Granny Crackers, and there stood Dixie Dawn, Granny Crackers's oldest and best friend. Dixie—now there's a woman who is kumquat crazy. Like bottled fruit, she's completely fermented.

A poem written by Savannah Jorja:

MEET AVA

She is twisting cucumber vines of confusion and chaos.
With rosebud lips she gives raspberry kisses.
Her soft green eyes cry fat blueberry tears.
Her hugs, warm sunshine embraces.
She is loud, red tomato cheers.

I'd like to introduce Ava, a garden-variety girl,
All blossoms and blooms,
But don't assume,
Because she'll change the minute you do.

She grows and she wilts.
Her pretty flowers make you tilt your head.
She wraps you in her choking vines of dread.

She is beautiful, fruitful,
Stunning; a peach
Out of reach,

Flourishing hotness,
Dazzling rain
And completely insane.

Meet Ava,
Strawberries and cream;
No apple pie dreams.

She's purple, red, violet, golden, and green.
Her sadness is black
And dips in between.

Her presence is large,
Though she makes herself small,
A teeny-tiny seed, not impressive at all.

She burrows deep down in the ground
Under soil and earth;
she longs for rebirth.

Hiding, fighting, waiting to thaw,
She withdraws,
Bursting with all
The beauty we cannot see.

Chapter Eleven

Granny Crackers, Ambrose, and Dixie chatted beside a garden bed. I strolled over, container in hand, and started picking green beans. I love picking green beans. It feels satisfying, snapping the long bean from its vine and filling an empty bucket. A full container is a yummy reward, and it makes me want to cook dinner. Collecting green beans is more methodical than plucking tomatoes or corn. Some beans are long and skinny, others short and fat. The fun part is discovering them. I enjoy combing through the stems, parting the leaves like hair, searching for ripe beans, and snapping them into my fingers. It's silent, time-consuming work, and it allows me to linger and listen to gossip.

Dixie is Granny Crackers's best friend; the two are longtime cronies. They became neighbors long ago, during a time when their houses and lives were messy, and they were young, pretty, and wild. They bonded over babies and billiards. Granny Crackers (or Rosie) had only two babies. Dixie had six little ones, not counting her late husband. Dixie claims all her kids grew up to be selfish assholes. At least once a week the women managed to escape home and shoot pool. According to Granny Crackers, pool used to be a men's-only sport. Dixie and Rosie upset many poolrooms back in the day. They'd enter a smoke-filled bar looking like Lucy and Ethel in flower-print dresses and bright red lips. They spent the first hour surviving sneers, jeers, and sexual insults, and the second hour commanding the room. Granny Crackers met at least two of her husbands in pool halls.

Granny Crackers has always been eccentric and unconventional. Dixie is just plain crazy. She's completely looney tunes. It wasn't hard to hear Granny Crackers and Dixie talking in the garden while I snapped beans, since they're both loud and animated.

"What do you mean you need a ride to court tomorrow?" Granny Crackers asked Dixie as Ambrose leaned in to be part of the conversation.

"Oh, it's really no big deal. I picked up a little misdemeanor, that's all."

"That's all? You weren't driving, were you? You know after that last fender bender you can't drive anymore."

"Damn it, Rosie, I know. That's why I just asked you to take me to court."

"Dixie, you know I hate to drive downtown. All them one-way streets and the parking stinks. Get one of your kids to take you."

"My kids don't need to be in my business. Besides, I know damn well you drove downtown the other night at dark to pick trash."

"That's only because they're remodeling the Federal Building, and they threw out a bunch of desk chairs. And I had my grandchild Montana drive me down, because she needs nightime driving hours to get her license."

"Rosie," Ambrose interrupted, his voice soft and kind, his thoughts rational. "Dixie is your best friend, and maybe this isn't about a ride." Ambrose looked over at Dixie with raised eyebrows. "After all, we got taxis and a bus. Perhaps Dixie needs you to be there as her friend."

Dixie flirted. "Thank you, Ambrose. You're such an insightful man."

"Cool your jets, Dixie Dawn," snapped Granny Crackers. "You knew I'd take you, or you wouldn't have asked. But if I'm going to be inconvenienced, I can give you a hard time. And don't you be so soft-hearted, Ambrose. We all know Dixie is just manipulating the system. Dixie, you don't need me cuz I'm your friend. You want me cuz I'm old. You're trying to get sympathy from the courts. Gonna have us looking like two helpless old ladies in front of a judge. What'd you do, anyways, solicit a police officer?"

Surprisingly, it was the last line that seemed to hit home, and Dixie became defensive. "It's not for solicitation!" she shouted. "It's inducing panic. And it wasn't a police officer, but rather a crew of paramedics."

Granny Crackers pulled off her big floppy gardening hat and fanned her face. "Woman, what'd you go and do now?"

Ambrose, every bit as curious, leaned in on Granny Crackers's shoulder so he could catch both the breeze and Dixie's story.

"It was that damn Life Alert button." Dixie sighed.

"Life Alert?" said Ambrose. "Dixie, you're about as feeble as an alley cat. What you got a Life Alert button for?"

"Oh, my kids got it for me. After I took that fall last summer, remember? That was the craziest thing. Doctors said that was due to low blood pressure. I was sitting on the toilet doing my business, and when I got up, the room spun and I fell to the floor. Hit my head on the side of the tub. They got me on so much Coumadin that I bled all over the damn bathroom. I was so dizzy I couldn't get up. My daughter Brenda happened to stop by while I was still laid out on the floor. Thank God she did. The bathroom looked like a homicide scene. She freaked out, called 911, and I went to the hospital for a day and a half of observation. Of course my kids got together and had 'the talk' about who's gonna start checking in on Mama. You'd think among six kids and fifteen grandchildren they could have figured out a schedule. Seems they're all too busy to drive into Paris Village and see how I'm doing, so instead they got me a Life Alert button. A perfect solution to clear their conscience while not being inconvenienced."

"That makes sense," said Ambrose. "But it still cracks me up. I just don't picture you as someone who needs a Life Alert button."

"Well, that's good, cuz I don't have one anymore. It was confiscated by the police, and I have been charged with calling in false emergencies and inducing panic."

"Spill the tea, Dixie," said Granny Crackers, placing her gardening hat back on her head.

"Oh, Rosie." Dixie let out a soft sigh. "It was a long winter. A real long winter." Dixie quieted for a minute, but so did everybody else, so she figured she might as well keep talking.
"The first time I hit the button," Dixie began, "I swear it was an accident. I had just got out of the shower and was drying off. Damn button was sitting on the sink. I didn't even know it was there. Placed my hand on it trying to steady myself. Next thing I know, four paramedics are standing in my home and I'm naked as a jaybird. I got so scared I dropped to the floor. Not an easy thing to do at my age, and I really couldn't get up. In hindsight I should have told them I accidentally hit Life Alert. Well, anyways, they wrapped me in a blanket, looked me over, checked my vitals. They were real sweet, pretty boys. No surprise, I was fine. When they left, I got dressed. But I had this tingling feeling all through my body. I wasn't quite sure what was wrong with me. Then I remembered, it was sheer excitement. Girl, I haven't felt excited in so long. I tried to hold on to the feeling as long as I could. I guess it got the best of me. So one day, I'm not sure why I did it, but I baked up a couple of pies."

"You don't bake," Granny Crackers interrupted.

"True enough, I don't. But Marie Callender does. I threw a couple of her pies into my oven and put on a fresh pot of coffee. I did my hair and makeup real pretty. Then I stripped down to my undies and put on an apron. Wearing only a floral smock, silk panties, and red heels, I pressed that Life Alert button. Lord, those handsome young men came barreling into my house, blue uniforms and medic bags; it was the sexist thing I've ever seen. I was sitting pretty on the kitchen floor, waiting for them. I said I twisted my ankle in my heels, and as they looked me over I offered them some pie and coffee."

"Mercy, woman, and they charged you with a crime?"

"Oh no, not that time; that time was fine. A couple of guys even ate a piece of pie."

"That time? How many times did you flash the emergency medical team?"

"Only once more. I'd been cooped up too long. Bored shit-less, needed something to do, so I got undressed, lay on top of my bed, and pushed the button. I suppose they don't like calls when the victim is lying comfortably on a queen-size bed. Anyways, it took them much longer to arrive this time, and by the time they got there, I had dozed off. Silly thing is, I painted my nipples with lipstick. I got the idea from a movie I'd seen years ago."

"Woman, you're insane!" Granny Crackers shouted. "Ain't nobody want to see your old, saggy breasts."

"I'll have you know I bought and paid for these tits a long time ago, and they've held up well, not too saggy. Plus they're still soft and supple."

"That's because every morning at the breakfast table, one boob is laying in your oatmeal and the other is floating in your tea."

"You're a mean old lady, Rosie."

"Maybe so, but I'm still the friend taking your nutty ass to court."

"So you can take me?"

"Honey, I wouldn't miss it if you paid me. Come over tonight so we can go through The Barrel. Somebody donated a whole bag of old lady clothes. I think I have two matching polyester pant-suits we can wear. Maybe we can find hats and ugly pocketbooks. Lord, this is gonna be a hoot."

"Thanks, Rosie. I'll be over after dinner."

"See ya tonight."

After Dixie left, the community garden seemed too quiet. I think everybody heard her embarrassing monologue, but nobody reacted. Kooky things happen in Paris Village all the time, so people are desensitized and pretend to mind their own business. However, Ambrose and Granny Crackers sure did have a laugh. They joked back and forth recalling Dixie's story. While they talked, I wandered to Kaleem's patch of green. He had arrived sometime in the last half hour without me noticing, and I wanted to say hi. I helped Kaleem tie up tomatoes while he talked about peppers and herbs. He gave me a fistful of mint. I can't wait to put it in my tea.

Going home the mood was much better than during this morning's walk. Granny Crackers whistled with each step, think-ing about Dixie and laughing to herself. I could tell she was excit-ed about going to court. Surprisingly I felt good too. The laughter in the garden had lifted my spirits.

I guess Paris Village isn't always terrible. There's the garden and Ambrose, the golden light on a shabby corner and people like Dixie, who bring comic relief, or Kaleem, with his friendship and kindness. Granny Crackers is always telling me to find happiness where I am, and that's what I'm doing. I search for beauty around every ugly corner and capture it. I photograph it, script it into a poem to remind myself it exists.

When we got home, Ava had returned. She was sitting in The Barrel with Mo, gluing buttons on a lampshade. Except for the shake of her hand and the sweat-bead mustache, she looked pretty good."

"Where did you go this morning?" Granny Crackers asked abruptly.

"Walking."

"Walking, huh? So did you stop by any salons on your walk and ask about a job?"

"Just one, Sexy Talons. They told me to come back when the owner is there."

"Hmm, and what the hell are you doing now?"

"Helping your store."

"How do you figure?"

"Well, Crackers, you got this old ugly lamp that's never gonna sell and a useless jar of buttons."

"Useless?"

"Yes, useless. Nobody collects and sews buttons anymore. That's not even a thing. So I'm gluing unwanted buttons onto an outdated desk lamp, and I guarantee you somebody will buy it."

"Well, I guess that's something," said Granny Crackers, walking away.

I stayed with my mother and Mo in The Barrel. I sat on the cool cement floor and watched Ava paste junk on junk trying to create something desirable.

Buttons are ordinary and homely, but they're also purposeful, and they hold things together. The collection of buttons reminded me of days, some shiny, most plain or dull, and several ugly as hell. When Ava placed the buttons in a random pattern, sides touching, they looked meaningful. At least they appeared intentional and each button significant.

Chapter Twelve

While Granny Crackers was gone all day at court making fun from dysfunction, I got stuck in The Barrel. Phoenix was at a swim meet, and Mo took off on his bike, so it was just Ava and me. Since it was a Friday, we stayed pretty busy. People came and went all day, a slow, steady flow of traffic. Honestly, my mother wasn't much help. She goes missing all the time, there one moment and gone the next. She's like a genie, popping in and out of a bottle. In her absence I sold the lamp. When she came back, I gloated. "I sold the button lamp," I sang to her.

"You did? That's great. How much?"

"Twenty bucks."

"Oh my god, that's awesome. Where is it?"

"Where's what?"

"My twenty dollars."

I was confused. The lamp wasn't hers, nor were the buttons. Was it her money, because she decided to glue the buttons on the lamp? True, neither thing would have sold separately, and it took her all morning crafting, but does she even deserve money when her children are being raised by Granny Crackers and she's living rent free? If so, should she get paid now, before the end of the day, and prior to Granny Crackers's return to calculate our daily sales?

Granny Crackers keeps most of the money made at The Barrel. In fairness, she always pays us for our time and a little extra for our finds. Phoenix usually makes the most money, because he's the best trash picker. However, we are never given the entire amount of the purchase. That money gets thrown into her bank account along with Social Security and rental checks. It all goes to pay the bills and put food on the table, clothes on our backs, and gas in the truck. We don't complain, because Granny Crackers always makes sure we have everything we need, most of what we want, and some spending money.

"Savannah Jorja, that ugly-ass lamp would've never sold without my help. I crafted a piece of art, making it my money. Give me the twenty!"

Fighting with my mother is a scary thing. She's relentless. I handed over twenty dollars from the cash box, and Ava vanished again. I have my suspicions about where Ava has been hanging out. I hope I'm wrong.

Around the corner from our home is an abandoned house. Actually there are a lot of deserted houses in Paris Village. Boarded-up homes sit on every street. It's an eyesore and a problem. Granny Crackers hates the orphaned houses. She and Ambrose have organized a community group of activists and protesters who want the properties torn down. They've put together a signed petition and attended several town hall meetings to voice their concerns. The mayor says he's addressing the problem, but we see no evidence.

The particular abandoned house that worries me has been taken over by squatters. Granny Crackers called the police to report it. They came out and questioned the people inside. One of the men told the cops the homeowner was letting him stay in the vacant property. The story must have checked out, because he's still there.

I think the squatters are drug addicts. It's easy to tell, with their skinny bruised arms and pockmarked faces. Besides that, one guy approached Mo and me and asked for money. Gave us a sob story about taking milk to a baby. I'm pretty sure it was bullshit. Junkies are liars and narcissists. They manipulate family and friends to near madness and then they go bug strangers. Addicts are tiresome. They wear you down with pleas and promises. If that doesn't work, an outburst explodes like a bomb. It's easier to give in than it is to survive the fallout.

At times the squatters' house is loud with people coming and going. And at other times, it's deadly silent. You think they are all gone, until the place gets loud again. I saw my mother at the house a couple days ago. She was standing on the back step, and then she wasn't. Like I said, genie in a bottle.

I stayed home all day stressing over a missing mother and twenty bucks, while my siblings ran around worry free, and Granny Crackers was out having a blast.

When Granny Crackers and Dixie left that morning, they looked like a couple of prudish church ladies heading off to court, unrecognizable to the folks who know them. It was strange to see them out of their distinct signature looks and wearing old lady clothes. Just like on Halloween, they were in costumes.

Granny Crackers, who resembles an aged Pocahontas, untwisted her braids and swept her silver hair into a bun. Dixie changed out of her bedazzled blue jeans and into a pair of lilac pants with an elastic waistband. A lavender jacket adorned in fat fabric buttons completed her pantsuit. Granny Crackers wore a similar outfit in mint green. The two turned Dixie's nine a.m. court date into an all-day adventure.

Granny Crackers and Dixie didn't return until dinner. By then everybody was home. We were all sitting on the front porch, plates balanced on our knees, eating leftovers. The two old ladies fell out of the Oldsmobile happy and laughing, as if they had been on an all-day excursion.

"Did you get your Life Alert button back?" Ava asked.

"Nah, they can keep it," responded Dixie with a flip of her hand. "Thanks to Rosie here, I was found innocent by reason of senility."

"Granny Crackers, did you play lawyer?"

"Well, somebody had to. Dixie was making a damn fool of herself."

"Do tell." Ava giggled.

Granny Crackers was delighted to talk about the day. It had been a blast, and she wanted to relish in it.

"Y'all should have seen Dixie feebly approach the judge." Granny Crackers laughed. Demonstrating, she hunched her back and took slow, shaky exaggerated steps toward the porch. "It may have been believable, if she hadn't begun to act like such a harlot."

"Harlot? Girrl, I never."

"The hell you haven't." The two started laughing.

It took a moment for them to compose themselves before Granny Crackers continued her story. "Well," she said, "when the judge read Dixie's charges and the complaint out loud, you could hear snickering in the courtroom. He asked Dixie if she had representation, and she said no. He told her she should come back with a lawyer, and she asked if she could proceed on her own. He allowed it and requested Dixie to tell her side of the story.

"Lordy, you should have seen her, it was a hoot. She started talking to the judge in a low, sexy drawl. She began licking her lips, batting her eyes, fanning her face, stroking her hair, and flipping her head about. She looked like a possessed seductress. She behaved tore up from the floor up. Her performance struck everybody speechless. The whole courtroom was staring at her with their mouths hanging open. As soon as Dixie unbuttoned the top of her ugly jacket and began stroking herself, I jumped up.

"Your Honor, Your Honor,' I said, 'please, can't you see this poor woman has old-timer's disease?' He asked, 'Who are you?' I said, 'I've been her best friend for nearly sixty years.' I buttoned Dixie back up, and she continued to bat her eyes at the judge. I said, 'Normally she is not like this, Your Honor. Her dementia is triggered when she sees a beautiful man. Please forgive her inappropriateness. She can't help it. How could she? When you're sitting there in that distinguished robe with your slicked-back silver hair. And your eyes, Your Honor, your eyes alone make a woman want to shed her clothes.'

"Well, he tapped his gavel, and everybody stopped chuckling. He tried to talk calmly to Dixie, give her a little lecture, and she continued to blow him kisses. So he kept her Life Alert button and told me to take her home.

"Hell, we had so much fun that after court we found a little dive bar and hustled pool. Made ourselves a nice chunk of change."

We were all in stitches by the time Granny Crackers finished her monologue, especially Dixie, who could barely hold herself up straight, laughing so hard.

"Hell, I'm 'bout to piss these ugly pants," Dixie cried. "Please, don't make me laugh."

"Can't help it," Granny Crackers said. "Shit's funny."

Dixie went to use the bathroom, and we all continued to laugh for another five full minutes. Granny Crackers, still in a performance mood, looked deranged as she imitated Dixie, batting her eyes and licking her lips.

It felt good to laugh. Before Granny Crackers came home my day had been full of frustration and worry. I needed the comic relief she and Dixie provided.

After Dixie left and everybody settled down, I went over the daily sales with Granny Crackers. To my surprise she didn't act too concerned about the twenty dollars I gave to Ava and was thrilled about the sale of the lamp.

"You owe me ten bucks," she told Ava. "And if you start making things that will sell, I'll split the profits with you."

I suppose I should be happy that the two worked out a deal and Ava will be contributing. But the truth is, I'm worried about my mom having money. With cash she's able to get high or worse yet, leave us again.

Chapter Thirteen

I have a Pinterest mom. Who'd think I could utter such a sentence? Ava accepted Granny Crackers's challenge to "make things that sell and we'll split the profits." Ava is excelling. My mother is up nights crafting and creating. She scrolls Pinterest for ideas and inspiration. By day she picks trash and thrifts, buying crap at Goodwill stores and flea markets to refurbish, repurpose, and sell for a profit. She's good at it. Her madness works in her favor, a cigarette in one hand, a paintbrush in the other. The spotlight attached to The Barrel lights up our back yard and permits her to work all night. She needs little sleep when her mind races with creative flow.

After the sale of the button lamp, Ava rummaged through The Barrel looking for another project. She found a stack of old window frames in various shapes and sizes leaning against the cement wall. All of them look distressed, glass panes framed in bare wood or peeling paint of black or white. Ava pulled a long white window from the collection. She cleaned it up with Windex, dusted away the cobwebs, propped it against the garage, and began painting. Using a chipped plate as her palate, she swirled circles of yellows, reds, browns, and white with fat and skinny brushes and painted vibrant sunflowers on the twelve panes of glass. The very next day the window sold quickly. The woman who bought it acted like she was getting the best deal ever.

"Oh my gosh, fifty dollars! You've got to be kidding me. Score!"

That night my mother stayed up recreating the window. Phoenix, Mo, and I sat outside in lawn chairs and watched her work. She flitted around the frame like a firefly, her yellow-tipped paintbrush dancing in the twilight.

My mother paints in the same manner she lives—carefree, childlike, and a bit reckless. Her work is bright. She likes orange and yellow. She has no fear laying color down. She knows how to mask her mistakes or accept them. A full moon and sucking on a vape pen filled with hash oil aided her exuberance.

"Look!" she said, pointing to the sky, laughing. "I'm painting sunflowers on a starry, starry night."

Ava does not track time. When she finished the window at 12:30 a.m., she thought it perfectly okay to haul her masterpiece to the neighbors to ask their opinion. Splattered in yellow paint, a midnight streak of sunshine racing across her forehead, she pounded on their door. The three of us, Mo, Phoenix, and I, curious as hell, watched from the front lawn. Fortunately Kaleem, who usually works third shift, was home and awake.

"Is everything all right?" his voice held a slight panic.

"How much should I sell this for?" Ava asked, holding the large sunflower window in front of her like a shield. Kaleem was taken aback at the sight of our family, but recovered quickly. I suppose if a whole family stands in your yard and bangs on your door after midnight, it might suggest an emergency. Clearly by now Jason and Kaleem have realized they moved next to a houseful of harmless crazy people, me included.

"Oh, umm, wow, that's beautiful," he said, opening the door wider. "Geez, Ava, did you paint that?" he asked, noticing my mother's yellow hands. "I didn't know you were an artist."

"Yeah, well, I guess I am. Usually I airbrush flowers onto acrylic nails. This was actually easier, not so intricate, much bigger surface than a fingernail. Anyways, how much should I sell it for?"

Kaleem stepped outside and gave it a closer look. "Well, umm, it really is lovely. I would think at least a hundred dollars, maybe two. But I don't know. Jason would be a much better judge than I am, but he's asleep."

"Two hundred? Are you shitting me? That's awesome!"

"Maybe you should stop by tomorrow when Jason is up. He could give you a more accurate idea."

"I'm up. I'm up," said Jason, stepping out onto the porch, a robe tied neatly around his waist. "Darling, did you do this?" he said, rubbing his eyes.

"Guilty!" My mother beamed.

"Absolutely a couple hundred, maybe more. We'll talk tomorrow, at a decent time. I'll do a little research and find out its worth. I may even have a buyer for that window. A friend of mine owns a little floral shop, and it would be perfect hanging in there."

"Thanks. See ya tomorrow, or I guess, later today at a decent time." She grinned.

"Goodnight." Both men nodded to my mother, and then "Goodnight!" they said again, waving to us kids standing in their yard.

After leaving Kaleem and Jason's house, my mother was pumped up. That night, using the same palette, she painted three more windows. She covered a six-pane window in yellow roses, another in daisies, and decorated a smaller window with bright lemons. High from hash oil, attention, and dreams of money, she couldn't stop. We three kids slowly drifted off to bed while our mother stayed lost in a yellow world.

The next morning I was the first one up and the first to go looking for Ava. The painted windows were lined up against The Barrel wall. The plate and brushes floated in a bucket of water. Ava's shoes were abandoned on the driveway, but she was gone. I sat on the front porch anticipating her return.

I fought tears as I watched my mother walk barefoot down the middle of our street, weaving toward our house, off-kilter. The sight of her was wild, a bit like her unbrushed hair. She was covered in paint, dripping shades of yellow and orange, as if she'd been holding the sun and it burst in her hands. Her sweaty, dirty T-shirt clung to her braless body. Her tiny shorts had climbed into her pubic crack. There was only one place she could have gone looking like that: the squatters' house.

"Hey," she said, looking upward toward me as she snaked up the front walk. "Do you think it's too early to knock on Jason and Kaleem's door?"

"Maybe you should shower first," I suggested.

"Oh, a shower." My mother laughed, glancing down at herself, possibly realizing for the first time that she was caked in paint. "A shower sounds good."

I was relieved when Jason and Kaleem knocked on our door before Ava was finished blow-drying her hair. It felt better knowing that they truly were interested and they had come to her, a thoughtful gesture. My mom was ecstatic. Her eyes were still beady from whatever she had ingested, but she was alert, perky, and making sense.

It's hard to tell when Ava is high or just manic. Perhaps the two coincide, living together like neurotic roommates. She functions moderately well at both levels. The best indicator of irrational behavior is her sleep pattern. She is either a dazzling insomniac, powdering her nose with stardust and pole-dancing with moonbeams, or unmotivated and sloth-like, lying comatose for days in a reclining lawn chair.

Jason and Kaleem brought their laptop with them, so it seemed proper to invite them in. After removing a sugar bowl, butter dish, salt and pepper shakers, two coffee cups, a pile of mail, and a stack of crossword puzzles and Sudoku books from the kitchen table, they sat down and turned on their computer. Granny Crackers and Ava pulled their chairs up next to them.

"This is Etsy," Jason explained. "It lists handmade items from independent sellers. Artists not nearly as talented as Ava sell their stuff on this site all day long. I typed 'wall art painted windows' in the search bar and found these."

"Jesus! That window is selling for two hundred and forty dollars, and mine is just as good!"

"I actually like yours better, " said Jason. "People love shabby chic, and honey, you got a knack for it. We can make you an Etsy shop and advertise the windows on Facebook Marketplace. You could even try selling them at art festivals."

"I want an Etsy shop," Ava shouted, leaping from her chair to prance around the kitchen.

Granny Crackers tried to talk her down, applying enough apprehension and questions to peel her from the ceiling. "How does she get paid?" Granny Crackers started. "And who is responsible for the cost of shipping? Does Etsy get a cut of the money? Does Ava have to sign any funky contracts? Who makes the rules about deliveries? Can she close up shop at any time?" Granny Crackers fired her questions rudely, sounding like an old grouchy person.

Jason and Kaleem continued to smile, patiently dealing with Ava's mania and Granny Crackers's cynicism.

Although Etsy sounds like a good idea, I'm leery. Honestly, it's hard to see Ava, a hot mess, and Granny Crackers, a computer illiterate, run an online business together.

Mo must have been thinking the same thing. Wanting to spare Jason and Kaleem from our loony family and save our crazy clan from itself, he sat down in Ava's abandoned chair and talked business. This behavior is typical Mo, as he is a rescuer. A journey through trauma and transition led Mo to be the man of the house, a role he's played since Mimi's death and our move to Paris Village. It's a position important to Mo, but not to Phoenix. It never occurred to Phoenix to step up, help out, and be the man, but then again, Phoenix is a thirteen-year-old boy. Mo has four years on Phoenix, plus the benefit of estrogen, making him a natural provider, nurturer, and caretaker.

"I do all the marketing for The Barrel," Mo began, a professional tone in his feminine voice.

I could tell Jason and Kaleem were impressed with Mo's tenacity, and by the end of the day, *Ava's Creations* was up and running.

Chapter Fourteen

$\mathcal{M}$imi always said, "Summertime flies after the fourth of July." Every Independence Day, her exuberance had the energy of a firecracker, the searing light of a Roman candle. She was a bottle rocket, clad in red, white, and blue, zigzagging the four of us from parade to cookout to carnival to fireworks. We hauled with us a cooler full of treats, blankets, chairs, sparklers, and glow sticks. We all were ecstatic to experience a day packed with summer festivities.

Every fifth of July, she was pensive, sitting at the kitchen table with a cup of coffee and notepad, contemplating time. "Summer will be over before you know it, and there is still so much to do. You need to help me make a list."

Montana, Phoenix, and I, sitting on mismatched wooden chairs, feet swinging under the table while eating bowls of Cap'n Crunch, would scream out our suggestions. She would jot them down.

"Zoo!"

"Baseball Game!"

"Beach!"

The next half of the summer, we worked on our agenda. Mimi always worried we wouldn't get it all done. "There's just not enough time to do everything you want to do," she'd explain, yet somehow she always managed to get through the list, making it a priority, drawing a line through the last activity on the day before school started. "We did it!" She would beam.

Mo, Phoenix, and I would skip around her, cheering. "Yahoo!" We were happy with ourselves, as if we had completed a triathlon. We basked in the glow of our accomplishment.

That was then. Nobody asks anymore how we'd like to spend our summer days or any other time, for that matter. It seems ironic now, that Mimi had a fascination with time.

"Stay little," she would command or jokingly scold. "You're growing up too fast."

My favorite Mimi line is when she'd look at us lovingly, and I mean truly look at us, absorb us, and then say, "I must remember not to blink."

Granny Crackers also talks about the speed of time. I guess that's your perception when you're old, or in Mimi's case, your days are shortly numbered. Mimi was fifty-seven years young when she died. Perhaps there was a subconscious part of her that always knew she would die too soon, and that's why she was transfixed on time.

For me, time is much more fluid, both a rushing river and a stagnant pond. It seems like forever since Mimi died, and I've been stuck, floating in a lake of grief, yet she was here yesterday, just beyond the bend in the stream.

Days without Mimi are difficult. Mr. Time, a master manipulator, slowly heals the wounds he causes, and soon the pain of each day becomes manageable. Holidays I spend missing Mimi are excruciating, and there is not a damn thing Time can do about it. Ambrose, however, helped make it better.

No swim practice on Independence Day, so Phoenix accompanied Granny Crackers and me to the garden early that morning. Ambrose was there, setting up a grill in the front lawn of the vacant house that borders the garden.

Every year on the fourth of July, Ambrose organizes a block party that's held in the community garden. By organizing, I mean he fires up his grill and people follow suit. It's become a Paris Village tradition. Within minutes of our arrival, he handed us his house key and put us to work. Phoenix and I made several trips up and down the street from Ambrose's house to the garden. We carried folded lawn chairs, a card table, charcoal, bags of stuff, and coolers full of ice, drinks, and meat.

Much like Ambrose himself, Ambrose's house is a charming structure on a ghetto street, a tiny pale-blue two-bedroom ranch behind a little white picket fence covered in climbing roses. On his front porch lies a Welcome mat, and on the door a wooden plaque reads Home Sweet Home. His living room is neat and sparsely furnished, devoid of the clutter that inhabits our home. A vase of flowers sits on the coffee table, and a picture of a brown Jesus hangs over the couch. His kitchen is retro, with avocado walls and burnt-orange countertops brightly lit by a large window, its sill lined with vibrant green plants in colorful clay pots.

"That's weed," Phoenix flatly stated, nodding his head toward a beam of sunshine streaming into the room.

"What?"

"Them plants in the window."

"It's not weed," I argued. "I'm pretty sure Ambrose doesn't grow pot in his kitchen."

"Oh ya, he does. Them are little baby bud plants. I know what ganja looks like, Savannah Jo. Jamal's daddy grows it in the basement. He got a whole setup with a long table and lights."

"Maybe it's herbs. You know, parsley, sage, rosemary, and thyme." I sang, remembering a song from Mimi's playlist.

"It's herb all right; good herb."

I hated that he compared Jamal's daddy to Ambrose. Jamal's

daddy is a lazy bum. I'm surprised to know he works at anything. Ambrose is the wisest, kindest man I know.

"Ambrose smokes dope." Phoenix laughed.

I didn't like that Phoenix had a positive connection to marijuana. He doesn't need any encouragement. "It makes sense," I said, rationalizing for the both of us. "Ambrose is organic. He grows vegetables, cans fruit, and makes his own salsa. If he needed cannabis for medical purposes, he would grow his own."

Phoenix shrugged his shoulders.

Satisfied with my justification, we loaded our backs like pack mules and headed to the garden.

As we set up chairs and tables, others came. Before you knew it, grills lined the grass. The smell of barbecue and ribs filled the streets. Kaleem left his patch of green and returned to the garden with a container full of kabobs and a hibachi. Jason followed with a large tray of cookies. Neighbors showed up with salad dishes, pasta, potatoes, chips, and sodas. Kids sucked on watermelon slices, spit seeds, and ate tomatoes off the vines. An old-school boombox played new music, and Beyoncé served lemonade. Tweens and teens jumped Double Dutch and danced in the street, while many artsy hands chalked the sidewalk.

The July sun, a white-hot light, beat down on the patch of vegetables and garden of people. With no escape from the heat, we were frogs in a terrarium. The first person to go into the Dollar General and come out with a large baby pool birthed an idea that spread like the measles. One by one plastic pools filled the backyard of the vacant lot. Grown people sat around basins of water like vacationers on holiday, soaking their feet and chatting. Blue tubs filled by the garden hose led teens to spray one another and babies to splash about.

Our assemblage, although peaceful and celebratory, alerted the police, who wandered through. Law enforcement always shows up when people gather in the hood. For the most part the people in my neighborhood don't like the po-po, simply because the cops don't like or trust the residents of Paris Village. Officer Miller is an exception.

Miller patrols the streets daily. He's friends with everyone. He passes out McDonald's bucks to the kids and gives bottles of water and toiletries to the homeless. Miller, a fortyish white dude with a mustache, is called Barney by the old people and Lite by the young. His real name is Michael, but he answers to all three. Mike Miller and his new partner hung in the garden all day.

Girls sat on a blanket braiding hair. I stood staring. I'm an observer. I love people watching. I take in their actions, interactions, style, and stance, collecting personas in the crowd with the same zeal one picks wildflowers from a valley. I snap photos of strangers and write my bouquets of people into poems.

"Come here, blondie," shouted a large dark-skinned girl who'd been braiding hair. For a moment I was scared. I felt my stomach tighten and my chest pack with anxiety. Perhaps I had focused too intently or snapped an unwanted photograph. People don't like you getting in their business or staring them down. Behavior like that will get your ass kicked.

"Yeah," I said, a nonchalant poker face hiding my fear.

"Let me braid you some golden tresses."

"You want to braid my hair?"

"What you think? Twenty dollars; you can keep the beads."

I stuck my hand in my pocket and pulled out three crumpled bills. "I only have twelve dollars," I said, straightening them out.

'That'll work," she said.

I sat on the blanket, happy to be surrounded by girls. Friends, another thing I've lost. A brush being pulled through my hair by another's hand felt good. She braided tight, slightly painful tugs at my scalp reminding me of days when Mimi struggled with my ratted mess.

"Knots, Savannah Jo," Mimi would quip. "Baby girl, stop twisting your hair. You've created a rat's nest."

Twisting my hair is a habit I don't think I'll ever outgrow. When the girl was finished, a hundred shell-colored beads hugged about fifty braided strands of my yellow hair. I felt pretty, happiness and self-confidence braided down my back.

Maybe it was my newfound confidence that caused the boy to toss the Frisbee in my direction.

"Is this yours?' he said, sailing the blue disc into my hands.

"No." I tossed it back.

"Savannah Jo?" he asked, throwing it again.

Oh my god, he knows my name. "Right," I answered, flinging it back.

"Mateo." Another throw.

"Nice to meet you." My return.

"Hey, kid. My Frisbee," shouted a shirtless hippie from across the lawn.

Mateo flashed me a blushing smile, flew the Frisbee to the man, and then off he ran to his friends. A total of six Frisbee tosses and a dozen spoken words sent me to the moon.

Honestly, I've noticed Mateo before. He's always busy, turning soil or chasing after younger siblings. I've watched him, mesmerized, as he talks to his mom in Spanish and his *amigos* in English. He speaks to me with shy glances and flirty grins. He's beautiful. Literally, the prettiest boy I've ever seen, black hair and beige skin. His smile is confectionary, sugary sweet, a smile that lights his entire face, all white teeth and perfectly shaped lips, deep dimples, and laughing eyes. I can't believe he noticed me. I was elated.

Feeling jubilant and hungry, I headed toward Jason and Kaleem, the smell of chicken kabobs and cumin spice pulling me along. Granny Crackers, Ambrose, and Dixie sat in chairs under a shade tree.

"Well, if it ain't Bo Derek," Dixie hollered as I strolled by.

"Hey, Bo," she croaked again, waving, a cigarette between two fingers, a can of Pabst Blue Ribbon in her other hand. "Rosie, your grandbaby looks just like Bo Derek. From now on it's Savannah Bo, not Jo."

I rolled my eyes in Dixie's direction and kept walking. She can be so annoying. How can one tiny woman have such a large, loud mouth and so many opinions? I ignored her the best I could, but she kept calling after me.

"Love me some Bo. See ya later, Savannah Bo." Dixie's got her nerve laughing at me, especially while wearing a red-striped miniskirt much too short to be worn by a woman of eighty years and a T-shirt with a large blue star on each boob.

I slumped into a chair next to Jason. Kaleem turned skewers of meat and veggies. I wished I weren't so sensitive. A minute earlier, I felt beautiful, stylish with my braided hair, and flirty, tossing the Frisbee to Mateo. Why had I given Dixie the power to change my mood with her ignorant teasing? I typed *Beau Derrick* on my phone and began a Google search.

"I love the hair," said Jason. "You look stunning, so why the sad face?"

"Dixie," I confessed. "It's stupid. I know I shouldn't care, but she keeps making fun of me, calling me Bo Derek."

"Do you know who Bo Derek is?" Jason asked.

"No, but I'm about to find out. No doubt he's some blond, cornrowed hillbilly country singer, the type Dixie likes, probably another old stoner, like Willie Nelson."

"Baby, you think Bo Derek is a redneck man?" Jason laughed.

"Bo may be a hottie, but she's no Willie Nelson." Kaleem chuckled.

The two people I thought would be the most sympathetic were laughing at me. I wanted to rip out my braids and run home. I hated being so emotional, my feelings hurt so easily. I sat speechless, pretending to focus on my phone, my gaze blurred by a pond of tears. I blinked twice, letting the water fall. A slow stream trickled down my face. Keeping my head bowed, I prayed for invisibility. Please don't let anybody see me cry. No such luck.

"Hush now, silly girl. Type the word "Ten" after the name, and it's spelled B-o-d-e-r-e-k." Jason consoled me, leaning over and looking at my phone.

I dried my cheeks and did as instructed. Sweet Jesus, there she was, the words "sex symbol" in a caption above her head. Dixie had been complimenting me, not teasing.

"That's lovely, luscious Bo Derek, a perfect ten, a timeless beauty. Gorgeous! Stunning! A goddess," said Jason, "and you, sweetheart, do look like her."

I took a screenshot of the Bo Derek photo and then took a selfie mimicking her expression. I scrolled back and forth between the two pictures, comparing our faces.

"Baby, look what God gave you," Jason whispered in my ear.

The hair and style were an exact copy thanks to Shania, the hair magician, but there were other similarities we shared, features I've always hated: freckles, a round face, square chin, and slim nose. To see your beauty for the first time is awakening, to realize it through the face of another is bizarre. I live in a family full of striking people and look like none of them. Their brand of beauty makes me feel ugly.

I am my father's daughter, and he is a stranger. From every photo I've ever seen, I know his hair was yellow, long, wavy, and feathered, much like the lead singer of a 1980's band. My dad, the lion king. Although he never held me above his head in the sunlight or introduced me to the world, he gave me his mane, the only thing I have going for me. Regardless, when you're the pale, plain sister stuck in between exotic-looking siblings, blond hair is not so spectacular. I imagine my father's hair is now short, a prison cut, but since my people burn bridges, rather than build them, I have no idea.

I posted the selfie on Instagram captioned Happy Fourth, and Mateo was the first to comment, using the emoji with heart eyes. Another rush of emotion. Oh my god, he is following me on social media. With the confirmation of my name he had found me on Twitter, Instagram, Facebook, and Snapchat. He had slid into my DMs, and once again, I felt pretty—Bo Freakin' Derek pretty.

Some people hung out in the garden all night. My mother may have been one of them; we didn't see her until morning. But not her children. Granny Crackers scurried us home at dusk. The block party had been a success. It was peaceful, family-oriented, and patriotic, with apple pie and American dreamers. We held ourselves together all day and had a hell of a celebration. But Paris Village has its limits, and like all dysfunctional communities, someone or something was bound to pop off. Our reality is that the day was long, the weather hot, and people had been drinking. These elements created the perfect formula for mayhem. Fireworks weren't the only things about to explode.

Tired, Granny Crackers went to bed early with no mention of fireworks. I shouldn't have been disappointed, but when you're fifteen years old, a Fourth of July without fireworks is like a birthday party with no cake. Besides, I had been on social media, a painful mistake, and seen posts from past allies. Old BFFs, my fair-weather friends were gathered at the park waiting for a brilliant display to light the sky. That clique of girls is proof of how easily one is forgotten. Sure, they still love my photos and send me hearts, but since my move to Granny's in the ghetto, they have invited me to nothing. Once inseparable, now we don't even text.

Mo climbed out our bedroom window and spread a blanket across the hot, rough shingles. Mo, Phoenix, and I lay in a horizontal slant on the high-peaked roof. By holding hands, palm to palm to palm, fingers laced, we made a pact: should one of us slide, we'd all go down. In the distance brilliant fireworks exploded into fluffy dandelions, heads gone to seed, blown against a black sky. On each one, I made a wish.

Chapter Fifteen

Sometimes I hate myself, thinking I'm a horrible person, weak and selfish. I should love my mother's art, be proud of her talents. I've prayed for years that my mother would stop disappointing everyone and screwing up. Now she's finally found her passion. Everybody loves her work. For the first time in my life, I've seen positive thoughts and praise tossed her way. I want to feel happy for her. Instead I'm resentful.

The thing is, I didn't even know my mother was crafty. Sure, I knew she could draw. She put designs on fingernails and doodles on scrap paper, nothing that impressed me. On the contrary, I remember the night she scribbled all over Mo's homework. Blue inked vines, crooked limbs, and leafy tree branches filled the margin of the notebook paper.

"My spelling words!" shouted Montana, snatching the paper off the table. "What did you do?"

"Oops, sorry baby."

"I'm gonna get in trouble."

"Oh, you are not. It's fine. You can still see the words. Besides, it will do your teachers good to see some creativity."

"No!" Montana wailed, large, impressive pipes held inside a tiny nine-year-old. "You ruined it."

"What's going on?" In rushed our savior and protector Mimi.

We had been living at Mimi's without our mother, but Ava had showed up again, begging for another chance, asking for one more vain attempt at sobriety.

My mother can blow promises like smoke rings, perfect little circles of hope that linger in the air and then slowly break apart, drift off, and disappear.

"She scribbled on my homework," Montana shouted, pointing her finger at Ava. "I had to write my spelling words five times each, and she drew all over them." Ava had turned the letters into flowers, w's into butterflies and m's into caterpillars.

Ava looked at Mimi and bowed her head. "I didn't know. I'm sorry."

Mimi's protective arms circled Montana's shoulders. "It's okay, sweetheart," she said, consoling the angry child. "You're just going to have to rewrite them."

"But I don't want to."

"Just think of the perfect score you're going to get, because you practiced your words so hard. Write them again, and then we'll go out for ice cream," Mimi promised.

Montana sneered at our mother, wiped her tears, and settled at the kitchen table to redo her homework. Ava went outside to smoke.

Mimi picked up the spelling page made into a jungle of climbing vines and decorative insects. The words, written in childish print, bloomed, blossomed, crawled, and fluttered off the page, being pulled by sketched snakes and swallowtails. "What a goddamn shame," Mimi softly said, crumpling up the paper into a ball and tossing it into the trash.

The next day my mother left. I always believed she had taken off, because she didn't want to be bothered by us. Later I thought she didn't feel welcome, and besides, I know now, there was no shame in a ruined spelling test, but in Ava's squandered talent.

Although we kids lived unimpressed by our mother's creativity, Mimi always knew. She often talked about Ava's artistic abilities, agonized over her lost potential. "Such a waste," she would say and then cry.

I never saw it. I do now. My mother is Martha Stewart on crack, geeking on acrylic paints and decoupage, each project another fix. She has an endless number of ideas for creations. When the windows proved difficult to ship, Ava began painting rocks for her Etsy site. Effortlessly she paints complex geometric shapes onto palm-sized stones. She uses colors with names like salmon, teal, mango, terracotta, sand, peach, periwinkle, and violet, turning smooth, flat gray stones into colorful mandalas. River rocks become beautiful, meditative kaleidoscopes that fill the center of your hand. Ambrose suggested my mother call her rocks *prayer stones*.

The artistry that Ava has unleashed would have been helpful years before. She could have been the best Girl Scout leader or coolest room mom. We should have had creative handmade Halloween costumes and themed birthday parties. She bestowed none of her talent on her children. It pisses me off.

Last week Ava came home from a walk and told me she needed help with a trash-picking find. Since Granny Crackers and Mo were gone with the truck and Ava was insistent, I helped her carry the large, heavy entertainment center three blocks.

"Are you sure?" I asked. "Nobody buys these anymore. Everyone wants a flat screen hung on their wall."

"Oh my god, yes! I have an idea I saw on Pinterest." That week my mother crafted, painted, and refurbished the big, ugly old TV stand into the cutest play kitchen I've ever seen. She painted it all bright white and flat black, turned brown wooden cabinets into a cupboard, refrigerator, and microwave. She painted a stovetop and stenciled on knobs and burners. She sawed holes in the space meant to hold a television and dropped in a metal bowl and small faucet, creating a sink. She attached a red plastic phone to the side of the cabinet and hung red-and-white checkered curtains on the back wall, giving the illusion of a window. With black chalkboard paint she created a place where a child could write an imaginary grocery list. Shiny spoons and teacups hung from little hooks, adding charm. The more accessories she included, the more adorable the kitchen became. I stood awed by each and every transformation. I had been unaware that my mother had the ability to turn trash into treasures and to do it with such ease. Mo photographed the little kitchen and posted it on our Facebook Marketplace, and it sold within an hour.

I was ashamed at the feeling of anger that I struggled with when the little girl and her mom showed up to pick up the play kitchen. At first I wasn't even sure why I was so mad. I tried to push it away and disregard my emotions. There was no way I was jealous of a six-year-old.

I'm a mature and sophisticated fifteen. I like poetry, photography, indie music, and Sundance films. Sure, as a child I played with dolls and Barbies and loved my plastic play kitchen, a gift from Mimi. Ava probably didn't even know how I begged for a kitchen that Christmas. Now I believe those toys to be sexist and infuriating. It's a chauvinistic play that teaches little girls to wash dishes and change diapers, so why did I feel so sad?

It shouldn't matter that my mother has never made anything for me. My play days were before Pinterest and DIY projects. Maybe Ava wasn't even aware that she could have been a crafty mommy. Besides, I should be happy for her. Two months ago she was panhandling on the side of the road. Now she's an entrepreneur, selling refurbished merchandise. Suddenly I understood the frustration and sadness that Mimi always felt. What a goddamn shame, indeed.

The yellow-haired child in a lemon dress danced around the kitchen on tiptoes.

"Look, Mommy, look!" She pointed out accessories and touched teacups.

"I know, Savannah. I love it too."

"Aww, you're Savannah? So is she," Ava said, pointing at me.

Savannah! The child's name was Savannah, proving God has a mean streak, sending a little girl with my hair and my name to buy the kitchen my six-year-old-self should have had. I watched Little Savannah prance around the yard, a happy little sunshine girl. I felt the tiny bitter tears of envy fill my eyes, spill over, and roll down my cheeks.

"Are you crying?" Phoenix asked, causing everyone to stop and stare.

"No!" I turned my face away.

It took Mo, Phoenix, Ava, and me to lift the heavy play kitchen and fit it into the back of the Ford Excursion. I imagine Little Savannah has a strong, groomed daddy to go with her well-kept mommy, who will unload the kitchen from the deluxe SUV, drag it up a manicured lawn, through the heavy front door of a beautiful home, down a hallway decorated with framed family photos, and into the pinkalicious bedroom of a pretty little girl living in a perfect world. No, I am not jealous of Little Savannah, I'm simply pointing out how unfair life can be.

The rest of the day I stayed quiet. No longer angry, merely ashamed and embarrassed by my mood. I played with my phone, taking Instagram photos of junk. Industrial Art is what I call it. Lowbrow pics of tools and Mason jars filled with bolts and screws.

I didn't know that Ava had witnessed my pain, but that night she crawled into my bed and wrapped herself around me, her legs and arms circling me like tentacles of an octopus. "Savannah

Jorja, my child made of sunshine, my sweet little peach," she cooed into my ear. "I should've made you a play kitchen."

"I'm a little too big for toys." I laughed, sounding phony.

"I'm a bad mommy," she whispered.

I could tell she was high. She is always most honest when high. I remained silent and emotionless, staring at the ceiling, arms pinned to my side. I wanted to roll away from her, wiggle out of her tight embrace. I dared not move.

"I'm a fuck up," she cried. "I don't deserve my babies."

I focused on the weight of her leg across my stomach, her unwelcome arms around my chest, a python mother, her hug fierce and constricting.

"Ssssorry, Sssavannah," she hissed.

I fought the urge to slither out of her arms. She was giving me my lesson in tolerance. I willed myself to endure her tight cuddle as well as her sobbing emotions. Give her no mercy, I told myself.

I closed my eyes and imagined her tears were pills. Little pink, blue, and white pills spilled from my mother's eyes, remnants of early memories, pills strewn across her dresser or bathroom sink, pretty drugs scattered like Skittles. It's a wonder we toddlers didn't eat them.

Children who live in messy houses are born with a sixth sense. Sheltered kids get into everything. My mother never had to call Poison Control.

I allowed Ava to cry on my shoulder and whisper unwanted confessions in my ear. I tried like hell to give back nothing, no anger, sadness, or sympathy. Eventually I grew weak and allowed her to squeeze the love right out of me, until I was nothing but a tall, cool glass of orange juice, forgiveness like pulp floating to the top.

I fought a hard battle, surrendered, and then fell asleep. When I woke I was no longer being crushed. She had gone out.

Chapter Sixteen

The five of us probably resembled a circus family. Phoenix, Granny Crackers, Ava, and I accompanied Mo to the Bureau of Motor Vehicles to take his driving test. In our family, imbalanced milestones are laid across a river of dysfunction, and each developmental step toward maturity becomes a sideshow.

Montana (the she, not he) always excelled at anything with wheels. Montana learned to ride a two-wheeled bike by the age of four, can flip-kick and ollie a skateboard with ease, and bunny-hopped her Razor Scooter down flights of stairs for fun. Add a battery-powered motor to any of those toys, and she was just as fearless. When the time came for Mo to get behind the wheel of a car, the passion he felt had the same intensity, the result effortless. Mo is a natural driver.

"Too bad those driving instructors can't see the way you handle the trash-picking truck," Ava said the night before the big test. "You'd impress them for sure. Ain't none of them would believe a sweet, pretty little thing like you could drive that big ol' vehicle."

" Ava's right," Granny Crackers said, suddenly standing at attention, a notion forming in her head like a cloud of gnats.

"Mo, you're gonna drive the truck tomorrow to take your test," she said.

"I can't drive that thing," protested Mo.

"The hell you can't, child. You have been driving it all summer long."

"But it's a clunker, big and filthy, with a rusted bed full of furniture and junk. Besides, it's probably prohibited, taking your test in a trash truck."

"I don't see why. The truck is legal. Gots its tags, two plates, insurance, working lights, rearview mirrors, and seat belts. The load is strapped down tight and secured."

"Granny Crackers, are you drunk?" Mo interrupted. "Everybody's gonna laugh at me." Listening in disbelief, I opened the fridge door to see if Granny Crackers had been drinking, but her forty-ounce was still chilling. Maybe Granny Crackers wasn't thinking about the condition of the truck, just that Mo could handle the hideous beast.

I know for a fact a person can get used to ugly things. I've seen the truck so many times that I don't notice it anymore. A year ago the very thought of sitting in the truck felt like a cruel punishment. Since then I've sat on its cracked vinyl seats a thousand times. I've climbed up its sides and back and flung trash over the high wooden pen extending the bed. I've smelled its exhaust, unloaded its treasures, hand cranked the windows down, and listened to its tunes on the radio and its melody of creaking and grinding.

Actually it was Mo who led me to embrace the offensive vehicle. He ignored the blue front side panel on the white truck, a redneck auto repair done by Uncle Ross. Mo didn't mind the clunky baby shoes that hung in the rearview mirror, and he laughed when Granny Crackers zip-tied the stuffed bunny to the front grill. The dirty, deranged-looking rabbit, once a soft, pretty blue Easter gift, was outgrown and tossed to the trash, only to be plucked from the pile and made into a trash-picker's mascot.

Mo drove the truck like a cowboy comedian. He laughed at

its vulgarity and was awed by its muscle. To Mo the trash truck was a recreational vehicle. He drove it with the same enthusiasm he'd had if he'd been mud running or competing in a demolition derby. Driving through our hood, he was proud. Everybody knew the truck and everything else Granny Crackers owned. Outside Paris Village, who cared what people thought? We were there to pick trash, and we held our own opinions. But to take it to the Department of Motor Vehicles for a driving exam seemed not only distasteful, but also insane, especially when you had a more appropriate car sitting in your driveway.

"Them driving instructors ain't gonna laugh at you," said Granny Crackers. "They're gonna shit their pants watching a tiny, young thing like you drive like a damn trucker."

Mo looked over at Phoenix and me. The three of us consoled each other by locking eyes, acutely aware that Ava and Granny Crackers were not only serious, but crazy enough to force Mo to drive the heinous trash truck to the DMV.

"Maybe if we unload it, the truck won't look so bad," suggested Phoenix.

"No, child. That would defeat the purpose," snapped Granny Crackers. "The truck needs to be stacked for the full effect. The whole point is for them instructors to view Mo's mobility skills. Child's a damn prodigy when it comes to driving. Prodigies show their best work. I bet you kids not one of them people at the Bureau of Motor Vehicles could pass maneuverability with a long-bed truckload, but Montana can."

"But what if I hit something?" muttered Mo, eyes filling with tears.

"You won't."

"How do you know?"

"Because I believe in you," Granny Crackers responded. "It's a lesson for all of you," she said, pointing to everyone in the room.

"In life, rare talents and great gifts seldom reveal themselves. It's up to you to seize the moments. There is a time to be humble and a time to be proud. Ya got to know the difference. When it's your turn to shine, do it big, bright, and completely unashamed."

"Granny Crackers is right." Ava stepped forward and cupped Mo's nervous face in her shaky hands. "Go ahead and shine," she said, planting a kiss on his forehead. "Go in the trash truck with Granny Crackers." She added, "I'll be there with the Oldsmobile just in case they won't let you drive the Ford. You can do this, baby!"

Granny Crackers and Ava were pumped. Although it was a crazy idea, arguing wouldn't make any difference.

"You got this!" I said, putting a hand on Mo's shoulder "Who gives a shit what it looks like? You've been driving it all summer for fun, and you handle it like a boss."

"Yeah!" said Phoenix "Show 'em what you can do."

The next day Granny Crackers agreed to close The Barrel so Phoenix and I could go and watch. The instructor assigned to Mo was a large, soft man who looked as if he were made from dough, constructed with rolls. I was proud of Mo as he bravely escorted the portly instructor to the truck. Two minutes later they walked back into the building. Mo pointed to Granny Crackers, who stood rocking on the heels of her moccasin feet, hands buried deep in the pockets of her overalls.

"Ma'am," called the driving instructor, waddling toward us. "Are you this child's guardian?"

"I am."

"And is that your truck out there?"

"It is."

"Do you have another car she can drive? Or perhaps you know someone with another car your granddaughter can test in." Mo ignored his gender mistake. We were picking our battles carefully, and pronouns weren't included.

"Is there a problem?" asked Granny Crackers.

"Well, ma'am, that's quite a load there. It seems highly unfair and more than a bit unconventional to allow this child to take her driving exam in a fully loaded, large-bed pickup truck."

"Is there a law that reads she can't take her test in a filled pickup truck?"

"Well, ma'am, no, I don't know of any law in particular that states it. It's just horse sense, if you know what I mean."

"Are you implying I don't have the sense God gave a horse?"

"No, ma'am, I'm not implying that at all. I'm just thinking you should probably reschedule your granddaughter's test and bring her back with a standard or small-size car. Something she can maneuver around objects."

"Thanks for your concern, but Montana can maneuver that truck like it's a small car, so I don't think we're gonna be rescheduling anything. If there's no rule about driving exams and pickup trucks, then she's good to go."

The driving instructor, dumbstruck, motioned Granny Crackers to follow him outside, so we all did. Casually he stood beside the truck and pointed out its contents, as if we hadn't just driven it up there ourselves and knew about its load.

"Look at this, ma'am," he said, "a patio table, chairs, large umbrella, dresser, lumber, crown molding, a door, a bed frame, a rake, and hoe. Now, ma'am, I'm just naming the stuff that's visible. No telling what else is in that bed."

Granny Crackers stood there peeved when the examiner pointed his fat fingers and talked down to her. She showed no emotion.

"Now, do you see that car over there?" he asked, nodding toward a little silver Honda Civic. "The last teen I tested drove that car. Looking at these two vehicles, ma'am, wouldn't you agree that it's highly unfair that your granddaughter has to pass a maneuverability test in this truck and somebody else gets to take their test in that car?" He talked to Granny Crackers as if indeed she did not have the sense of a horse.

Finally, after a moment of silence and a steely gaze, Granny Crackers responded. "Life is unfair," she began. "It's unfair that you gonna look at me and my truck and then talk to me like I'm stupid. It's unfair that what comes naturally for some is a struggle for others. It's unfair that you, sir, a driving instructor who thinks he knows everything, will never be able to drive as well as this child here. Now if there is nothing in the guidelines about hauling a load during a driving exam, it's time for Montana to take her test."

"Have it your way, ma'am."

By the time the two had finished their exchange, the parking lot held curious onlookers. Word about Mo, Granny Crackers, the examiner, and the F-150 had spread. People waiting patiently at the bureau for tags and titles came outside, eager to watch the pretty trans boy maneuver the load.

Mo quickly jumped behind the steering wheel and waited patiently while the instructor slowly and laboriously hauled himself up into the passenger's seat.

Once situated, the two headed toward the tall white coordinated poles, and people followed. They flowed from the flat gray cement building like they were about to watch an after-school fight and formed a circle a few feet from the course.

The onlookers laughed, talked, and pointed at the truck. I kept my eyes on Mo. He pulled forward through the poles with ease and off to the side for a momentary stop. In thirty seconds or so he had checked mirrors and made an innate calculation of distance, space, and speed. Biting his bottom lip, he palmed the top of the steering wheel as if giving his hand to a dance partner and effortlessly swam the truck backwards, like a fish in the current. It was a complicated choreographed double twist between two obstacles made in one swift, graceful movement.

It was over almost as soon as it began. The crowd roared, nobody as loud as Ava. If Mo started out as a spectacle, he ended a pro. He gave a half grin and quick wave to the cheering fans in the parking lot, and with the smirking instructor by his side, he headed out into the streets for the road test.

Although his full name, Montana, is printed on his driver's license and under *sex* it says *female*, Mo couldn't have been happier. She/he exited that truck a conquering hero.

"Ambrose is making a celebratory dinner for Mo," Granny Crackers said when she hung up the phone. "Everybody needs to be ready to go at six."

I could tell she was pissed off at Ava when she backed out at the last minute. My mother—Ava, Ava, quite contrary, beamed with pride for Mo one minute and opted out of his party the next. She makes no damn sense.

Dixie opened the door when we got to Ambrose's house and led us into the kitchen. On the table sat a homemade chocolate cake in a rectangular pan, the words "Go Mo" were piped out in a shaky scrawl.

"Look here what I made ya," Dixie said to Mo, pointing at the dessert.

"Wow, Dixie, you made me a cake? It's awesome." It was obvious Mo was touched.

Dixie had taken a matchbox truck and pushed it across the top of the cake, making toy tire marks. She parked the toy on a heap of chocolate icing in the bottom right corner. "I love cake," said Dixie. "It's probably my favorite food, so any excuse to make one is fine by me."

"Let's go see what Ambrose is cooking," Granny Crackers said, following the smell out the backdoor. A scrumptious white fog rose from a tall rectangular metal black box, setting my mouth watering.

"What's in the smoker?" asked Granny Crackers.

"A pork butt. Been smokin' twelve hours." Ambrose grinned.

"Ambrose, you've been cooking this meal for twelve hours? For me?" Clearly Mo was overcome by the generosity of Granny Crackers's two best friends.

"Sweetheart, you deserve a slow-cooked feast. You've made history as the first and last child to take a maneuverability test in a long-bed F-150 overloaded with cargo."

"Well, I didn't have much of a choice," said Mo, eyeing Granny Crackers.

A shiny little red Mazda was parked in Ambrose's drive, and on a table sat a tub of Turtle Wax and a polishing cloth. Ambrose must have been busy all day.

"You get a new car?" Mo asked.

"Well, no, it's not mine," said Ambrose. "A friend bought it used, paid me to look it over, do some repairs and clean it up."

"That's dope." Mo circled the vehicle, checking it out. "It looks good. Real nice."

"Yup," agreed Ambrose. "It's plenty nice."

An hour later we sat on lawn chairs, plates balanced on our knees, and ate pulled pork and coleslaw sandwiches with cabbage and carrots picked from the community garden. We talked about the day. Mo, Phoenix, and I took turns mimicking the driving instructor, acting out the scene. When Granny Crackers pantomimed her version, we all roared. Laughter fell like rain, flooding the backyard. A downpour of snorts and chuckles came from Ambrose and Dixie as they slapped their knees and sipped their Pabst. Ambrose's rich, thunderous voice guffawed until tears fell from his eyes. We waded through giggles, eating chocolate cake. When the mosquitoes came out, it was time to go in.

As we said our goodbyes, Ambrose pulled a set of keys from his jeans pocket and placed them in Granny Crackers's hand. The gesture silenced the rest of us and caused a hopeful anticipation. Granny Crackers handed the keys off to Mo.

A surge of emotion filled his eyes with tears. Phoenix and I shared a look, both knowing that the same milestone in our lives would not create the same stir. No second little Mazda will be in the driveway when I get my license a year from now. A deep-center understanding overpowered any jealousy, and it was okay. This rite of passage was truly a Mo moment. That solemn and pretty trans-boy deserves something good. Besides, if you're forced to take your driving exam in a big, ugly, fully loaded trash truck, you should be rewarded with a little red Mazda.

"Wipe them tears, child. What's the matter with you?" scolded Granny Crackers.

"You bought me a car?" squeaked Mo, wiping at his eyes.

"Goodness, no, don't be crazy. I bought myself a car that you may drive."

"Oh?" said Mo, clearly confused.

"Y'all kids run me ragged," Granny Crackers explained. "School's 'bout to start, and things are just gonna get worse, activities and errands, and all three of you needin' to be somewhere all the time. I can't keep up and run The Barrel. Mo, I'm expecting you to help out. Y'all know how selfish I am with my Oldsmobile, and the trash truck is for trash-picking. I bought this little car to taxi everybody around, and I'm making you my taxi driver."

I'd never seen Mo so excited. He was glowing, haloed in an exuberant aura, caught in a bubble of happiness.

"Let's take the long way home," Granny Crackers said,

opening up the passenger door. Mo drove up and down the one-way streets, zigzagging through our neighborhood, circling block after block. A country song sailed out our open windows, the evening air drifted in, and I was thinking I wish every day could be this good.

As we neared the squatters' house, life suddenly stalled. In slow motion our beautiful day came crashing down. Mo eased the Mazda to a stop just as Ava tumbled out the front door of the forsaken house. We watched in horror. Our mother—a zombie, half-dead—stumbled across the porch on tiptoe. Her head was slumped to one side, long brown hair covering her face like a veil, her limbs loose and limp. Ava spilled down five cement steps, a ragdoll in a waterfall, cascading over concrete. She landed, face smashed, onto the pavement. Granny Crackers was the first one out of the car, her purse in hand. She rushed to our mother, flipped her on her back, quickly checked her mouth, and began compressions.

"Help!" she screamed to the three frozen kids in the car.

We jumped from the vehicle. I called 911.

"My mom," I said, "I think she's dead." Bright red blood from the fall dripped over her baby blue lips, and her olive skin was white.

"My bag! My bag!" Granny Crackers shouted.

"What? What do you need?" cried Mo.

Granny Crackers was focused on Ava, pumping her chest, breathing into her mouth. I imagine it's hard to talk when performing CPR. "Nasal spray," Granny Crackers said between breaths. Mo upturned the full purse onto the walk and frantically rummaged through the contents.

"There!" Granny Crackers said when Mo's hand touched a small white bottle.

He handed the bottle to Granny Crackers, who stopped doing compressions, looked it over, and then shoved it up my mother's nostril and sprayed, filling her nose with Narcan. The four of us froze again, watching, waiting for Ava's breath to return, as if waiting for a loved one on a train.

The sirens approached as my mother's eyes fluttered open. Behind the ambulance, trailing in his police car, was Officer Miller. The paramedics surrounded Ava, quickly moving around her stone-statue children.

"Congratulations," said a medic to Granny Crackers. "You just successfully reversed an opioid overdose."

"Well done, Rosie."

The sad fact is my mother nearly died. Just as tragic, my great-grandma carries overdose spray in her purse while other grandmothers tote around Rolaids.

As two paramedics checked Ava's vitals, another checked Granny Crackers.

My mother was loaded onto a stretcher and disappeared into the back of an ambulance. Granny Crackers was still on her knees, crouching where Ava had lain.

I stared down at her, my gaze riveted. I couldn't help myself. Silently I pressed her image into my mind, taking in every characteristic of my newfound hero. Her gnarled fingers like claws pressed the ground. Her white hair lifted in feathery wisps above tired and watery seafoam-green eyes. Her face reminded me of dried cracked earth, her story written in the deep wrinkled lines on her brown, suntanned skin. I had never seen anyone look frailer yet more fierce.

"You take this house down or I will," she said, looking up at Officer Miller.

"I got this, Rosie," he said, helping her up.

We Crackers solemnly climbed back into the Mazda and headed home just as more police cruisers were arriving.

A poem written by Savannah Jorja:

MY GREAT-GRANDMOTHER'S PURSE

She's a ragtag,
A curmudgeon,
With a purse like a dungeon,

A deep, dark cavernous bag
Weathered, leather
And full of treasures.

She carries odd and ordinary things
Teabags, a gold ring,
Scraps of paper, old receipts,
Cough drops, and butterscotch sweets.

She collects Altoid tins.
Only one is full of mints;
The others hold Band-Aids,
Rubber bands, and paper clips.

She has three tubes of color for bright red lips.
She cuts clippings; likes her folded news:
Obituaries, coupons,
And political views.

Has goats-milk lotion for her hands
And an old ticking watch with a broken band,

A bingo dauber, talcum powder,
A bottle of Windsong from Prince Matchabelli,
A little container of petroleum jelly,

And in her bag is a little purse
To hold coins and spare keys;
Claims her face cream is priceless,
Yet it's a Dollar Store container of vitamin E.

She has wadded tissues and denture glue,
A pack of Freedent, a bag of cashews,
And a slew
Of many other extraordinary things,

But my very favorite treasure of all
Is a small
Nasal spray of Narcan.

Like an old medicine man,
Her behavior
A savior,

Strong and calm
As she saved my mom.

Yes, they call her Crackers;
Say she's whackers,

But I know Rosie
Is cozy
With God.

Chapter Seventeen

*A*va was hospitalized for two weeks, not because she was sick physically, just mentally. Her erratic behavior in the first twenty-four hours led to a transfer to the psych ward. Mo, Phoenix, and I visited Ava every day at seven p.m. during family hour. Granny Crackers stayed home. During our visits our mother was quiet and ashamed.

She reminded me of the vacant houses that have taken over our neighborhood, ghost structures with boarded-up doors and crumbling walls. No longer strong, she was like a memory, or rather a silhouette of the spirit that used to live inside her, before the light in her eyes went out.

We took her sweatpants and T-shirts from home, along with chewing gum, a sketchpad, and some pencils. Withdrawn, she quietly thanked us for our visits and gifts with half smiles and whispered gratitude. Each visit was awkward and painful. Still we went, simply because if seven o'clock came and we weren't there, the guilt would be excruciating.

Granny Crackers, on the other hand, freed herself from obligation and pity. "I don't do hospitals," she said.

I wish I could adopt that attitude. Hospitals are no fun unless you're visiting a new baby. All the other rooms are full of sickness and pain. No matter how sad a floor is, the psych ward has a different sort of gloom, hemmed in by dismal white walls and cold dingy tile.

The psychiatric wing is behind locked double doors. Attached to the wall is a buzzer to ring you in. We shyly wave through the small window to the gatekeeper. He smiles back and pushes a button. The heavy door clicks, and we heave it open, entering a commons area with patients young and old, male and female wandering about. We can easily distinguish the patients from the visitors. We have shoes on our feet, while the patients wander around in socks.

The nurse's station is directly inside the room. It's a watch-tower, really, guarding the mentally ill. The first thing you must do is sign in, and before leaving you must sign out, every visit recorded, down to the minute. Beyond the nurse's station are three couches framing an ugly square of carpet. The sofas are angled to watch the same television, which is usually airing some stupid drama or an inappropriate reality show, which makes me believe the patients control the TV.

Tables and chairs where families sit together having uncomfortable conversations face one another. We took a pizza once. Our mother nibbled on the same piece for the full hour. We started taking Uno cards, playing a game or two; it helped fill the uneasy time, giving us something to focus on. Two hallways jut from the commons, one on each side. To the west are the men's rooms, and to the east are the women's. To the north, hidden away, are padded rooms for anyone who needs a time out.

The people milling about are as bland as the decor. Everything looks depressed. There is no art adorning the walls on the psych ward. No sparkle or interior decoration. Personally I think it would be appropriate to hang up a van Gogh or maybe Edvard Munch's, *The Scream*. I mean really, what could it hurt? And it would add some color to an otherwise colorless world.

While we played cards I couldn't help people watching. Honestly, I was completely captivated by the anguish. Although it was wrenching on my tender heart and sensitive soul, I didn't look away. I pushed through my empathy, fought tears and fears, ignored pathos and pity, and challenged my mind. It was a vain attempt to make myself hard and strong, so life didn't hurt so much. For the most part the patients looked normal, just sad and displaced. It made me wonder what the hell happened that landed them in an insane asylum. Some can't hide their crazy, and it's scary. They wander in circles, talk to everyone, talk to themselves, pick at their skin, pull at their hair, bother the nurses, beg to use the phone, and inappropriately talk, cry, laugh, swear, or shriek.

I took long walks during the day, before going to the hospital. We all needed an escape. Mo sped off in the Mazda, Phoenix on his bike, and me on foot. We went our separate ways in the daylight on solitary journeys, feeling depressed and alone. We were like sad lushes, boozing on sunbeams, propelled strictly by solar energy and the primal need to move.

Somehow Mateo joined me. The first time was accidental. I was walking by the corner store as he was coming out. He was loaded down with bags, so I offered to carry the milk.

"I'm sorry about your mom," he said scuffling his feet "Is she doing okay?"

"Yeah, she's better." Everybody had heard about Ava's collapse, her brush with death, her resurrection by Granny Crackers, and the raid that brought down the squatters' house.

During the rest of the time, Mateo thought up random things to talk about. He told me stupid jokes, complained about his brother, talked shit about his neighbor, and said anything at all to relieve the uncomfortable silence wrapped around me like an itchy blanket. I appreciated the gesture.

The next day I found myself strolling by Mateo's house, a subliminal route change. As I passed his front lawn, he came skipping down the front steps of the crowded porch, waving back to his family and friends as if he were leaving a party.

"Hey, wait up," he called. We strolled down the cracked and uneven sidewalk of our rough neighborhood with no particular destination. We walked past rows of eclectic houses and oddball yards, lawns as distinctly different as their residents; a family of garden gnomes behind a picket fence; an open patch of green strewn with toddler toys, balls, and bikes; a garden of political signs, opinions lined up like tomato stakes; a honeysuckle-covered fence, high grass, and trash.

We turned the corner by the coin laundry and bar, walked the perimeter of the community garden, passed the Dollar Store, barber shop, and beer drive-through, stopped at the 7-Eleven for an Icee, and then cruised down the railroad tracks. Mateo skipped from tie to tie as I walked the rail like a balance beam. Shyly, he reached out and took hold of my hand.

Mateo and I walked hand in hand every afternoon for the two weeks my mother was in the hospital, and he talked the entire time. That boy rambled on and on, jumping from subject to subject, asking questions and then answering them, telling jokes and stories, waving to strangers, and skipping over cracks. Honestly, I think he's ADD and probably off his meds for the summer. Regardless, he's charming, cute, and funny, and he took my mind off Ava and all the drama.

Mateo was honest and interesting, an open book, narrating his story. My pages were glued shut, so I quietly listened. Sadly, Mateo and I have common ground. Like my mother and biological father, Mateo's dad is locked away. He's an undocumented immigrant. He made a left turn at 4:10 p.m. from a lane that prohibits turns during the hours of four to six p.m. Monday through

Friday and was pulled over. With no driver's license and no papers, he was put in jail and placed on an immigration hold from ICE. Now he's waiting for mercy, a court date, or deportation, whichever comes first.

Since his father's arrest, Mateo's mother lives in constant fear, despite having her working papers. Mateo and his family live with his aunt. The house is crowded and everybody's scared. They moved because without his father they could no longer pay their rent and because Paris Village is nestled inside a sanctuary city. Still, his mother lives her life like she resides in a horror movie, anticipating a boogieman around every corner. She no longer goes to church or picnics and refuses to have quinceanera for his sister. Mateo's mother cries all the time. Mateo says she's not rational.

"She has papers to work here. They can't take her away, but she hears stories about kids in cages and people with papers being detained. I don't know how she has any tears left," he said.

"If only you could bottle them," I replied, trying to lighten the mood. "Sell her tears as sorrow water to masochists and poets." The look on Mateo's face reminded me that I don't speak like my peers, perhaps because I'm fixated and perplexed by suffering. However, this I know: regardless of the shit I've been through, I can't imagine what it's like for Mateo's mom or dad. To live undocumented must be a sentence from hell, being horrified that at any moment your family will be taken, imprisoned, and torn apart. Mateo's mom starts and ends every day terrified. She is walking a nightmare, hiding in the shadows. She lives with relentless panic. She must miss her husband terribly. She fears her babies will be ripped from her arms and placed in foster care and she will be shipped back to a hellhole she courageously escaped. Her troubles are an ocean of crashing waves, too deep and vast for me to fully grasp.

Unfortunately I do know what it feels like for Mateo and his siblings, the heartbreak of waking up one day to find your parent gone. I cannot imagine an ache worse than the pain of losing Mimi. As far as our parents, the difference is Mateo's dad is a tireless and talented construction worker, a faithful and loving husband and father, a devout Catholic. My dad was a drug dealer. Mateo's mom is a lioness, who believes her sole purpose is to protect her cubs. My mom is a misguided free bird, who flies off to get high and nearly dies.

The reality of these truths pierced my heart and caused me to cry, prompting Mateo to lean in and kiss me. His touch ignited a spark on my trembling lips that stopped my tears and aroused my smile.

I carried that smile inside me all day and to the hospital in the evening. I gestured to the gatekeeper, who looked hesitant, maybe confused or something. He waved before buzzing us in.

As Mo was signing in, a nurse approached with hesitation. "Um, I'm sorry, kids, but your mother has been released."

I looked to Mo, waiting for him to say something, but he was speechless, completely deflated. I watched him as he slowly slid down the wall, slumping below the counter. He looked like a marionette, lifeless after play, with wobbly wooden limbs held together by strings. He folded into himself, sinking into a puddle of hopelessness, his shaven head bent to the ground, his pretty, feminine face hidden in his small hands.

With Mo broken beside me, I was the one who had to speak up—me, the weak one. "Released?" I questioned. "To who? Why didn't she call us? Who picked her up? Where did she go? What do you mean, our mother was released?"

The nurse gently spoke. "Oh, sweetheart, I'm so sorry, but I can't tell you that."

"No!" wailed Phoenix, standing behind me, his icy scream freezing the room. My hysterical baby brother, only thirteen years old, yet nearly six feet tall and beautifully brown; a boy like that can get in trouble. My frantic thoughts raced for his protection, whispered pleas and prayers. *Stop, Phoenix,* I thought. *Please don't go off. Hold it together, man. You're on a psych ward. They will lock you up, drug you.*

"That bitch!" he yelled. Picking up a blue plastic chair, he hurled it up against the double doors. "I fucking hate her!" His rage echoed between the drab walls.

Mo stared up from his lotus position, but said nothing.

"Hey, son," hollered a big, bald, black security guy, approaching on the run, charging Phoenix like a bull, his wide nostrils flaring, bulging muscles popping out of short sleeves.

"Don't hurt him," I breathlessly mumbled, praying over and over. Within seconds the security guard wrapped himself around Phoenix in a restraint, or at least I thought Phoenix was being restrained. Instead he was caught in a bear hug. The black man rocked back and forth with Phoenix pinned inside his giant arms, slowly swaying, as if soothing a baby. He held Phoenix like a father would, the father missing from Phoenix's life, from all of our lives.

My brother broke down in the stranger's arms, sobbing like the child he actually was, and that grown, muscular, dynamic man cried too. He held my brother in his arms, tears rolling down his black face like oil droplets, and every nurse, crazy psychopath, lonely, depressed, drug-addicted, paranoid freak wept along with him.

When it was over three minutes later, we walked out the double doors—three misfit children: a caramel-colored mixed man-child, a beautiful broken trans boy, and a lanky blond girl, leaving behind scattered pieces of our broken hearts that were quickly swept up.

Chapter Eighteen

After my mother left, sadness moved into our home like a rude, unwanted houseguest. Depression was more than a feeling; it was a presence. Depression lounged on our furniture with its feet up, took over the TV, and invaded our space. Days felt monotonous and long. Everything was dull.

It may seem ludicrous to miss a bad mother so much. It's complicated. Yes, Ava is erratic, unstable, and crazy. She's also witty, creative, beautiful, and loving, and she appeared at a time when she was desperately needed. Unreliable Ava, spinning out of control, crash-landed in our lives while we were stranded on an island of mourning. We were sad, missing our Mimi, and then our mom showed up with a backpack full of problems and a sto-len dog and painted our blue days yellow.

My mother reminds me of her painting palette. Her vibrant moods are swirls of color. She is witty, kooky orange one minute and reckless, sexy red the next. She is shades of sunshine and sunflower petals, and she is a circle of black, burrowing in a deep hole of depression and sadness. My mom is sincerely flawed and beautiful, making it hard not to fall in love with her.

Ava's abandonment flipped my emotions upside down. Rejection turns love to hate. I took my anger to the communi-ty garden. I tilled my fury and pain into the soil, clawing at the ground and pulling up weeds. I turned gardening into a street fight. My bare hands dug up potatoes and carrots, snapped beans and cucumbers from vines, deadheaded the marigolds. Ambrose didn't question, lecture, or judge my mood. Instead he gave me laborious jobs to do and took advantage of my aggressive energy and the need to tear something apart.

"Come here, Savannah. I'm gonna teach you how to properly weed the beds," said Ambrose, handing me a hoe. "Always hoe the garden before you water. You want the earth to be as dry as it can be. And stand up tall. Good posture will make it easier on your back."

I stood straight, holding the long-handled tool, its thin, sharp metal blade resting on the ground.

"The trick is to sweep the ground with the hoe, like you're sweeping the floor. That's good," he said, "Make broad fluid strokes right over the tops of those weeds. Slice off their heads."

I did exactly as Ambrose instructed. I liked swinging the hoe back and forth. Soon my momentum picked up. It felt good expelling energy.

"Now you're gonna do the weed stems," Ambrose said. "Aim to sweep just below the surface of the soil. Careful now, you're gonna chop off your toes, swinging like that. Accuracy, Savannah Jo. You got to be precise, or you're gonna take out plants you want to keep."

I slowed my aggression and focused my aim. I switched hands, rubbed out the soreness. Ambrose brought me gloves, and I began swinging again. I worked on the earth until sweat ran down my face. Once I cleared a bed, Ambrose pointed me to another. I weeded bed after bed, thinking of Ava, swinging the hoe back and forth like a pendulum. If only I could turn back time.

My swaying arms felt as heavy as my thoughts, my back

ached, my hands blistered. I talked to myself in affirmations. Push through the pain, keep going, be strong. When I could endure no more, I stopped hoeing and cried. Ambrose brought me lemonade. I watered the garden with my tears. Ambrose sat silently beside me.

"Were you raised on a farm?" I asked Ambrose, regaining my composure.

"A farm? No, baby, I was raised in an apartment in the city."

"Who taught you to garden?"

"Now that's an interesting story," Ambrose said, smiling. "Fact is, Savannah Jo, I learned it when I was in prison." A silence fell between us as Ambrose locked his milky brown eyes on my watery blues.

I sat speechless, afraid to talk. His truth had spun me into a vortex of confusion. My mind raced with thoughts, my emotions with anxiety. How could Ambrose have been in prison? He is the wisest, kindest, and most gentle man I have ever met. I asked him nothing. I didn't want to know. I wanted to have one pure soul in my life, one untarnished being, one guru. Ambrose told me his story anyway.

"It was 1968, a tumultuous time in history. I had just come home from Vietnam. Martin Luther King, Jr, had just been shot. I was mad as hell. My very soul burned with fury. One night I got in a bar fight with two white men. I didn't care much for white folks, cuz as I seen it, they didn't like me. Any contempt or prejudice they gave me, I returned with a vengeance. Those two men started a fight, and it ended with me beating them both to near death. I was charged with attempted murder and felonious assault, which was crazy, since it was two against one, and in my mind I had not attempted to kill anyone. However, if they had died, I wouldn't have shed a tear. I had no remorse, just more anger. Ironically it took ten years in prison to cool my temperature and change my perception. I guess you can say I'm rehabilitated."

"Did you find religion?" I asked.

"No, baby, I discovered humanity, the pure goodness of human beings."

Ambrose took a moment before he began speaking again, as if pulling forth a memory that was sacredly tucked away. "Down the road from the prison lived a family, a farmer, Samuel Merritt, his wife, Eliza, and their slew of towheaded children. Sam was a big guy, strong, tough, ruggedly handsome. He was the kind of man who wasn't afraid of criminals. Eliza had a natural beauty, a round and curvy figure, the sweet smile of a mother, and long blond hair she kept hidden under a straw hat. Eliza was as fearless as Samuel, and she could outwork any man. The two were not the flowery, psychedelic sixties hippies you hear about, yet they were free spirits, unconventional, and they had made an agreement with the warden.

"Every day Sam would pick up a few choice prisoners and take them to his farm to work. One day he took a chance on me. I must have done something right, because the next day he asked for me by name. It was wonderful to get away from the confinement of a prison wall, to walk in fields of gold, and see farm animals and running, laughing children. It felt as if Samuel Merritt had taken me from hell to heaven. Of course, in the evening he drove us back to the underworld. You'd think it would be hard to return to the penitentiary after being on a farm all day, but I landed each evening in my cell tired, completely worn out. And for the first time in years I slept good.

"Sam and Eliza had a poultry farm, sold chickens and eggs. I guess prisoners aren't supposed to mind snapping the necks of chickens. It bothered me. Sam noticed. Instead of taking me back to prison and getting someone else to do the job, he put me to work in his massive vegetable garden. There I fell in love with agriculture and the backbreaking, laborious task of cultivating the earth and growing food.

"I helped in the garden throughout the summer and into harvest. When winter came, Sam stopped asking for me. I thought my days on the farm were over, but as soon as the ground thawed, I was once again handpicked.

"In a garden, you can lose yourself and find yourself at the same time. Problem was I didn't like the man I found. Poverty, prejudice, and Vietnam had ingrained hatred in my heart. I stopped thinking about myself and started to ponder Eliza and Sam. I found it astounding that they put faith in convicted criminals and gave unfortunate souls a chance. This white couple showed no judgment, trusted me—a black man accused of attempted murder—near their home and around their children and worked me no harder than they worked themselves. They were true humanitarians. They never preached or tried to save souls. They weren't earning brownie points or trying to get into heaven. They had no agenda. They were just morally kind and altruistic. Their mercy didn't send me to my knees begging for salvation or professing my sins. Our relationship was not that dramatic. It simply made me a better man, and no longer angry.

"Ya know, Savannah Jo, Buddha said that anger is a hot coal, and by holding it to throw at someone, you end up burning yourself. Baby, you can't take your mama's leaving as personal. Nothing others do is because of you. People have their own reality and perceptions. And sometimes things need to be broken so they can be fixed."

"What if she can't be fixed?" I asked.

"Them what if's are dangerous thoughts, Savannah Jo. The road of what if's leads to the state of misery."

Ambrose patted me on the head and walked away, leaving me

sitting alone in the dirt with a tear-stained face. I know Ambrose told me his story to impart wisdom or teach me a lesson. Honestly, I found the man as confusing as Jesus, talking to me in parables. I was still having trouble getting past the fact that Ambrose, my touchstone, had been in prison.

Chapter Nineteen

$\mathcal{E}$ ach summer Mateo's aunt pitches a tent in the backyard and sends her houseful of children outside to sleep. They love it. They spend every night wishing on stars, catching fireflies in Mason jars, playing flashlight tag, and roasting hotdogs and marshmallows in a bonfire. It's summer camp at home.

Whenever the opportunity arises, Mateo and I hide in the tent and kiss. Mateo didn't give me my first kiss. Still, I never knew kissing could feel so good. There was a boy from my old school named Mitch McCurdy. Mitch and I would linger after lunch, waiting around until the coast was clear, hiding behind the gym door after the bell rang, to practice French kissing. It was a game he thought up and I unenthusiastically played. He was an eager boy excited to have a willing mouth to rehearse on, and I was a fourteen-year-old girl with a dying Mimi, trying to feel something. Mitch's tongue was quick and aggressive, probing my mouth like a dental tool, foreign and uncomfortable. It was nothing like kissing Mateo.

Mateo slips me the tongue slowly and cautiously, as if asking for permission. I'm now the eager one, opening my mouth wider, welcoming the intrusion. His sugar plum lips are full and sweet, his butterfly wing touches send tingles down my spine. It's way too much and not enough. We lay in the hot tent, sweaty and sticky, listening to the chatty Spanish voices of his siblings. As we kiss, I hear their unleashed play and boundless energy circling the yard. Our hidden caresses feel risky, sneaky, exciting, and fun.

I love kissing Mateo. I could do it all day long, needing nothing more than the feel of his honeyed lips on my neck and ear, his mouth pressed to mine. It's not the same for Mateo. His hands have started to wander. At first it was over my clothes, a barrier of cotton between our flesh; now it's under my shirt. His fingers brush across my nipples, which are suddenly brought to attention. His touch sends sensations through my body. I feel a startling and shameful pulse between my legs. It's terrifying, partly because it feels good.

The first time Mateo stuck his hand up my shirt, neither one of us knew what to do. I lay motionless—a stiff corpse—as he palmed my boob like he was squeezing a tennis ball. He's gotten better, and I'm more compliant; however, I have put up unvoiced caution tape, forming boundaries. Mateo's fingers trace the top of my cutoff jean shorts and the outline of my zipper. I move his hands, push them back up to my chest. Mateo hugs me tighter, pushes himself up against my hip. I feel his hardness through his nylon gym shorts. Alarms sound. It makes me tense, anxious, unsure of myself. Still, I keep kissing.

I talked to Mo about Mateo. It may sound odd to go to a sexually confused trans boy with my intimate secrets on sexual flirtations and frustrations, but before he was Mo, she was Montana, my big sister and best friend, and I went to Montana for everything. It's a hard habit to break.

"I think I'm a tease," I confessed.

"Why would you think that?"

"Because I love kissing Mateo," I said, smiling.

"So?"

"No, I mean I really like it."

"Yeah well, what else do you like?" Mo inquired with a smirk.

"He's gone up my shirt." I blushed. "He gave me a hickey." I pulled the collar on my T-shirt down and showed Mo the small purple mark at the top of my breast.

"Savannah Jorja!" He scolded me.

"I liked that too," I admitted. "I didn't at first. In the beginning I was nervous to have him touch me. Honestly, he wasn't very good at it. He squeezed my boobs like they were water balloons."

Mo laughed. "Girl, you crack me up."

I raised my eyebrows, a shit-eating grin plastered on my face, insecurities lined up like naughty children hidden behind my smile. "But I don't want to do anything else," I said, turning serious.

"Does he try?"

"Yeah, a little bit. I mean he's nice and sweet, but his hands wander, and I push them from private places."

"Don't be afraid to tell him no when he strays into forbidden territory."

"I do," I said, hesitating a moment before I whispered, "but I can feel him grow. We're just kissing and hugging. That's all. I swear. Then suddenly a hard bulge in his shorts is throbbing against my thigh. It scares the hell out of me."

"Well, he can't help that," Mo said tenderly. "Truth is, the boy probably gets a stiffy just by looking at you."

Mo's bluntness caused me to look down.

"But that ain't your fault, Savannah Jo, no more than it's his. That's just hormones. However, we're not animals, and you don't have to do anything you don't want to do."

"Yeah but, does it make me a tease or slutty, to kiss Mateo, let him go up my shirt, get him all worked up, and then tell him no?" My question triggered a moment of silence.

Mo responded with a cocked head, furrowed brow, and pouty

lips, a sure sign that a lecture was coming. "No, it doesn't make you a tease," Mo began, "it makes you innocent. So you like kissing. Guess what? Everybody does. And just because you let someone on second base doesn't mean they get to touch your mound or steal home. It's your body, your rights. Girl, don't you pay attention or watch the news? There is a Me-Too movement going on right now that states you don't have to let someone in your pants just because they want to be there. You're never obligated to have sex with anyone. Do you understand that?"

I slowly nodded my head, alarmed at how annoyed Montana had become.

"And guess what," Mo continued. "It's perfectly normal for you to like making out. If guys can like it, why can't girls? You can enjoy kissing and touching all you want. Hell, it feels good. And you can stomp the brakes when things start moving too fast. You're allowed to slow down or even stop. There is nothing, you hear me, nothing wrong with kissing a guy and then telling him no."

When Mo stands on a soap box, he reminds me so much of Granny Crackers. They both have a way of making a justification sound like a closing argument. Mo's speech alleviated my regrets. I had been feeling ashamed, and honestly I don't need another reason for low self-esteem. I took my newfound freedom and needy lips down to Mateo's house to play.

A poem written by Savannah Jorja:

HIS KISS

Sweet as clover honey,
Isn't it funny?
I dreamed of his mouth
Stealing my tongue,

Leaving me speechless.
My heedless curiosity,
His generosity,
Is more than I had planned

But he's a boy becoming a man,
And I'm full of sugar and spice,
A-not-so nice virginal girl,

No pearl
Of wisdom,
Just a pink empty shell

Who fell
For the taste of desire,
His mouth my pacifier.

Babies
Young and dumb
Having fun.

I'm elated.
He's frustrated.
Kissing.
Why does it have to be so complicated?

"That's crazy about the squatters' house," Mateo said as we sat talking and kissing in the steamy tent.

"What are you talking about?" I said, pulling back.

"You didn't hear? A dude was killed there last night."

"What?"

"Yeah, seventeen years old, shot straight in the head."

Half the neighborhood had watched the raid on the squatters' house the night my mother turned blue. A handful had seen Granny Crackers bring Ava back from the dead, and their voices soared like birds. Tweet, tweet, they pressed into their phones. Instagram pics were taken. "This shit is crazy" captioned one photo. One had a distant shot of my weathered great-grandma, crouching down, looking strong and fierce and my mother, weak as hell, being placed on a stretcher. I've seen the Facebook video, a blur of red and blue lights screeching up to the house. The line of handcuffed junkies paraded down the front grass and placed in the back of a paddy wagon. I thought the house had been cleaned out. I guess they're back.

Raiding one house in Paris Village isn't gonna make much of a difference. You will still be able to get all the drugs you want. It simply sends a message. Problem is, people here don't take warnings seriously. If there is a convenient place to sell or do drugs they'll take advantage of it. The squatters' house needs to be boarded up like the other vacant houses that line the streets, but that house must have an owner who pays its taxes and allows random folks to stay, or they just do.

I didn't feel much like making out after Mateo's news. Instead I sat up and cried.

"I hate it here," I said.

"Me too," responded Mateo, gripping my hand.

When I got home Granny Crackers was on the phone, talking furiously. Mo and Phoenix were stretched out on the couch, holding chihuahuas and eavesdropping.

"Russian roulette, my ass! That boy was a goddamn mule!"

I knew what a mule was—someone who carried drugs back and forth.

"Can you believe the police are saying that child killed himself in a game?" Crackers said to us, hanging up the phone. "A game! This ain't no damn game!" she said, storming out the door.

Granny Crackers stayed gone for hours. I made dinner, and we ate without her. After supper, Mo, Phoenix, and I went out on the front porch to sit. Jason and Kaleem saw us and brought over three bowls of strawberry shortcake. They're the best neighbors ever. They always seem to be looking out for us. I'm guessing they thought that a death at the squatters' house would bubble up memories of a blue mother. Wanting to comfort, the two compassionate men fed our emotions angel food, strawberries, and cream. They stayed on our porch filling the silent space between us with corny jokes and awkward laughter. I imagine it wasn't easy, trying to elevate the moods of three solemn vampire children. We sucked the energy from their very souls in an hour's time. They gathered their dirty dishes and left.

When Granny Crackers got home I offered to heat up the cheesy-mac Hamburger Helper, but she said she felt too hot and angry to eat. She said she had gone to the police station and fought with Officer Miller for an hour. Officer Miller had told her,

"Rosie, I understand your frustration but the truth is, three teens played Russian roulette last night with their daddy's gun, and one boy lost." Granny Crackers told us she responded, "That's bullshit, Miller, and if you believe that, then you wouldn't know the truth if it sat on your face and farted."

Mo giggled. "Oh my god."

We all burst out laughing.

"You actually said that to a cop?" I asked.

"Of course I did. He needs to do his damn job and lock up the thugs who come to our streets to feed the addicts and bully the children. I told him that too. He asked me to leave or he'd have me arrested for being disorderly. Total bluff. I was so mad I knocked over a chair heading to the door. 'How's that for disorder-ly?' I shouted on my way out. Now don't any of you go mouthing off to the cops like that. I'm an old woman who's already earned their respect. Y'all ain't nothing, but the kids who live here; they call y'all Paris rats. Being sassy to the police is wrong. It'll get you locked up, sure as shootin'."

"Where did you go after that?" Mo asked, looking toward the clock.

"Over to Dixie's. I needed to vent. Then we called Ambrose. The three of us consoled one another, talked about the good days, when this town wasn't so poor and broken. And now I'm going to bed. All my energy's been spent. I'm just tired, very, very tired."

Granny Crackers slept, covered in a melancholy quilt, head resting on a pillow of nostalgia. Mo, Phoenix, and I stayed awake. We talked about our mother, wondered where she was and if she was doing alright. We talked about our Granny, her torrential strength and her commitment to family, friends, and community.

"I thought Granny Crackers liked Miller," I said. "Officer Miller and her have always been friendly and respectful of each other."

"She does," said Mo. "She's just pissed off, watching her neighborhood go to hell. She needs someone to blame. Granny Crackers is loyal. Think about it. She's lived in the same damn house forever, has had the same best friends for years, and will never give up on her family. Even when she's too old to be raising kids, she's doing it. And she saved Ava, literally brought her back from the dead. And how is she being repaid? By Ava's rejection and the police's denial. Still, she's up for a fight. She's a feisty bitch. I hope I'm just like her when I'm old."

"You're just like her now," Phoenix said, taking the words right out of my mouth.

Lying in bed, we were shaken by sirens. The blaring and whistling of truck after truck, red lights flashing, and voices filling the night, a neighborhood being awakened.

"I'm gonna see what's going on," Mo was brave enough to suggest.

"I'll go with you," I said, matching his courage.

Jason and Kaleem were outside on their front porch, called forth by the same sounds. Phoenix and Granny Crackers plowed out the door behind us.

"Well, let's go check it out," Granny Crackers said, leading the way toward the sound of sirens and the smell of smoke. Down the street and around the corner, the squatters' house glowed red. The entire back end of the house was ablaze. Firefighters fought the flame, a red-orange forked tongue, licking the black sky. Neighbors stood on the street cheering, videotaping, watching the infamous house turn to ash. Mateo appeared beside me. Hand in hand we felt the heat, inhaled the choking fumes, and witnessed the tall white structure become charred to a crisp, like watching a kabob of marshmallows catch fire.

"I was at the E. R. when that boy was brought in last night," Kaleem said, breaking the silence that awed and gripped our small circle. "Dead on arrival."

I looked over at Granny Crackers, a silhouette illuminated by a ghetto fire, her face once savagely beautiful, now starkly old, glowing red and yellow.

Chapter Twenty

$\mathcal{J}$t's been more than a week, and talk of the fire still hasn't died down. Usually things here are short-lived. Drama has an unexpected, exciting birth followed by a fast death, making room for more tragedy. The charred, forsaken house has kept its fascination. I hear mention of the house everywhere I go. At The Barrel people converse over old VHS tapes and paperback books. In the garden, myths flutter by on the wings of butterflies. Folks gossip while digging up carrots and gathering hot peppers.

The cause was blamed on candles. Without electricity, the people who squatted used wax and wick to light their home. Nobody was in it when it went up in flames. Perhaps they fled when flames became unmanageable, or maybe candles burned in an empty house for hours. Regardless, the cause is unbelievable. Cops accept the conclusion of candles, because nobody was hurt and now there's one less drug house in Paris Village. But candles make about as much sense as Russian roulette. Nobody believes that seventeen-year-old Quenton Harris was playing a game, and most think the fire and Harris are connected.

People say the inferno was retaliation by a rival gang or perhaps a heartbroken loved one avenging Quenton's death. Others say it has nothing to do with Que Harris and they suspect the homeowner. He was tired of his property being invaded by lowlifes and junkies, so he burned it to the ground. Maybe there's insurance money to collect. Everyone is playing detective; they rationalize and strategize all day long. Although their theories differ, the cause is always arson.

"Candles?" I heard Ambrose say. "The house was a damn crime scene with plastic tape surrounding it, Quenton Harris's brains still stuck to the walls. Wasn't nobody sitting in there with candles."

Gossip drifts down the street like plastic bags, whirling in the wind. Theories are being tossed to the curb like litter. My very own Granny Crackers has become a suspect. I've heard discussions where the name Rosie floats by like a red kite. They call her sharp and sly. Their opponents argue that she's at least eighty years old, ornery but harmless. Still, they've heard of the rumored threat to Officer Miller, "You bring down this house or I will."

Granny Crackers is immune to slander. She ignores the accusations. She has no problems keeping to herself. If she is bothered or saddened by the gossip, she shows no emotions. She says she doesn't let herself get worked up over chitchat.

"Thems just sticks and stones, Savannah Jo. Ain't nothing but sticks and stones." And of course she has Dixie, her best friend, to provide comic relief.

Next to Dixie's big brick house is a little blue monopoly-sized house. The tiny home sits farther back off the street than the others in Paris Village. Its size and location makes it look out of place, like it was accidentally dropped by a crane on its way to a retirement village. The little house is rental property. People move in and out every year. Dixie normally hates her neighbors, usually a fighting couple, or a single mom with badass kids, so Dixie was really surprised when the nice, quiet, respectable man who lived there most recently cleared out unexpectedly. Dixie watched him out her window through a stream of moonlight. He and another guy loaded his stuff into a truck. They were gone by morning. Dixie, never one to miss an opportunity, approached the landlord the minute she saw him snooping around.

"Yep, he's gone," she told him. "Packed a U-Haul in the middle of the night, must be running from something. But if you're worried about renting it, I know someone looking for a place. My granddaughter, Twyla, sweet girl, works hard, keeps a clean home."

With a referral from Dixie, a woman who has lived in Paris Village for more than sixty years, the landlord didn't hesitate. Twyla left husband number three and moved into the tiny house the very next weekend.

"She's a good kid," Dixie told Granny Crackers. "Just a little flighty with a bad picker. Switches out men like underwear. Each one ends up being a weirdo. Child is like a magnet for crazy, attracting nothing but screw-ups and oddballs. Thank God she doesn't have any children."

Granny Crackers claims Twyla is a young version of Dixie, without the litter of babies to keep her grounded.

Twyla is the grandchild Dixie talks most about, simply because she was born in the Save-A-Lot. I've heard Twyla's birth story a hundred times. Brenda, Twyla's mother and Dixie's daughter, had a strange and constant craving for La Choy Chicken Chow Mein. Twyla was born in aisle nine at nine p.m. It's not just Twyla's birth story and failed marriages that make her intriguing.

Twyla is the type of person who lives in constant change, forever reinventing herself. Mimi and I saw her three summers ago at the Dockside Grill. She and her husband wore matching Harley Davidson shirts, and her denim-blue eyes sparkled. A year later we saw her again in a Hallmark Store at Christmastime, wrapped in a joyous smile, waving a marquise-cut diamond, engaged to a banker, and getting her real estate license. Then, on a mellow, yellow day last September, she came to the hospital. Sitting bedside, she took Mimi's hand in hers and softly rubbed the palm, told her she was back in school to be a massage therapist, and that her new guy was a gem. Twyla's life has numerous chapters of contrasting seasons, yet she's always happy, until she's not, and then she changes directions like the wind and soars off to find something new. Twyla's move next door to Dixie was good for both of them. Sure, family can be awful and irritating. Still, we need each other.

A week after Twyla moved into her new home, FedEx delivered a package. Dixie and Twyla returned home from running errands just as I was passing by. A massive box sat on Twyla's front stoop. I stopped to be courteous. Twyla and I pushed the big box through the front door.

"What did you buy now?" Dixie inquired.

Twyla's a shopper, and she's been known to go on Amazon after a few glasses of wine to make a purchase.

"Lord, I don't know," she said as she grabbed a knife and sliced through the tape. "What the hell?" Twyla opened up the cardboard flap and pulled out a large can.

"What is it?" asked Dixie.

"Pork and beans!" Twyla said. "The entire box is packed with cans."

"You ordered a shipment of pork and beans?"

"No, Grandma, I wouldn't have ordered beans, even if I was drunk. Hell, I don't even eat pork and beans. This makes no damn sense." Twyla pulled down the cardboard flap. "There's my address, but no name."

Dixie reached inside and pulled out another can, shaking it up by her ear. "This can't be beans; it's too light. That box should be heavy as hell," she said, sliding it with her foot. Dixie marched into Twyla's kitchen and grabbed a can opener. "Girrl, what did you get yourself into now?" she said, pulling a bag of weed out of the can.

"That ain't mine," cried Twyla, clearly confused.

"Lordy, if all them cans are full of pot, we're in deep trouble," said Dixie, shaking the baggie of weed.

"Jesus, take the wheel," Twyla wailed.

Dixie turned to me. "Savannah, go get Ambrose. He'll know what to do."

I bolted out the door and to the garden. I found him and Granny Crackers chatting over cherry tomatoes. "Come with me," I said. "Dixie needs your help."

"This can't be good," Ambrose said to Granny Crackers. The two walked beside me to Dixie's house. I said nothing, fearing my words would be carried off by songbirds. It's best to keep quiet and act normal.

"Holy shit!" Granny Crackers said, peering into the innocuous-looking box, cans lined up neatly in a row.

"Must be two ounces in each can," Ambrose said, holding up the baggie. "That's about five hundred dollars a can. And you got a shitload of beans. Brother must be messin' with the cartel. No wonder he packed up in the middle of the night."

"Cartel? But he was such a nice guy," said Dixie.

"Twyla, you need to call the police," insisted Ambrose.

"Oh, my god," Twyla cried. "I'm going to prison or getting killed. My life is over, prison or death."

"Child, you gotta calm down," said Ambrose. "Everything is going to be fine. You're gonna turn this box in and tell the police the truth, that you just moved into this house and opened it by mistake. Then you're gonna record the cops taking it away."

"Record?"

"Baby, when they come looking for this box, you need to be

clueless, a blonde bubblehead. Tell them the cops showed up and took a box from your porch. You didn't know what it was or what was going on. You have it all on video."

"I'm gonna die."

As Ambrose consoled a hysterical Twyla, Granny Crackers phoned law enforcement. I looked over at Dixie and watched her calmly pick up a can of beans and put it on the pantry shelf, like she was putting away groceries.

"Shhh," she whispered, noticing my stare. "It's for my glaucoma."

A total of three cruisers and six cops showed up to remove one big box. I thought they would just haul it away, but instead they created a spectacle. They opened the box and emptied it on the front lawn. After lining up and counting forty-nine cans, they re-packed the box. With all the cans neatly put away, the blank space stood out like a missing tooth. We stood shocked, volleying a ball of anxiety and fear back and forth, as cops wandered around the yard, seeking the hidden can.

"Okay," said one cop, heading toward Twyla, "where's the can?"

"I didn't take any beans," Twyla cried. "Oh, my god, I swear. Who's got the beans? Please, please give up the beans!" Twyla was back in a fit of hysteria, completely unhinged, a sobbing wreck. Her crazed blubbering worked in her favor.

I was the next person they approached, I suppose since I'm a teenager.

"Okay, girly, where did you stash the beans?"

"I didn't." My voice trembled, head nodding back and forth, eyes filled with tears. If Twyla looked like a hysterical nutcase, I resembled a neglected and abused pet. I shook, terror snaking through me. Should I tell them Dixie took the beans? As I tee-tered on the truth, about to fall, Granny Crackers spoke up.

"Where do you think she stashed a can of beans, in her short-shorts or tank top? Please, leave that child alone. She's innocent, shy, and naive. And Twyla, well she's too damn scared." She waved an arthritic finger in the air. "Perhaps it was one of you."

"Excuse me," said the most aggressive cop, lumbering toward Granny Crackers. He stopped toe-to-toe, hovering over her small frame in an attempt to intimidate an old woman.

"You heard me." Granny Crackers stood as tall as she could on moccasin feet, face pointed to the sun. "I said maybe one of your men took the can."

"That didn't happen, Granny," he said, unintentionally getting her name right.

"Well, then, that leaves you with three old-ass people to harass, doesn't it? But as I see it, we called you. We put our lives, families, and homes in danger and handed over about twenty-five thousand dollars in marijuana, probably from a drug cartel. So maybe you can forget all about one little can of beans."

The bully-cop looked around to the other officers, pointing his thumb at Granny Crackers, a cocky gesture that stated, "Get a load of this old lady." Although he kept up his arrogant persona, I could tell her punch had knocked him off balance. Granny Crackers remained grounded, chin up.

"Maybe you're right," he finally said, not knowing what else to do. "Let's pack up, men," he called to the officers.

The police put the box in the cruiser, and we quickly returned to our lives, encouraging the crowd of onlookers to disperse. Ambrose walked to the garden, Twyla and Dixie scrambled into the house, and Granny Crackers and I headed home.

"Does Dixie have glaucoma?" I asked, stopping Granny Crackers in her tracks.

"That crazy coot! Did she tell you that?"

I slowly nodded.

"Well, I ought to kick her old ass," she said, putting her arm around my shoulders and leading us home.

Two days after the cops confiscated the box, a big scary dude knocked on Twyla's front door and questioned her about a delivery. Twyla played stupid, just as Ambrose instructed. She had video of a front yard full of police and the box being unpacked. So did others. Folks had lined up across the street watching the drama unfold. Like sportscasters, they know how to get close enough to capture footage, yet far enough away to stay out of the game. If he went snooping it would be the same replay on everybody's phone. He left in a hurry, probably thinking it best if nobody knew he was associated with the box of beans.

Chapter Twenty-One

*T*he last days of summer and the start of a new school year create a collage of emotions. My feelings were visible, as if they were pasted on a poster board. I'm excited about the changing of seasons, summer into fall. I love back-to-school shopping, a pair of new Nikes and skinny jeans. Schedule pickup and orientation fill me with anxiety, though. I dread the thought of days at Paris High, where I am an alien in a foreign land.

Summertime ends for Phoenix with his name etched into gold on a giant trophy. My little brother broke the longtime butterfly record held by the swim team.

"This young and talented athlete, new to our team, has the fastest butterfly stroke this city has ever seen," Jason announced at the awards banquet, calling Phoenix up to collect his victory prize. I knew my brother was a good swimmer, but I had no idea he was a champion. We missed most of his swim meets, spending our time working at The Barrel or trash picking, but Mo, Granny Crackers, and I were there for Awards Night.

The reception was held at Northside Pool, where Phoenix and Jason spent their summer mornings. We swam at dusk under a pink sky and played volleyball and Marco Polo. The evening air filled with *Billboard* songs, the music drifting from speakers that resembled rocks. Jason and Kaleem planned the party, organizing it through head and heart, which is how they do everything.

They had a buffet fit for kids of kings: pizza, subs, chips, fruit salad, cupcakes, and cookies. Kaleem created a slideshow of vivid photographs of happy sun-kissed people submerged in blue sky and water. Jason presented a special award to each swimmer along with a heartfelt monologue, full of inside jokes, making me feel envious and alone, desperately wishing I was part of the team.

By the end of the evening Phoenix was draped in medals, carrying a colorful bouquet of ribbons in one hand and his trophy in the other. We followed behind him, splashing in his glory, the proud family of a stellar athlete. We left the pool with a high, supplied by happiness and sugar cookies. We crashed hard on top of made beds, bodies half nude and sticky, cooled by an open window and box fan, quilt marks imprinted on our faces.

We were pulled awake by the sound of sirens and the smell of smoke. Two blocks away a house went up in flames, another wildfire in Paris Village. A second infamous house was torched, the charred structure reportedly the site of a rape. It's been more than a year since the assault was reported. The victim was a loose girl with a slutty reputation, a fact that made some question her story. She claimed to have been lured into the house and raped on the floorboards. For a short while women were scared and men were angry. Free self-defense classes were offered at the recreation center. Girls carried rape whistles, mace, or a gun. The rapist was never found. Eventually everybody stopped thinking about it. The police put the girl's file on ice and boarded up the vacant structure. It's clear somebody remembered. They reminded the community by setting the porch on fire.

For the second time in two weeks we gathered at a ghetto bonfire, Snapchat photos of yellow-orange flames clawing the night taken like paparazzi. We watched in awe, choking on dust, as if a lump of charcoal was stuck in our throats. Drenched in soot, we walked home in a rain of embers, wading through cinders, ash swirling at our feet.

Come morning, our bright blue summer sky had turned slate gray. We had fallen asleep in Paris Village, but awoke in Gotham City. A vigilante was all anyone could talk about.

I'm not sure if the police thought the two fires were connected, but the community sure as hell did. The hype is arson by an avenging superhero, a mysterious night watchman hiding behind a moon shadow, his secrets kept by alley cats. Neighbors pieced together guesswork like a gigantic quilt and covered the hood in speculation.

On the very last night of summer break, Mateo, Mo, Phoenix, and I hung out in the park. Paris Park and Recreation Center sits in the middle of our zip code and stretches from block to block. The park, once spectacular, as shown by the photographs that adorn the rec center walls, now looks old and worn.

The playground is decorated in graffiti, mostly names; so and so was here. In bad taste, a giant penis is drawn in permanent black marker on the metal slide. A broken baby swing hangs crooked from one chain. Shards of glass litter the ground around the trashcan. You would think the mayor would see the benefit of a park and rec center in the inner city and put some money into rebuilding, but then again, if the city isn't going to restore our abandoned houses, why would it clean up an unkept park? Regardless, it doesn't stop the kids from playing there.

The park was full. The shouts of happy voices rang with the beat of rap music. A blinged-out ride sat in the parking lot, a car with large gold rims, an under-glow of neon lights, and speakers that shook the ground it drove on. Accompanied by the thrumming music, we watched an exciting game of basketball. It was shirts versus skins. Skins won. Once the children were called home for dinner and bath time, we took over the swings and debated over suspected superheroes.

"Maybe it's Enzo setting the fires," Phoenix suggested.

"Enzo, the Italian slumlord?" I questioned.

"Yeah, why not? He kind of looks like a superhero, strong, good-looking, and a bit thuggish."

"But why would he burn down houses?"

"Well, a vacant house makes the neighborhood look bad. Nobody wants to rent a house on a sad-looking street. If he burns them all down, they'll have to build more, and he could buy the new ones."

"It's a thought," I agreed.

"Enzo The Igniter!" Phoenix yelled, running around the playground, arms extended like an airplane.

We all laughed.

"It's Enzo's rundown rental properties that depress the neighborhood. It's not him. He doesn't care enough," said Mateo. "I think it's Marjuan. The dude owns the corner store, lives in the neighborhood, knows everybody, is always pissed off, talks about how the area has changed. And I heard he once shot a man who tried to rob him. Never did one day in jail."

"What's Marjuan's superhero name?" I asked.

Mateo stood in superman pose, feet firmly planted, fists on hips, chest pumped out. "Captain Blaze," he shouted.

"I got one," I said. "How about Flame-Thrower?"

"Yeah, whose superhero name is Flame-Thrower?"

"Leo," I said proudly.

"Leo, the crossing guard at the elementary school?" Phoenix asked.

"Yeah, he's already in costume, wearing his orange vest and twirling his flag like a baton. He's always doing tricks for the little ones. And he's already protecting the children. I think he cares a lot about us kids, and I bet he'd burn down a house or two if he thought it would help."

"That's a good one," Phoenix agreed.

The others nodded.

"What do you think, Mo?" I asked.

"I think it's a woman," said Mo seriously. "Think about it. It's 2018, the year of the woman. They've taken over grassroots organizations, started movements, and created the Women's March, the largest protest in U.S. history. Women are born advocates. Now lots are running for political office. Women have been pissed off for the past two years, and they're not taking shit anymore. Besides, I think women care about neighborhoods an awful lot more than men. It's where they raise their kids."

"A Wonder Woman." I smiled.

"Nah," said Mo. "Smolder Woman, cuz that girl is hot."

We all cracked up, and then threw out a bunch of names of suspected crime fighters. We finally agreed Smolder Woman was Rochelle, owner of Rochelle's Beauty Bar, a brown girls' hair salon that specializes in weaves and permanents. We liked the thought of Rochelle, simply because the look fit. She's a thick girl, a curvaceous, bodacious diva, all done up in sparkle and bling. Rochelle is dark brown with a blond weave, sassy as hell, and she would look badass in a superhero costume.

Talked out and satisfied with our crime fighter, I began swinging. I love swinging. My hands gripped the rusty chain and I leaned my head all the way back, legs pumping in the sky. My long blond hair brushed the earth and my toes dipped into the twilight. I wanted to tell my siblings and boyfriend what I truly thought—that Granny Crackers and Ambrose had something to do with the fires. But I didn't.

Maybe they were thinking the same thing. I hope not.

Suspicion is a disturbing sensation you feel in your gut. I live with a stomach full of flutters. Unsettling thoughts swarming in my center have me unfocused and obsessing. It sucks knowing Ambrose has been in prison.

On the last night of summer break, we stayed in the park until the first stars appeared, made our wishes, and headed home.

Chapter Twenty-Two

J began my sophomore year attending Paris High without a sibling by my side. We are in three different places this year. Phoenix is in eighth grade, his last year of middle school, and Mo, a senior, has decided to go the vocational route.

Mo has never been much of a student. School's a chore that he plods through. For the first time since kindergarten, Mo was excited about the start of a new year. He will be at the career center all day, taking a few core classes and concentrating his talents on auto mechanics. Mo is thrilled to have his face removed from the pages of a book and stuck under the hood of a car. After all, he thinks reading sucks, and he can pretty much fix anything. I'm happy for Mo. He needed a change of scenery, especially after his transition from sister to brother. It's complicated for people; maybe new faces will make it easier. Instead of dreading a school day, he can spend it learning something that interests him. Selfishly, I will miss Mo. Last year we ate lunch together every day. Thank God I have Mateo. He is my only friend at school. Without him it would be a lonely place.

I suppose I could have more friends if I tried, but the truth is, I haven't. Last September Mimi died. We changed schools, moved to Paris Village, and I began high school cloaked in sadness, a closet full of sorrow and a backpack loaded with grief. I walked the halls invisible, which was good, because it's best to lay low at an inner city school. Last year I clung to Mo, and together we learned how to survive: choose the seat closest to the window, stay silent, avoid eye contact, and don't stand out. This year I feel alone.

My tenth grade classes are difficult, burdened with lots of homework. I have a study hall, but can already tell I'm going to struggle with geometry. It doesn't help that the teacher is as boring as shit, unenthusiastic, and speaks in a monotone. Thank God I have an art class. The teacher, Mrs. Gypsy Honeywood, is awesome and as pretty as her name. Mrs. Honeywood is a middle-aged brown woman who relates well to the young. Her hair is shaved short like Mo's, but not because she wants to look male. On the contrary, I think Mrs. Honeywood loves being a woman. Her face is perfect, eyebrows on fleek, full lips painted red. She reminds me of an African princess, with her long dangling earrings that nearly touch her shoulders; necklaces carved from wood: giraffes, lions, and wooden beads strung on black cords; and a wrist full of bangles that jingle while she works.

Besides her cool fashion sense, I like Ms. Honeywood's style of teaching. Her curriculum combines art with art history, and every few weeks she introduces a new artist. She said that this year we will learn painting, sculpture, architecture, ceramics, drawing, printmaking, and photography. I'm excited. The first artist we've started with is Vincent van Gogh. We are working with watercolors, trying our brushstrokes at post-impressionism. We are talking about van Gogh's brilliance and his illness. It's so interesting—the truth, theories, and lies.

It's rumored that Vincent van Gogh ate yellow paint. The belief is he ate the paint, because he wanted to feel happy inside. Ms. Honeywood says this is not exactly accurate and that van Gogh had a condition called pica, an eating disorder. People with pica crave nonfood items, like soil, metal, and chalk. Sadly pica has been turned into a reality TV show called *My Strange Addiction*. It's crazy the things we exploit. Vincent had a taste for turpentine. Ingesting paint may have led to his hallucinations. In the asylum, van Gogh sucked on the tip of his brush and painted madness into sunflowers.

Vincent reminds me of Ava, who likewise painted sunflowers, and when I think about it, she also eats yellow paint. Her sunshine droplet comes in the form of an opioid. Both Vincent and Ava attempted to paint their insides happy, or just numb the pain.

Perhaps I shouldn't be so judgy. I think I might be another yellow-paint connoisseur. I digest yellow paint when taking photographs. My Instagram has a theme. The motif is my search for beauty in ugly places and sad things, and the tolerance tests I put myself through, like standing barefoot on hot asphalt or pinching my arms till they bruise. It's the same as scarfing yellow paint. I do these things, because I want to strengthen my endurance for all things unpleasant and decrease my emotional sensitivity. I'm way too sensitive.

I want to be strong like Mimi. She fought a war with cancer that lasted four years. Every day Mimi woke and dressed her mind for combat. She battled chemo, radiation, sickness, and pain with a barrage of optimism. She shot cancer with cannonballs of hope, forcing it to retreat. Cancer would wave a white flag and trick Mimi into thinking she had won. Hiding in Mimi's corners, cancer would plan its sneak attack, silently waiting for the perfect moment. When Mimi felt healthy, happy, and whole, cancer would pop up, metastasized to a new organ, and the fighting would ensue.

I could not have done it, fight a hideous beast with courage and strength. I am weak, so I eat yellow paint by turning my depressing surroundings into raw Instagram photos and writing sadness into poetry. Why do I do it? Because I'm exploring life's quandaries in a pursuit to happiness? Not really. I'm actually just trying to learn how to be content in a world that's fucked up. My mother swallows pills to figure out the same thing. Sad, isn't it, all the people struggling to be happy?

A poem written by Savannah Jorja:

EATING YELLOW PAINT

I'm eating yellow paint,
Turning my mountains into molehills.
That's what control is,

Because lemon days
Make lemonade,
And I'm tired of being afraid

Of the monsters under my bed.
It's all in my head.
Mind over matter.

Keep sadness under flatter,
Give laughter instead of tears,
Hide your fears

And turn winter into spring.
Suffering
Is cured by guzzling

A gallon of canary hue.
It's what a saint would do,
Digest yellow paint

Without complaint
Or restraint,
Smile through the pain,

Because each drop of rain
Helps the flowers bloom
In a garden of gloom.

Grey things look pretty.
I don't need your pity.
I'm fine.

Drinking sunshine,
I swallow my hurt,
Bat my eyes and flirt

With woe,
Just like van Gogh;
That's how I flow.

Chapter Twenty-Three

A meeting is scheduled at the community center tonight. People are in a tizzy about the fires. They think police aren't doing enough to protect us. The Paris Village Facebook page is full of angry posts. "It would be declared a state of emergency if the empty houses in a rich neighborhood caught fire. Nobody cares if we burn up."

Granny Crackers says folks have a right to be worried and angry. "Fires jump," she told us. "No telling where it may end up. A dancing blaze is likely to twirl and spin from house to yard to another house, or roof to roof. The entire street could go up in flames while we're all sleeping. The very least the police can do is tell us how they plan to handle it."

We all bounced down to the community center after dinner and watched people scream at the cops. The place was packed. This neighborhood's full of people who love drama. They gobble it up. Folks here cook up saga like it's a pot of community stew, add a little bit of tragedy, a pinch of shocking, sprinkle it with melodrama, and eat that shit with a tarnished spoon. People were going off, one by one, each argument fueling the next one. Neighbors that live beside vacant houses were the most concerned. They complained of sleepless nights, frightened their house would catch fire. Their fear was real.

Officer Miller did his best to calm the panic, but he was vastly outnumbered by drama-stew-eating gluttons.

Ambrose finally stepped forward, the voice of reason. He calmed the residents and defended the police without starting a riot. That's no easy thing. It takes a man like Ambrose, sensible and charismatic, a reverend among ordinary people. Ambrose is a shepherd with a flock of black sheep. He's working with the police and fire department, organizing a block watch in Paris Village. "It's our job to help keep things in check," he told the crowd of angry neighbors. "We need to be a community that looks out for each other. We need to walk our own streets, keep watch for clues and signs, and alert the authorities if we see something."

If you think Ambrose's suggestions are common sense, you don't live in Paris Village. We don't snoop around the streets looking for reasons to call the po-po on people. Just the opposite. We're taught to mind our own business and not get involved.

Mateo found me after the meeting and asked me to take a walk around the park. He'd skipped school, and I hadn't seen him all day. I wanted to be angry at Mateo. He'd been ignoring me, not answering my texts; he had me left on red. But his pretty-boy face and delicious smile softened my anger.

We circled the park hand in hand. Mateo stayed quiet. I didn't really notice at first. It's hard to register somebody else's mood when you're talking a mile a minute. Granny Crackers says I have the gift of gab.

During a minute of silence when I had paused to catch my breath, Mateo stopped and looked at me, his face molded into the large frown of a sad clown. "My dad is being deported," he softly said.

"Why?" I asked in disbelief, adopting a frown of my own. "When?"

"Now." He gently kicked at a mound of dirt. "We went to court today. ICE has held him for six months. Today they tore us completely apart. I didn't even get a chance to hug him before they led him away." Fat gemstone teardrops fell from Mateo's black agate eyes. It broke my heart.

"Oh, my god, Mateo, I'm so sorry." I tried to hug him, but he pulled back. I understood. Embraces are tricky things. Hugs can crush a sad person. A little distance forces you to stand strong. It's probably best not to crumble on a shoulder in the middle of a ghetto park.

Mateo's voice was an audible whisper. "They say they're sending him back home. But this is home. He's lived in this country for twenty years, worked all of them, always paid his bills and helped others. This is where he met his wife, fell in love, and created a life. All of his babies were born here. My mother isn't strong enough for this, Savannah. She won't recover."

Tears fell from my own eyes as Mateo and I stood facing each other, the space and energy between us thick with sorrow. I was speechless. I had nothing but my presence to give. No words could soothe such a deep sadness. Every thought and phrase that entered my mind sounded clumsy and awkward. Talking would be like drinking from a dribble cup. I pressed my lips together to keep stupid utterances from spilling out of my mouth. I squeezed Mateo's hand, leaned in with a light kiss, and then we began walking again, both of us silent.

We passed the jungle gym where happy kids swung from their arms like monkeys. We shuffled by the crowded swings, rounded a game of basketball, wandered over to an empty ball diamond and then back to the community center. We walked in circles, lost in our heads. With each lap the sun dimmed and the park emptied. The crowd of busybodies left the community center and took their children with them. The game of basketball slowly disintegrated to one lone baller shooting hoops against a purple sky. Mateo and I still walked. A sprinkle of light rain dampened our hair. Mateo ignored it, so I did too. I figured it was a metaphor from God. It made sense that Mateo's and my stroll would include rain. Besides, the drizzle was good company for our tears. Water dripped down our cheeks and noses. I kept my gaze down and focused on how the street lights shone on the wet pavement.

"Savannah! Mateo!" The shout came from the other side of the park. In the indigo light stood a figure, slightly hunched, a tiny frame holding an umbrella. It was Granny Crackers. "It's time to go!"

As we walked Mateo to his house, I anticipated a lecture, but Granny Crackers respected the silence that encased us. She knew about Mateo's dad. Otherwise, I would be in trouble for being in the park after dark, out in the rain.

"How did you hear?" I asked as the two of us headed home.

"Mateo's aunt called. She was really worried."

Granny Crackers's words brought me fresh tears and a trembling chin. I sniffled. "Why do terrible things happen to good people?"

"Baby, I don't know," she answered honestly. "I've been asking God that same question for years."

I peeled off my wet clothes and laid them in the sink to drip. I stepped into a hot shower, more water to drown my sorrows. I lathered my hair with cheap, pink strawberry shampoo, inhaled its perfume, and exhaled tension. I stood in the tub breathing slowly until the water turned cold. When I got out I wiped every droplet from my body. I blow-dried my hair and face. My blue puddle eyes, now two empty droughts. For bed I dressed in gym shorts and a shirt that was three sizes too big.

"Can I lie down with you?" I asked, stepping toward Mo's bed.

"Sure," he said, pulling aside the sheet. "Get in."

Montana and I have shared a room my entire life. Countless times I've abandoned my own bed to crawl into hers. All that stopped with a change in pronouns and a shaved head. I was excited Mo said yes. Plopping down quickly, I bumped his arm. Mo flinched, a sudden flash of pain.

"What's wrong? Are you okay?"

"I'm fine," he lied.

Chapter Twenty-Four

Mo has been unusually silent for the past couple weeks. I can tell he is trying to avoid me, taking off on his skateboard and staying gone for hours. When he is home he's in the backyard tossing a ball to Granny Crackers's three neurotic dogs. I know something is wrong, but instead of telling me, he's whispering his secrets into the perked ears of tense chihuahuas.

At first I blamed Mo's cranky mood on his period. I know when he's menstruating. We share a room and the same cycle. Mo's period comes with cramps, irritability, dysphoria, and the rude reminder that he has a vagina.

Lying in bed with a heating pad across my stomach, watching Mo angrily toss our room looking for a lost book and then cry into his pillow, I thought periods truly are a curse. The days kept moving, though. My cramping stopped. My bleeding slowed and then disappeared. The boxes of tampons and pads remained half full, and the bathroom trashcan stood empty. I was running around again, dancing in my bedroom to Lizzo and practicing my front flips in the backyard. The prior crippling week was gone from my mind like the stains in my underwear. Mo's mood didn't improve, revealing his troubles were other than hormonal.

I honestly thought this year was going to be great for Mo. He's got so many things going for him: being a senior, a new school, classes in auto mechanics, a driver's license, and a little red Mazda. He's still just a lost boy. I try to get him to talk. Mo is like opening up a new toy. His emotions are all pent up and sealed inside a box. Once you get the box open, you discover his feelings are zip-tied into place. You have to get your fingers in there and really work at untwisting the binding around each mood, discard all the cardboard and plastic, and uncover the real stuff.

Since I can't get him to tell me what's wrong. I spy on him. I've stalked his Finsta. That's a fake Instagram account meant for a chosen few. It's a place to share depressing stuff. I don't have a Finsta, although a lot of teen girls do. I don't need one. I put my dismal days out there on Instagram for everyone to see. I just edit them first so I appear artsy and not sad. I wish I knew what was going on in Mo's unfiltered life, but that's just it; we used to be so close, and now we're connected by wishes and prayers. I wish we were still best friends. Mo prays I'd leave him alone.

Montana has pulled so far back, she's fading, like an old pencil sketch on paper. First she erased her boobs and hair. She blew her girlishness right off the paper, along with eraser bits. It was fine, because Mo remained beautiful and whole. Now he's gone and erased his mouth, so he doesn't have to speak or smile.

Granny Crackers has also noticed Mo's silent and solemn mood, and since she tackles everything in an unconventional way, she took us bowling. "Get in the car," she told the three of us just as the day was ending and we were preparing for the next one.

"What?" I said, flipping through my closet, picking out tomorrow's clothes.

"You heard me. Get in the car."

"Why?" asked Phoenix, rummaging through his backpack in search of missing homework.

"Because we're going bowling."

"Now?" Mo asked. "But it's a school night."

"Yes, Montana, right now. I feel like knocking down some pins. Don't you?"

"No, I'm not going."

"Yes, you are. Get in the car."

Mo moped out the door. Phoenix and I were excited and happy to go bowling, and on a school night too.

Granny Crackers circled through the neighborhood, stopped in front of Dixie's house, and honked three times.

Dixie stepped out on her porch wearing a housedress, her hair rolled in pink curlers. "Where are we going?" she asked, proving Dixie's always ready for a change of scenery.

"Bowling!" Granny Crackers yelled.

"Hell, yeah! Give me a minute."

We idled in front of Dixie's house, Granny Crackers's Barry Manilow CD blaring in our ears. Granny Crackers is a terrible singer, but it doesn't stop her from belting out her favorites.

"At the Copa, Copacabana," she screeched. The Oldsmobile had turned into a torture chamber for the three of us teens stuck in the back. Finally Twyla stepped outside. She held the door open for Dixie, who emerged dressed in bedazzled blue jeans and a black T-shirt adorned with rhinestones that spelled out WILD, curlers gone, white hair teased into a frenzy. Twyla squeezed into the back seat, where four sets of bony legs crushed up against each other, while Dixie comfortably rode shotgun.

"Oooh Barry!" she said, pushing the arrow to song number four. "At the Copa, Copacabana," she crooned.

I figured the night would get better once we got to the bowling alley.

Stardust Lanes was packed. To my surprise Jason and Kaleem stood near the food counter.

"Hey!" Phoenix said excitedly. "Jason and Kaleem are here."

"What are the odds?" I asked.

"Pretty damn good," responded Granny Crackers, "since I called and invited them. I figured we'd have ourselves a little party."

"Rosie," said Jason as we approached, "it was a nice thought. Thanks for the invite, but we can't bowl; tonight is reserved for leagues only."

"Of course it is," said Granny Crackers. "Every Wednesday night is league night. Y'all stay right here. I'll get us a lane."

As Granny Crackers negotiated the only empty lane with the manager, we stood off to the side talking doubt. "There's eight of us," Twyla counted. "I don't think they even allow eight people to bowl in one lane."

"They do if they want to make money," Dixie said. "Besides, Rosie can talk her way into anyplace, anytime." Dixie was right. Five minutes later we were picking out our balls and shoes.

"How did she do that?" Kaleem asked, clearly impressed.

"Rosie magic." Dixie smiled. "See why I've hung out with that lady for sixty plus years?"

For the first hour, bowling was a riot and good for us all. The energy and crowd elevated gloomy moods. Happiness was fueled by the sound of laughter, banging of pins, high fives, claps, and shouts of excitement. I stopped thinking about Mateo and his family, a two-hour vacation from heartache. Granny Crackers and Dixie bought pizzas and pitchers of pop. We laughed and joked, none of us taking the game too seriously, except for Granny Crackers, who bowls like she shoots pool, competitively. Her biggest challenge was Jason. It's good, because Granny Crackers likes a serious opponent as much as she likes her fun. It must be Jason's strong arms that make him such a good bowler.

Same with Phoenix. He played well for a beginner, but then again, Phoenix has natural athletic ability. It doesn't matter what kind of ball he's throwing—baseball, football, bowling ball—he's pretty good. Sadly I was leading Twyla by only four measly pins. Twyla was the worst bowler with the loudest laugh. What she lacked in sport she made up in spirit. Her mood was contagious, and she reminded me of Ava.

Eventually Mo's stone face softened and a faint smile appeared. Although Mo no longer looked as pained, he still threw the ball like he hurt. Granny Crackers can usually count on Mo as a competitor, but instead he bowled like a cripple. His aim and accuracy were fine, but his arm was lame and limp, a red flag we pretended to ignore.

Halfway through the second game, Dixie's mind must have wandered twenty years back. Nursing a beer, she lit a Pall Mall and blew her smoke down our lane.

"Grandma, you can't smoke in here," Twyla scolded.

"Sure, I can. It's a bowling alley. The walls are faux painted with cigarette stains. Besides, I've smoked here hundreds of times."

"I bet not recently." Twyla rolled her eyes.

The rest of us kept quiet. It's hard to tell Dixie what to do and best just to let life happen.

The manager, a middle-aged, hard-looking white woman, watched Dixie from behind the shoe counter for several exasperated minutes before approaching. "What the hell do you think you're doing?"

"What?" a clueless Dixie responded, spilling a little beer on her shirt.

"Lady, this ain't the 1970s! Stamp that out!"

"I told you," Twyla growled as Dixie tapped her cigarette on the bottom of her bowling shoe.

"I'm sorry," Dixie said, looking past Twyla and over to Jason and Kaleem, who politely smiled. Once the woman walked away, Granny Crackers took her turn reprimanding Dixie.

"You know you can't smoke inside. What the hell is wrong with you?"

"It was a senior moment, Rosie. My mind slipped back in time. It was a nice trip. You remember that winter we joined a league? We wanted to get away from the house another night, away from husbands and babies. You had a one-night stand with Bernie the night he bowled a three hundred."

"Hell, I hadn't thought about Bernie in years," Granny Crackers said, snickering. "He was on fire that night. And here I was married to Charles the cheater, husband number two. Charles and I had a big fight that day over a bimbo named Loretta. Then I watched Bernie bowl a perfect game. I figured if I was ever gonna have revenge sex, that was the night and that was the man. Lawdy, I was not wrong."

I hate when Granny Crackers reminiscences about her sexual affairs. It makes me completely uncomfortable and a little freaked out. However, I could tell Jason and Kaleem loved it. They are completely awed by Granny Crackers and gripped by her stories. They stood listening with perked ears and cocked heads.

I looked over at Mo, rubbing his shoulder. Lifting his arm, the sleeve of his T-shirt inched up, revealing a line of hidden purple flesh. I quietly stared.

Twyla noticed the same thing and impulsively shouted out, "Oh my god, what happened to your arm?"

Granny Crackers's head snapped to attention.

"Nothing." Mo patted his sleeve down. The air in the room abruptly changed, and it felt as if our group were encased in a bubble, suddenly quiet, the faint crashing of pins echoing deep in the background. The eight of us stood frozen in our snow globe, all eyes on Mo.

"Show me your arm, Montana," Granny Crackers softly demanded.

Mo bit his bottom lip, his eyes brimming with tears. He slowly lifted the sleeve of his right arm, exposing a bruise the size and color of an eggplant. The sight of his purple bicep caused us to cringe and sucked the oxygen from our bubble.

"Jesus, child, what happened?" Granny Crackers asked.

"Nothing," Mo cried.

"It doesn't look like nothin'."

Granny Crackers's questioning felt for Mo as painful as the bruise. He was having trouble speaking.

Kaleem was the first to approach Mo. He tenderly picked up his arm, pushing the sleeve higher, uncovering more pain. "Looks like you're bruised to the bone." Kaleem turned Mo's arm, inspecting all sides. "Did somebody hit you with something?"

Mo looked down, said nothing.

"Somebody get an ice pack."

Both Twyla and Jason headed for the concession stand. Jason returned with a plastic bag filled with crushed ice.

Twyla handed Mo a Coke and then rummaged through her messy purse until she found a bottle of Aleve. "Here," she said, handing Mo a little blue pill.

Kaleem led Mo over to a table. They both sat. Mo sipped his soda and Kaleem held the bag of ice to his arm.

"Okay, Montana," Granny Crackers said, "spill the tea."

"Really, it's nothin'." Mo wiped his eyes. "It's just guys trying to be funny."

"What guys?"

"At school, in my auto mechanics class. It's how they greet me."

"They greet you by pummeling the shit out of your arm?" Granny Crackers asked.

"Yeah you know, like 'Hey Man,' punch to the arm or 'How's it going dude,' punch to the arm. They're just a bunch of rednecks trying to see how tough I am."

"Bullshit, Montana," Dixie interjected. "They're a bunch of little pricks pissed off cuz your dick is bigger than theirs."

Dixie was right, but Granny Crackers raised her hand as if to stop everybody from talking. "I'll handle this," she said. "How many times a day do you get punched in the arm?"

"Well, there's twenty-four in my class."

"And all of them take turns hitting you?"

"Not all, just most."

"You gonna give me some names?"

"No, Ma'am. I can't."

"You mean you won't." Granny Crackers stopped talking, leaving a space for Mo to fill with names, but he just looked down. After several seconds of painful silence, Granny Crackers began again. "Mo, I'm gonna tell you something. This bullshit is stopping tomorrow, and don't you ever again take a beating in silence. Do you understand me?"

"Yes, Ma'am."

Granny Crackers turned to our neighbor. "Jason, can you go up to the school with me in the morning? I'm going to need a sanity check, someone who can help me advocate for Montana and keep me from throwing a chair at one of those little bastards."

"Absolutely, Rosie. I'll be ready by seven in the morning."

We left the bowling alley with three frames left, laid our shoes on the counter in a heap, paid our money, and walked out sadder than when we had walked in. I'm glad Granny Crackers asked Jason for backup. As a teacher he has more leverage than a poor great-grandma raising ghetto grandchildren. I'm sure nobody understands Mo's pain better than Jason and Kaleem, two sensitive, caring gentlemen who learned to fight bullies the hard way. That night I tried to talk to Mo, but he pretended to be asleep. Instead I wrote him a poem and laid it on his pillow.

A poem written by Savannah Jorja:

LET'S FLY AWAY

I wish you and I could fly away
To the place where lost boys play.

We'll go out through our window and into the night
Past the second star on the right,

Soaring on happy thoughts and pixie dust
With gypsy hearts and wanderlust.

We'll travel long and journey far,
Just like Max in Where the Wild Things Are.

Our path guided by a starlit compass,
Upon our arrival, a royal rumpus

With Tinker Bell and Peter Pan,
Queen and King of Neverland.

Leave our shadows and worries behind
To live on an island that's undefined,

Make our home in a house, in a tree,
On the edge of the forest, close to the sea

And sleep soundly on a pillow of moss
Dream of riding an albatross,

Throw a welcome party and play charades,
Invite only dolphins and pretty mermaids.

We'll feast on mud pies, wear coonskin caps,
Keep sacred possessions in burlap sacks,

Take our baths in the blue lagoon lakes,
Fill our pockets with crystals and snakes.

We'll have a pretend battle, acorns in slingshots,
And sail a ship at fifty knots,

And Captain Hook can't spoil our fun
Because he's just a guy who's come undone,

And we're not afraid of crocodile tears
Because we've had to battle much bigger fears,

So let's never grow up. Ignore the clock.
Pay no mind to the tick and the tock

And live together in never-ending time,
Sweet sister-brother of mine.

Let's fly away.

Chapter Twenty-Five

Mo's eggplant arm has faded to yellow. Granny Crackers and Jason assume that the bullying situation has been resolved since they reported it. Adults are like that. They believe you can fix any problem by going straight at it with a little aggression and some political correctness.

The political correctness came from Jason, the aggression from Granny Crackers. The two met with the teacher, principal, and student counselor before school. The meeting lasted well into the beginning of the day. Before leaving, Granny Crackers made sure to excuse herself and step away, perhaps making a trip to the bathroom. However it happened, she made a detour down the hall and looked into Mo's classroom, which is actually a big garage.

"Have a good day, Montana," she shouted into the room, making sure to catch the attention of the entire class, the space full of redneck boys with greasy nails and no couth. With all eyes on Granny Crackers, she calmly and methodically aimed a finger at a few students. She then blew on the tip of her pointer and patted her pocketbook.

"What the hell?" said Mo, coming into the house after school. "You threatened to shoot my class?"

"I did not," argued Granny Crackers, her face like a storm

cloud. "I simply wagged my finger at the bad boys. Shame on them."

"That was not a shaming wave; it was a finger gun. You even gave a wink like you're Clint Eastwood or some shit. You can't do that, Granny Crackers. It's called a threat."

"Calm down, Mo. I didn't threaten anyone."

"You patted your purse like you're packing heat."

"Oh, don't be silly. I don't own a gun."

"I know that, but those guys in my class don't. And now they think you're a wacky old coot, crazy enough to shoot 'em."

"Well, that might solve some problems. Don't ya think?"

Mo's mouth dropped open. Unsure of what to say, he stomped into our bedroom and slammed the door.

Granny Crackers tried to subtly put the fear of God into Mo's classmates, but the bullies didn't change. They are still mean, foul individuals, now playing a new game, fuck with the trans boy without getting caught.

Mo spends his school days taking fragile steps across a rickety foundation of anxiety. He wipes the eggshells from his shoes before entering the house. It's not the school's fault. With twenty-four students in auto mechanics and Mo's refusal to call out the abusers by name, there wasn't much they could do. Who knows? Maybe life is also difficult for the idiots picking on Mo, a bunch of homophobes attracted to a trans boy. His femininity screws with their manhood.

Montana is like a sunset. Regardless of how the day is dressed, you cannot steal her beauty. In work coveralls and grease, Mo is still gorgeous. The outline of his slight yet curvy frame tantalizes both the opposite and same sex. You can bind big tits only so tight. His shaven head and olive skin, wiped clean of makeup, makes him look like a woman of natural beauty and not like a man at all. It's easy for a person to get lost in his green bedroom eyes the color of juniper and forget which side of the fence they're on.

Life for Mo would be easier if he wasn't so damn sultry, but the same sensuous blood that flows through the generations of women in this family courses through Mo's veins as well. He can douse himself in men's cologne, but that doesn't stop him from reeking of estrogen, a fact that causes him to hide within.

Since Mo's emotional absence, life has been lonely. I wish I could see more of Mateo and fill my lonely moments with sweet honey kisses, but he's busy. With his father's deportation and his mother's mental breakdown, Mateo thinks he needs to be the man of the house. He got a job at the soul food restaurant two blocks from home. He buses tables every evening after school and all day on weekends.

Mateo doesn't mind the long hours. His home is now a structure furnished with sadness. Besides that, they need the money. Mateo says Solomon, owner of The Sol Shack, is cool. He gives Mateo free meals and lets him sit in a back booth to do homework when business is slow. Each night after ten o'clock, when Mateo is finally free, he and I talk, but by then he's so tired he usually falls asleep, phone in hand. I've become accustomed to the soft snoring I hear over FaceTime. Mateo's phone resting on his pillow gives me a clear visual of the crack in the ceiling above his bed. Staring at peeling paint and water stains, I feel close to him. I drift off listening to the hum of his breath.

I guess it shouldn't be too surprising that the fatigued people living in my house and Mateo's slept straight through the apocalypse. On one night in Paris Village, two more houses burned to the ground.

Since we moved to the hood, alarms no longer alarmed us. We ignored the sirens and incorporated the blaring into our dreams, as bugles and bells. I guess it's the same as living next door to the airport. Eventually you become immune to the roar and vibrations of planes.

In the morning Granny Crackers sat, a cracked porcelain doll, staring at the flat, dusty television screen. The anchor, a debonair dude in a sports coat, was reporting live from a place I knew by fractured heart.

"Is that Paris Village?" I asked, alerting my siblings.

"Armageddon," Granny Crackers replied. Mo, Phoenix, and I, three curious kittens, pounced on our cell phones, scrolling to find the most exciting coverage. I had two missed calls from Mateo and a picture of a charred house taken that morning.

The first to catch fire was the abandoned structure that sat next to the community garden, a tall, pale blue shack with a collapsing roof and a rat infestation that Ambrose battled alone. The house burned like a torch, the pirouetting flames attracting an audience. The police controlled the crowd as firefighters fought the blaze. The arsonist, also an opportunist, took full advantage of everyone gathered in one spot and set another house ablaze on the opposite end of the village.

The second inferno was a large white corner ranch. Granny Crackers loved that house. She knew its original owners, the Daltons. They had twelve children. Granny Crackers ran with the oldest ones. She said that every time Mrs. Dalton had a new baby, Mr. Dalton built a bedroom. The house consisted of cubicle-sized rooms and stretched the full block. Granny Crackers used to talk of buying the Dalton place. She dreamed of fixing it up and renting out rooms.

"It would make a perfect boarding house," she'd said. Granny Crackers went inside once, to check it out. The place reeked of homeless tenants. All the copper piping had been stripped out. With no electricity and no water, a five-gallon bucket of shit sat in a bedroom. She fled the house to puke in the yard. Realistically the cost to restore the home was too much. "It would be cheaper to build new," she said.

Eventually the doors and windows were sealed. The boards and ugly siding were decorated with spray-painted graffiti and ghetto art. The once-lively Dalton house was a forsaken eyesore. It sat two blocks from our home, on the corner where I caught the school bus.

I walked out of the house into the dawn, the morning sky the color of bruises and streaked with ash the shade of bird shit. Kids, their parents, and half the neighborhood gathered around the desecrated home. Caution tape and men in uniforms attempted to hold us back, but they couldn't stop us from taking cell phone videos. The volcanic smell of hell's fire filled our nostrils. There was a buzz of excitement comparable to the year of the cicada. The handsome anchor I'd just seen on TV held his microphone in the faces of those wanting to be on the news. I found Mateo, and we chatted. Both of us had missed the actual burning.

The bus arrived ten minutes late, and the Paris Village kids went to school hyped after a sleepless night, fueled by a steamy cup of havoc. Adrenaline pumped like petroleum through the veins of teens. Everybody was high on drama. By ten in the morning you could feel a collapse of energy. Paces slowed, and emotional crashes were on the verge. With an astounding lack of insensitivity our nerves were shaken awake.

The powers that be, in their infinite wisdom, chose to enact an active shooter drill. I helped my classmates barricade the door with tables and chairs and then found my hiding spot. Armed with a sharp pencil and crammed in a storage closet with ten other kids, one being a large asperger's boy having a full-blown panic attack, I thought, "Jesus, where have all the safe places gone?"

When I got home from school, Officer Miller and his partner were standing on our front porch talking to Granny Crackers. I stopped on the steps, opening my ears wide like a catcher's mitt, straining to snatch bits of their conversation.

"Go on inside, Savannah Jo. Start on your homework," said Granny Crackers.

I walked past the three yapping chihuahuas into my room. Mo was there, going through his clothes, organizing his drawers. He's much neater than me.

"What's Miller doing here?" I asked.

"Talking to Granny Crackers."

"Duh. I can see that. What about?"

"Who knows? Could be about our mother, who ghosted us. Maybe they found her dead somewhere."

"Montana! Don't say that."

"Why? You know it's a possibility." Mo stopped long enough for an awkward silence to split us in two before continuing. "I'm guessing he's asking her about the fires."

"Oh, no! Do ya think she's torching the neighborhood?" The words ran out of my mouth before I could catch them.

"Whoa, what? No! I didn't say that. Jesus, Savannah, they're not questioning her like a suspect. I meant checking with her to see if the block watch reported anything unusual."

"Oh," I said, biting my lip.

"Damn, Savannah, you can't really believe our eighty-year-old grandmother is running around in the middle of the night setting houses on fire. That's just crazy."

"Yeah, no. I know." I giggled, acting like I hadn't just accused Granny Crackers of being an arsonist.

Mo gave me a glare, said nothing, and continued folding his white V-neck T's and boxer shorts.

I plopped on my bed and unloaded my backpack, silently

sorting through homework. My mind whirled. The truth is that my head had been spinning since the fires started. I was obsessing, really, with the same train of thought revolving over and over like a hamster on a wheel. I remembered all the times that Granny Crackers raged about the abandoned properties. "The village has gone to hell," she'd say. Last winter she actually put together a petition about the vacant houses and circulated it through the neighborhood. She took her signatures to a town hall meeting, spoke to the mayor, demanded the city either tear the houses down or fix them up.

I wanted to be able to talk to Mo and tell someone how I really felt. I wanted to spill all my anxiety, drain my cup, and have it filled with calming thoughts. "I don't know, Mo," I breathed, breaking our silence with a whispered confession. "She hated those houses, called them unsafe and unsightly. She blamed them for half the neighborhood problems—prostitution, drugs."

"Everybody hates those houses, Savannah Jo, and they all say exactly what Granny Crackers says."

"Yeah, but she's louder."

"That doesn't make her guilty. Besides, Granny Crackers and Ambrose are working with the firefighters and police. Remember?"

"I know. It's just Ava . . . and the night of the Narcan." I looked up at my sister/brother with teary eyes. I had thought an empty cup would make me feel better, but it only left me hollow.

"Look," said Mo, taking pity on me, "Granny Crackers may not like those vacant properties, but she doesn't like fire any better. In fact, fire scares her more than empty homes. You heard her at the community center. The tremble in her voice as she thanked God that nobody has been hurt. The frightening theories she tossed about, like a homeless person could be inside sleeping when the fire is set, God forbid a stray teen. And how she talks about fire jumping, a domino effect. Half the people in this town don't have working smoke detectors, or at least they didn't last week."

"Yeah, no, you're right," I said, wiping my eyes. "I'm sorry, I know she would never do anything that could end up hurting someone. I don't know what I was thinking."

"Stop crying. It's fine. You just have a sensitive mind, that's all. You always think too hard and too deep. You always have, writing your sad poems. But maybe, Savannah Jo, just maybe . . . not everybody is as fucked up as you think they are."

After shaming me into submission, Mo walked out of our bedroom with a pile of dirty clothes and ran straight into Granny Crackers, standing outside our door.

"I'll do that laundry," Granny Crackers said. "You kids have been packing my washer too full. You're gonna break my machine."

"If you insist," Mo said, handing over the basket and looking at me.

Our gaze locked, both of us nervously wondering if she had overheard our conversation.

Chapter Twenty-Six

Our watercolor paintings are hung on the wall of Mrs. Honeywood's classroom, clipped to a string like colorful sheets on a clothesline. After weeks of painting we've moved on to photography. We're a poor district, so none of us have cameras; however, we do have school-issued Android tablets, and some of us have cell phones. We can use either one. Mrs. Honeywood says we don't need cameras. Her class is not a photography class. It's an art class, and the assignment is to take pictures that stir emotions. She says we can edit, alter, and, use filters on our photos; it's all part of art.

Just as Gypsy Honeywood lectured on van Gogh while we painted with watercolors, she's been introducing us to photographers whose images are nothing less than stunning. Artists like Lee Jeffries, Lisa Kristine, and Rehahn, photographers who capture the souls of their subjects. I think of their work as visual poems or portraits that sing. Their photos, soundless prints that speak volumes, move me in the same way as words and music do.

I want to be a photographer someday and travel the globe taking pictures that are raw, real, and humanly beautiful. As for now, Paris Village is my canvas and the folks here are my stories. I snap pics of everyone.

I took a close-up of Granny Crackers in The Barrel, shelves

of clutter and antiques as her backdrop. Mirrored in her eyes are the echoes of time and beauty. Her ruddy skin, gray braids, and high cheekbones give her a Native American vibe. Whether it's authentic or not, she plays into it by wearing a chunk of turquoise around her neck and moccasins on her feet.

I got a great shot of Ambrose, dwarfed by sunflowers and standing in his spun-to-gold garden. He holds a sharp spade in his gnarled hand and a soft look in his milky brown eyes.

I nabbed a candid of Dixie and Twyla coming out of Bob's Bar into a stream of sunlight. Twyla looks happy, squinting eyes, her bright red lips split into a large smile, laughing with her whole face. Dixie resembles a living Muppet, her head of blue-gray fuzz teased into a hairy monster, a Pall Mall hanging from puckered, stitch-marked lips.

I crossed the street to The Sol Shack. Inside I snapped pics of happy patrons and of my sweet Mateo busing tables. Another photo shows him sitting in a back booth doing homework, while the waitress, an older black woman, leans over his shoulder, helping him with his English.

Solomon didn't mind the photo shoot because I took some great food porn to share on social media. I posted scrumptious pics of fried fish, fried chicken, collard greens, and peach cobbler.

I also took a shot of Montana that looks like an ad for Abercrombie and Fitch. Mo can't help being photogenic. His beauty is crippling. Mo was sitting on his bed, a James Dean poster hanging on the wall behind him. He was freshly showered, so his breasts were unbound. His thin white T-shirt clung to damp skin, faint nipples pressed against cotton.

In a ballsy move I used a stepladder to catch Jason and Kaleem sitting in their serenity garden. The Japanese maples are turning red. The two men lounged side by side in Adirondack chairs, soaking in the beauty.

"Can I take your picture?" I asked, peering over the cedar fence.

"Uhh . . . sure." Their surprised response was spoken in unison.

"It's homework." I tried to explain away the awkwardness.

"Really? What's the assignment?"

"Take pictures that stir emotions."

"Well, in that case." Jason grinned and reached for Kaleem's hand.

The two clasped onto each other like lovers, dark and white fingers interlaced like piano keys. Kaleem smiled and tilted his head toward his partner, who leaned in. The men touched forehead to forehead. I took several shots of them looking lovingly into each other's eyes and then a few more while they smiled at me. In the pics Jason resembled the all-American-man: blond and blue-eyed, an athlete dressed in an Adidas jogging suit, a silver cross hanging around his neck. Kaleem looked every bit a Muslim, sparkling and luminous in his crisp, white tunic top and matching pants, gold bracelets wrapped around each naked ankle, his bare feet crossed. The Japanese garden is a beautiful backdrop. Maybe I should convince Mo to have me take his senior pictures in their backyard.

I was excited about the photos I had taken and stayed after class to show Mrs. Honeywood.

"Savannah," she cooed while swiping through my phone. "You're an artist."

I don't believe I have ever impressed a teacher prior to Mrs. Honeywood. I'm not mistreated at school. I've never been in trouble or treated unfairly, nor have I been a pet. I don't receive attention for bad behavior or good behavior. I'm simply a kid who exists. Her praise flipped a switch and flooded me with light.

"Honey, you have a gift."

Her sugary compliments melted my armor. I began showing her all my photographs, digging through my library in search of treasures. I got excited and dug too deep, began uncovering rubies and gems. The photo of Ava panhandling, Sarge at her side, caused my mouth to parch and my chest to feel empty, like a cave. A rock lodged in my throat. My voice cracked. "That's my mom." I'm not sure why I said it. It was a confession that escaped my lips while my guard was down.

"Oh baby," she whispered.

I grabbed my phone and swiped some more, trying to change the subject. I came upon the photographs of Mimi. The first showed a room of light, sunbeams streaming through glass, illuminated potted plants lining the window sill. Mimi is lying center stage in a hospital bed, sleeping, blanketed in a ray of light. Another photo shows her sitting up in bed. Her hair, a new growth of spiky silver blades standing on end like spring grass, accompanies a big smile under cracked lips. A selfie taken on the same day, Mo, Phoenix, and I had climbed into her lap, all of us laughing. I have so many pictures of Mimi.

Granny Crackers bought us our phones the Christmas that cancer came back with a vengeance, so she could get hold of all three of us at any time, and vice versa. Montana loaded her phone with music and placed earbuds in her ears, drowning out the hospital sounds. Often Montana played songs for Mimi, downloading our grandmother's favorites : the Eagles, Elton John, and Van Morrison. Phoenix played games on his phone. He escaped long hospital days by transporting to Fortnite. Me? I took photographs.

That's when my search for happiness began, during stage-four cancer. I spent all my time looking for light in the darkness, hunting for a silver lining. I captured painful moments, trying to discover anything good going on. Where was the grace in dying? I wanted some sort of proof that peace lives in pain. I think I was looking for God. Sometimes I found him. Now it's become an obsession. I look for God all the time, in every dark and dingy corner of my world, in every sad moment of my life. When I find him or her I take a pic and write a poem.

A teardrop clung to Mrs. Honeywood's bottom lash like a dew drop on a leaf as she stared at my photographs. Excitement was replaced with vulnerability. I felt uncomfortably naked. Shamefaced, I looked at the clock. I'd spent so much time uncovering my soul that I'd missed the bus.

"I'm sorry." I snatched my phone. "I gotta bounce." I fled the building. Standing on the sidewalk, I thought about what to do. I could call Montana to pick me up, but Mo has been so angsty lately. I couldn't stand any more heartbreak, having to sit close to someone who's so distant. I decided to walk over to the middle school. Phoenix should be getting out soon, and maybe he'd walk home with me. It was only a couple of miles.

Phoenix was standing against the corner of the building acting chill with a group of guys, sucking on a Juul. He's so much stronger and bigger than the kids his age. Phoenix is an athlete, boy, and thuggish man-child all rolled into one. He's a ball of clay, pliable, and not yet formed or fired. There's no telling how he's going to be cast. He's tall and good-looking like our mother, dark and mysterious like his father, and full of leadership qualities. At home he's the baby. In sports he's naturally athletic and fast. At school he's just another inner city kid from a broken home, and in the streets, he's a little gangsta.

"Hey!" I shouted to Phoenix, causing the cluster of boys to swim off like a school of fish.

"What's up?" Although he acted calm, I could tell Phoenix was surprised and happy to see me, which made me feel better.

"I missed the bus. I'm gonna walk. Come with me. We can stop at The Sol Shack, and I'll buy you a piece of cornbread and a sweet tea."

"Hell, yeah, let's skirt."

Phoenix and I took the tracks toward home. We followed the railroad ties, two unsupervised teens on a freedom trek, off the school bus and away from others. A few trees had begun to morph from green to yellow. The cool morning had developed into a bright, beautiful day. Queen Anne's lace, daisies, and blue chicory grew alongside the tracks, a splatter of beauty in the ghetto.

I talked Phoenix into a photo shoot. We had fun. I took photographs of him walking the tracks ahead of me, and Phoenix took pics of me posed, sitting on the rail, and another standing in the wildflowers. I got a gritty shot of him sitting on the slanted cement of the underpass, freeway traffic above his head, graffiti below his feet. In between photos we laughed, ran, and played.

We left the tracks and walked down alleys bordered by back lots. A dirty yellow stray cat crossed our path. Unlike most feral cats, this one stopped and looked up at us with helpless, hopeful gold eyes.

"Hey, kitty, kitty." I leaned forward to pet its back.

The cat, scared, pulled itself in, but did not move. It allowed me to stroke its fur.

"I bet she's hungry," Phoenix said. Reaching into his backpack he pulled out a turkey sandwich. I looked at Phoenix, wondering why he wasn't eating.

"It was pizza day," he explained, laying his lunch in the dirt. "I brought my own money and bought food."

The cat began scarfing the sandwich in ravenous, noisy bites, the whispered roar of a hungry lion coming from a yellow alley cat. Within minutes the meal was devoured and the cat was begging us for more.

"Sorry, kitty." Phoenix was kind. "I'm all out."

As we walked, the cat followed. She was a small stray, thin except for her misshapen belly with nipples that nearly dragged the ground.

"Poor thing. I bet she has babies. No wonder she's hungry."

We began following the pathetic creature, wondering where she would lead. It felt as if the cat had planned our meeting, stopped us, grabbed our attention—and in good fortune a meal—and then invited us to her home. The cat pranced up the back-yard of a deserted house as if she were the owner. Two blocks from home, Phoenix and I knew the house well. It had been empty for as long as we'd lived in Paris Village, a bright red sticker taped to its front door.

The cat jumped onto the back-porch railing and sat on the weathered board, staring at us. Above its head was a four-paned window missing one piece of glass. "Meow!" she pleaded, before leaping through the opening.

Phoenix, who is much taller than me, stood on tiptoes to peer inside. "Savannah, you're right. She has kittens."

"I knew it." I smiled.

"She's smart," Phoenix said. "She found more than an empty box to have babies in; she found a whole house."

"Yeah, smart, until it goes up in flames."

"Aww, shit, Savannah, somebody's gonna torch this house, ain't they?"

"It's possible."

"We need to save them." Phoenix was insistent. "We'll take 'em home. Hide 'em in my closet. I can take care of them. We can give the kittens away to friends when they get bigger and put the mama cat back outside."

It sounded like a good plan. First thing we needed to do was check around the house, make sure the cat and kittens were the only squatters. We walked around to the front and peered into the dirty windows. The inside of the small house looked vast and empty, devoid of the things that fill a room. We tried once more to open the locked doors. Satisfied that we were the only humans on the property, we returned to the back window.

"I can fit through there," I said confidently. "Give me a lift. I'll unlock the door and let you in."

"Get on my shoulders," Phoenix said, bending down.

It was an easy solution. Phoenix is tall. I'm light and I've been on his shoulders hundreds of times, playing chicken in the swimming pool. I plopped on his shoulders, and when Phoenix stood up, I was three feet taller. I pulled myself through the window head first and landed on my stomach in a tiny kitchen. The yellow cat curled around her babies. Three balls of greedy fur feasted at her belly, sucking her dry, draining her of all nourishment. Being a mom must suck, I thought, before rising and letting Phoenix in.

We sat on dirty linoleum watching the kittens nurse. I stroked the mama cat, not much more than a baby herself. She purred loudly, like a broken-down car revving its engine, desperately wanting to go. Finally the kittens were satisfied.

"Let's bounce," I said to Phoenix, watching a spider creep up the wall. "You get the kittens. I'll bring the mama." Phoenix gently picked up the kittens and stuck them one by one into his thin windbreaker, lining the inside of his zipped jacket with fur babies. He stepped outside. As I was about to scoop up the mama cat, I heard a deep baritone voice shouting.

"Halt! I said stop! Get your hands up! I said get your fucking hands up! Get your hands out of your jacket! Out of your jacket!"

I sprang to the door. Phoenix stood petrified, his hand deep in his windbreaker, calming kittens, unable to speak or react. A red-faced cop was screaming, pointing his gun at my brother.

The weapon went off in his hands like a bomb. Instinctively I jumped. As Phoenix went down, I did too. He hit the ground. I flew from the porch and landed on top of him, covering his body with mine, his brown face hidden under my long blond hair.

"Don't shoot! Don't shoot!" I screamed over and over. "He's my brother! Don't shoot!"

"What's in his coat?" shouted the officer standing over top of us, his gun still smoking. I slowly lifted myself up and stared into the shocked and pained face of my baby brother.

"Kittens," I said, unzipping his jacket with shaking hands. "He was saving kittens."

Chapter Twenty-Seven

This is what I remember: the kittens poking their heads out of Phoenix's jacket, unharmed, and softly mewing, a slow spread of red on a white T-shirt, my brother's face with a shocked stare, the whispered word "Savannah" gurgling from his mouth, spit and blood dripping down his chin. Standing behind me is the officer who shot my brother.

"Jesus Christ, what have I done?" I recognized a second voice, Officer Miller. "Code eight, juvenile down, dispatch squad to three one two Monet Avenue."

Both men sound faraway, voices traveling three dimensions before reaching my ears. Phoenix and I, in our own universe. I place my hand on his chest, and warm red blood seeps through my fingers. Our world spins. We're floating, Phoenix and I, kittens swimming between us.

"You're going to be okay," I tell him. "I promise. It's gonna be fine."

I hear approaching sirens, see a blur of blue lights. Medics swarm in on Phoenix, surround him, their urgent voices speaking code. Somehow I am suddenly standing.

I have been removed from the scene and tossed into time, where I am suspended. Everything around me moves in fast forward. Phoenix disappears into the back of an ambulance. It screeches off and leaves me standing in the grass.

Never in my life have I felt so alone. My gaze follows the lights until the emergency vehicle turns the corner. My heart, a red balloon, drifts down the road chasing after it. As the space between Phoenix and me expands, the sounds of piercing sirens decreases. The separation between my brother and me feels vast and stretches quickly.

Just moments before, I'd slammed into him, tackling him to the ground, like our games of wrestle. My body covered his body. When he exhaled, I inhaled, swallowing his fear. His blood was still on my hands. The smell of gunpowder lingered in the air. As if planted in one spot, unable to move, I felt the crowd growing around me.

Life was surreal. I was in a haze, caught in a fog. I sank to the ground, empty and cold. The sun had evaporated, everything golden was gone and streaming down my face in tears. My eyes rained large droplets of yellow paint, bleeding every bit of happiness that I'd ever ingested and left me sitting in a mustard-colored puddle of pain.

Within my aura of yellow and gray only sadness existed. Outside the bubble, life was chaotic. A crowd of people and police, a news van, cameras, and reporters appeared out of nowhere. Cops kept talking to me, but I had no language. Mouths opened and closed, lips flapped like wings. The only thing I heard was the ringing in my ears and the echo of gunfire.

I felt the familiarity of her fingertips. Her arthritic hands, sticks and stones, pressed on my soft flesh. Her touch allowed me to fully surrender and sent me deeper to the earth. My head bent, rested on her moccasin feet, and my arms encircled her thin ankles.

"Get up, baby," she said. "Phoenix needs us at the hospital."

At the sound of my brother's name, my strength slowly returned. I pulled on Mo's hand to get to my feet. Granny Crackers wrapped her arm around me, and I crawled inside her pit, nestled up to her side.

She stuck out her old hand, warding off reporters, as we walked. "Shame on you!" She spit anger as they approached. "Shame! Shame!" She stimulated their conscience and repelled them with words of disgrace. We made it, un-assaulted, to the Oldsmobile. Mo drove steadily, shaky hands gripping the wheel, eyes fixed on the road.

At the hospital we were escorted from the emergency room through double doors and down a long corridor to an empty waiting area with ugly blue chairs and a TV airing Fox News. With Granny Crackers's comforting sweater smelling of sassafras tea and wet wool thrown over my shoulders, her old hand in mine, and Mo by my side, I answered the questions posed by policemen. My family made me feel strong, but my answers sounded weak and simple, as if Phoenix and I are young and ignorant. Perhaps, because we are.

I told them I followed the cat inside. I climbed through the opened window and let my brother in. Our intent was to keep the animals from burning up in a house that was bound to catch fire.

"Am I in trouble for trespassing?" I asked.

"No," Miller answered.

Officer Miller waited with us, but not too close. He came and went and walked the halls. His presence remained in and out of my peripheral sight. I began counting, a human metronome, his steps, my pulse, the ticking of the clock, everything moved with the steady beat of my heart.

Time travels slower in a hospital than anywhere else on earth. We waited for hours that felt like years to hear if Phoenix was alive or dead. Lost within the minutes, I filled each second with prayers.

"Oh, Heavenly Father, Sweet Jesus, Hail Mary, Dear God, Holy Spirit." I strung prayers together like pearls. Prayers ran out of my mouth, a jumble of words dumped into God's hands, sifting through his fingers. Phoenix, a grain for God to catch in the center of his palm and blow on him the breath of life.

"Dear Mimi," I begged. "Wrap your heavenly arms around Phoenix, mend him with a sweet kiss, and send him back to us. We need him, Mimi, even though he was your baby boy, perhaps your favorite. Please, Mimi, I don't think I'm strong enough to live if Phoenix dies."

While I frantically prayed, so did Granny Crackers and Mo. All three of us, engaged in whispered conversations, calling forth Jesus and Mimi with mumbled hopes and frantic negotiations. When I looked up, Ambrose stood in front of me.

"You okay, sweetheart?" His face crumpled with caring.

"Yes, sir."

Sometimes a touch says it all. He ran his thick fingers over my long hair, rested his hand on my shoulder, and gave it a squeeze. He then took a seat next to Granny Crackers. Words unnecessary, she leaned into his shoulder, and he laid his large brown head on her silver braids. I got up, feeling an urgent need to move. I stared at the two of them. Their eyes closed, bodies pressed together, old bones holding each other up. I couldn't help myself; I snapped a photo.

"You wanna walk?" I asked Mo.

"Yeah," he said, getting up. We strolled the hall, back and forth, up and down, our steps covering miles, going nowhere.

"I'm sorry." I eventually cried.

'It's not your fault, Savannah Jo. It's not your fault."

We saw the doctor approach Granny Crackers and Ambrose. Anxiety stood between Mo and me like another person; the three of us grabbed hands and rushed to hear the news. I embraced the words and squeezed. Phoenix was going to be okay. Shot point blank in the chest, he suffered a cracked sternum and two broken ribs. The bullet had missed his heart and lungs. They removed the fragments and bits that lodged in his upper chest and under his left armpit.

A collective exhale burst aloud. We had been living among ghosts, knowing the possibilities, expecting the worst. Bound by our sorrow, we stood united in glory. The positive energy of our communal sigh birthed relief as visible as an apparition. I wore worry like a corset, fastened tightly around my chest, crushing me, halting each breath. The diagnosis of a cracked sternum and broken ribs loosened the strings and allowed me to breathe easier. Not so much for Phoenix.

"He's extremely lucky," said the surgeon. "He must have an angel."

"He does. Her name is Mimi," I told him.

We'd thrown our prayers to the heavens, scattered them across the sky like stars, and they'd been answered. Our wishes were pinpoint lights, shining against the vast darkness. Mercifully a Phoenix had been mapped in the constellation of our desperate pleas. My brother, a galaxy king, had been blessed.

After the doctor left, Kaleem came running down the hall. He'd been working second shift in the ER, three to eleven p.m., and had just gotten off the job. He had been able to keep tabs on Phoenix and already knew what we knew. He explained further, calming our concerns. "Chest injuries heal on their own," he said, "but it takes time, and it's painful. The most important thing is to make sure he doesn't develop an infection. He needs to cough. He needs to take deep breaths. He won't want to. It will hurt. It will take at least a couple of months for him to mend. I'll be there to check on him every step of the way." Leaning in closer to Granny Crackers, he continued, "More importantly, Rosie, is care for his mental health." Kaleem looked at me "Both of them. They've been through a horrible trauma."

I was thankful for Kaleem's bluntness. The way he put it out there opened the door, laid it on the table. The truth was that Phoenix, especially Phoenix, and I were going to be screwed up for a while.

"Can you take the girls home?" Granny Crackers asked Kaleem.

"Yeah, sure, no problem."

"But I don't want to go."

"Me either," said Mo.

"You guys go. Get some sleep," Granny Crackers insisted. "I'm gonna stay here till Phoenix wakes. Tomorrow I'll need rest and Phoenix will need his sisters. If we're gonna be in this together for the long haul, we'll have to work in shifts." Granny Crackers is good at making her case. The car ride home was quiet, hushed by mental fatigue. Kaleem filled the silence with Taylor Swift's new album. I low-key appreciated his efforts.

Pulling onto the streets in Paris Village felt eerie. I could sense the electricity. A current of adrenaline flowed down the avenues like the blood in veins. Emotions were sparked. High voltage moods were walking about. It was nearly midnight, and people were everywhere.

"What's going on?" I cluelessly asked.

"Sweetie," Kaleem explained. "People are upset. They're worried about Phoenix. They're angry at the police."

"Oh." The realization of the ripple effect hit me like a wave.

Kaleem pulled into the driveway. On his porch sat Jason, Twyla, and Dixie, each one of them holding a kitten, waiting for our arrival.

Chapter Twenty-Eight

a thirteen-year-old unarmed African American boy was shot by a white police officer. It's all over the news, on every channel and in every paper. Phoenix Dale was rescuing kittens from a vacant house when he was shot down in broad daylight. Savannah Dale, Phoenix's sister, who is Caucasian, covered him with her body.

Phoenix's eighth-grade school picture is being aired on every news station. Social media is burning up with the story. Somebody we don't know started a GoFundMe. Phoenix is described as young, handsome, smart, and athletic, a star swimmer who is already breaking city records. The fact that I laid on top of him and the shooting stopped doesn't make me a hero; it just proves that racism exists.

For someone who doesn't like hospitals, Granny Crackers spent all night with Phoenix. In the morning she came home, sat down on the couch to talk to us, and promptly passed out. I covered her up with an afghan. The chihuahuas jumped onto their mistress and quickly found their resting spots alongside her body. She napped not knowing she was draped in dogs, one at her feet, another across her legs, a third on her shoulder. She was compelled to sleep by pure and raw exhaustion. Mo left a note on the kitchen table, and we took our shift at the hospital beside our brother.

Phoenix's pain is visible, etched across his face. His suffering shows in the way he holds his body, stiff and flat, like a board. Phoenix can barely move to change positions. It hurts him to breathe.

Kaleem told us Phoenix would feel discomfort, his insides bruised and battered. Kaleem said it would take several weeks, maybe months, for Phoenix to heal. A speeding bullet ripping through your chest leaves shock waves. Lying in bed bandaged and broken, he looks every bit thirteen, no more a man-child, just a child. His number of years are no longer masked by his height, maturity, and cockiness. Phoenix looks young and small. His name is gigantic.

My brother is headline news, suddenly the poster boy for police discrimination. Phoenix is dealing with things his white siblings can't possibly understand. Still, I had been there. I heard the angry command, "Get your hands up!" I saw my brother shot. I tried to protect him. All I got was blood on my hands.

Feelings of shame and sorrow bounced between Phoenix and me, unspoken words scattered like jacks at my feet. It's strange to feel so distant from a person and yet so close. Phoenix and I had been through a trauma together, and he had been hurt. I felt like the X over the whY in the formula of racism. I was part of an equation that couldn't find a solution.

I never thought about color before the shooting. We are a mixed-race family living in a diverse neighborhood where homes and families line up like a giant box of crayons. Yes, Phoenix's skin is darker than mine. So is Montana's. We have different fathers, making the three of us varying shades, with our own distinct heads of hair, yet we have spent our entire lives sharing toys, meals, beds, baths, and germs. Raised together by three generations of women, we have lived the same fairytale story.

When Devious Addiction swooped in and carried off our princess, the queen took us to her haven. There we laughed, loved, and played together until our dreams turned to nightmares. Our majesty was slain by cancer. We had to leave our gingerbread cottage and go live with the little old lady who lives in a shoe. And we were doing just fine until the big bad wolf shot my brother.

Mo, Phoenix, and I have been through hardships as one, and now a giant color wheel stood between my brother and me. As I wiped the dew from my eyes and the snot from my nose, Phoenix peered at me.

"Good tackle." His voice cracked. "Mo, you should have seen Savannah dive. It was badass."

"We gonna start calling you Flygirl," Mo teased.

The tension shattered. Mo and I stood at Phoenix's bedside, joking with our brother, and he tried not to laugh, because it hurt. It occurred to me that even though the rest of the world compared the shade of his skin to mine, Phoenix didn't.

It's simple. We are siblings, birds with different feathers, flocked together in one nest. The thoughts and opinions beyond our branch didn't matter. Our family quilt, created by strong women and different fathers, presented varicolored patterns stitched together by strands of DNA much stronger than racism.

"Look at this," I said, pointing my phone at my brother.

"The kittens." He smiled.

"They're at the house waiting for you. Mama cat too, sleeping in your bed."

"You can thank Dixie and Twyla," said Mo. "They caught them one by one. Sat on Jason's porch till midnight with a box full of cats, waiting for us to come home. They even bought us cat food and litter. They're good peeps."

"The best," Phoenix whispered and again drifted off to sleep.

When he awoke, Mo and I were still there, sitting beside his bed, and we picked up our conversation like he hadn't just napped for two hours.

"What do you want to name the kittens?" I asked.

"Yeah," said Mo, "we have to name them before Granny Crackers thinks something up."

It was true. The chihuahuas have terrible names—Inky, Stinky, and Parlez Vous. I don't know what she was thinking. Chihuahuas are Mexican dogs, and *parlez vous* is French.

"Mama cat is Tupelo," Phoenix said, his voice weak.

I nodded. "Tupelo! That's a great name. I love it."

"I love it too," said Mo. "It's perfect. A yellow mama named Tupelo."

Both Mo and I knew where Phoenix had come up with the name. There were two reasons, curled around Mimi. First, her favorite song was "Tupelo Honey" by Van Morrison, and second, Mimi's yellow lab was named Honey. Every Sunday morning Mimi would play the whole Van Morrison CD as she sang in the kitchen making pancakes. When "Tupelo Honey" came on, the volume went up, and she'd scoop up in her arms whoever was closest and dance around the kitchen.

I added, "We can name the kittens after honey too. Like Clover—you know, clover honey?"

Phoenix nodded at my suggestion.

"How about Wildflower?" Mo said. "There's wildflower honey."

"Tupelo, Clover and Wildflower." I was excited the names were coming so easily. "Those sound good, don't you think?"

Phoenix's pallid smile was an unvoiced "Yes."

"What should we name the last one?" Mo asked.

"I don't know. What other types of honey are there?"

Mo Googled *honey* on his phone.

A voice answered me from the hallway. Her words drifted into the room on stardust and dandelion fluff. A thousand times we had wished for her return, there she stood.

"Buckwheat," our mother said. "Buckwheat is a popular honey."

Ava stood in the doorway. She looked clean, refreshed, healthy, and very pregnant. Her thin pink T-shirt stretched over a basketball belly, her belly button poking through the cotton like a small nose.

We stared in shock. I knew my mouth was hanging open. It felt like my heart stopped.

What the hell? She'd disappeared less than three months earlier. She had vanished a sick, sad, skinny drug addict and returned resembling the Virgin Mary, full of child. Who was the father? And how could she be close to giving birth?

Chapter Twenty-Nine

Our front porch is covered with gifts. We can't even get in the front door. Bouquets of flowers grace the steps; balloons crowd the railings; families drop off letters, cards, and children's heartfelt artwork. People are thoughtful. Plush toys—fish, dolphins, and butterflies in bright hues—sit on the porch waiting for Phoenix, the butterfly swimmer, to come home.

Phoenix has been in the hospital five days, and Ava has visited each and every one. She saw the news, her baby boy shot in the chest rescuing kittens. She couldn't stay away. She gathered all the courage she could find, tossed copper coins of strength into a well of wishes, put on her big-girl panties, and rushed to save her son.

I suppose the epitome of child neglect would be failing to know when a child is growing inside of you. Ava had no idea that she was incubating a little chick when she showed up on our porch that first day of June. She remained clueless that month and the next as she played in paints and snorted drugs. Not until her overdose that horrible night did she learn of her pregnancy. When she argued with the hospital staff, an ultrasound revealed she was four months along. The confirmation caused the hysterical meltdown that landed her on the psych ward, and when we visited her every night in the hospital, she couldn't look at us.

Dressed in institutional pajamas and shame, socks on her feet, and a tear in her eye, she kept her face turned toward the wall,.

Ava, too far along to terminate the pregnancy, knew her baby would be taken from her. Four months in utero and already a victim of child abuse. Sad, depressed, ashamed, heartbroken, and suicidal, she had just enough strength to disappear.

When Ava left the hospital she was sent to the Healing House, a rehabilitation facility that helps women get clean. Her vow of secrecy and HIPAA kept us from knowing where she was.

No penance can take away her guilt. She says that the only thing she could do was self-nurture through the rest of her pregnancy. She embraced treatment and recovery at the Healing House. She planned to come home to us after the baby's adoption, detoxed and desperately needing to mother someone. She'd hoped we'd never know that out there, somewhere, was another little extension of us, and we'd be spared the pain of loving someone only to lose them.

Then Phoenix got shot. It was all over the news, her baby's face splashed on the flat screen in the Healing House, a shelter full of broken women, young and old, doing their best to mend.

"Tsk, tsk," they all said. "Look at that, another little brown boy shot by a cop."

Ava gasped. "That's my boy."

She showed up at the hospital drenched in humility, a pathetic, bedraggled stray standing on the other side of the door, desperate to enter.

Ava has confessed her story bit by bit. She shows up to see Phoenix each day, wanting to be next to him. He allows it. He lets her camp beside his bed. He asks her no questions. She holds his hand, and he sleeps. Sympathetically I understand. Phoenix is a young, scared boy who needs a mom. It doesn't matter that she's reckless. She's there.

Phoenix's body is slowly healing, I'm not quite sure what was going on in his mind. I know I've been having nightmares and ugly daydreams. My quiet moments are rudely interrupted by vivid flashbacks, the red, angry face of a white policeman; a black gun; my brother frozen with fear. In the center of my brain lives the echo of "Get your fucking hands up!" BAM! The wailing of sirens. I can only imagine that Phoenix's PTSD is ten times worse than mine.

Getting Phoenix to talk is a struggle, like deep-sea fishing. In the depths of blue, his words are hidden in the abyss. My baby brother was tough and chill, cocky and bold, strong, sporty, kooky, and fun. Now he's quiet. He's submerged his personality in those deep waters. His toughness and strength silently combat the pain. His bold cockiness helps him ignore his trauma. Coping with his internal fears requires that he swallow his external forces, and I see their energy depleting. Phoenix's strength of character has just enough vitality to keep him sitting upright.

Granny Crackers is a neutral river, a viewless stream. She wades ankle deep in the shallows with Ava, keeping her eyes on the island Phoenix has become. She doesn't say much, which is surprising. Usually Granny Crackers is a woman who holds nothing back. She scolds with coarse humor and frank wisdom. A beer in her hand, mockery in her voice, Granny Crackers has no problem shaming someone into good behavior. With this shooting, she hasn't even attempted it. No sarcastic reprimands will change anything. What's done is done.

Mo, on the other hand, is ruthless. He doesn't want to be in Phoenix's room if Ava is there. The sight of our mother, one hand clutching Phoenix the other hand resting on her baby bump, sparks a fire inside Montana that cannot be extinguished. Mo's fury burns like the houses in Paris Village. Nothing but contempt is reflected in his eyes. Mo's laser-gun pupils focus on Ava. She is the prey caught in a target of disdain. He shoots loathing toward her with silent beams of insult.

"How could you be four months pregnant and not know it?" Mo finally asked, disgusted.

I felt sorry for our pathetic mother. Her shameful, vulnerable response was spoken in a trembling voice. Mo's hardness made Ava look even more fragile.

"I don't know, Montana. I'm not even able to explain it to myself. I was in bad shape... My period was spotty, my cycle erratic. Wasted days turned into forgotten weeks and lost months. I didn't pay attention to my body. I gave it no time or love. My body provided no sign."

"That's so fucked up."

"It is. I was. I'm sorry. I love you all." A stream of tears ran down her face. "I love this little guy too," she said, rubbing her belly. "And I've hurt you all. I'm a terrible person."

"You said it, not me." Mo walked out of the room.

"Who's the father?" I don't know why I asked. "Is it the dude that killed Sarge?"

"Could be," she whimpered, shamefaced. "Could be someone else. It doesn't matter."

And it didn't matter, because in the hush of that moment, a nurse walked into Phoenix's room. She checked his bandages and rewrapped his chest. He winced. She told him to cough. He moaned, groaned, and recoiled. The nurse persisted, and Phoenix coughed up thick yellow-green mucus streaked with blood. The nurse left the room, Phoenix lay back, struggling with a sigh, and Ava returned to his side. Mother and son, hand in hand, closed their tired lids. A crushing silence filled the room.

Phoenix and Ava are connected by blood and recovery. Both of their bodies are fighting a battle. As his body labors to restore itself, she grows life in arid soil.

Chapter Thirty

*M*y brother is loved by a nation of people pissed off by police violence. Phoenix's name is painted on cardboard signs and heard in chants and cries. It's been written in activist's blogs and slam poetry and shared on social media. On the same day Phoenix was released from the hospital, Black Lives Matter organized a protest. Mo, Jason, Kaleem, Ava, Twyla and I participated. Jason custom-made us matching shirts; a swim-team photo of Phoenix was printed onto a light blue T with "Phoenix Strong" written across the back.

The response to the protest was overwhelming. Hundreds of people showed up to march. They came from all over, diverse and united, black, white, brown, and yellow. They stood happily jammed together, side by side and hand in hand. There were old and young people, dogs on leashes, bike riders, rollerbladers, strollers, wagons, and scooters. Everybody carried signs and smiles. "Justice for Phoenix Dale" was stenciled, colored, and glued onto cardboard, written on poster board, scripted with fabric markers on sweatshirts, and painted onto fabric and flags. His name was hollered and chanted. It was sung to the heavens and it drifted on the breeze. Phoenix was not just a name but a hymn, an anthem.

Resounding voices filled every corner of the city. Streets

vibrated with energy. We marched from the house on Monet Avenue, a long seven miles to Police Headquarters, belting my brother's name. The crowd and chaos shut down a major roadway. We made national news. It was the first time since the shooting that I didn't feel alone.

Police lined the streets of our walk, anticipating riots, but hoping for none, and although we demanded that one of their own be fired, nobody was arrested. We are peaceful people, after all.

Police Officer Brian Martin is suspended, with pay, pending an internal investigation. We want his badge. Authorities say they are examining the incident from all sides, studying footage from the body cam, taking into account extenuating circumstances, the recent fires, and a 911 call that reported two kids (yes, she said kids) snooping around a vacant house.

I read that police anxiety is high in Paris Village. It's a neighborhood of mostly poor people. Many of the residents own guns, and some carry their weapons concealed. Felons, drugs, and domestic violence live here. But so do happy couples, small children, loving families, and elderly folks.

Bigoted minds believe that people in my neighborhood are lawless, that we live in mayhem and anarchy, but I will tell you what I know. It took Brian Martin less than ten seconds to decide to fire his gun into Phoenix's chest. A shot to kill. He made a snap decision to shoot a thirteen-year-old boy armed with kittens, frozen with panic. If Officer Brian Martin truly feared for his life, it was only because Phoenix is brown.

On Sunday, a day after the protest, Ambrose took Mo and me to church. We accepted his invitation, and we were the only two white people in attendance. Sitting in the pews, I was by far the lightest person. My white skin and yellow hair made me stand out like a taper candle in a dark room, but it didn't stop people from being kind. They called me Sister Savannah. They gave me hugs and handshakes, referred to me as brave, and raved about my courage. They credited me for saving Phoenix and they did it without making me feel bad about my color or the way I was underdressed.

The minister, a majestic and verbose man, wove his scripture lecture around Phoenix and me. I was a part of the gospel. The choir dedicated their songs to Phoenix. The animated sermon, upbeat hymns, dancing, stomping, clapping, amens, and hallelujahs, all part of a black church experience, were meant to lift the spirits of the congregation. Every last one of them felt the attack on Phoenix's life as a personal threat. Their sons and grandsons might be shot while doing something as innocent as rescuing kittens. Black men are stopped every day by police for no reason at all. Black men cause suspicion; they entice fear and they do it simply by living. It's an unfair truth, and it adds to my white guilt.

The people at Ambrose's church showed me no judgment, although I'm full of guilt and shame. I am the cruel validation that racism exists. Instead of giving me their anger, they gave me kindness.

They lit candles for Phoenix. They lit a candle for Mo and me. They included our family in their prayer. They invited us back to church services. I guess it's true that when two or more gather in his name, there is love.

Chapter Thirty-One

Kaleem and Jason come every day to see Phoenix. Kaleem checks his wound, takes his temperature, makes him cough, and coaches him with deep-breathing exercises. Jason brings his assignments and tutors him along.

"Godsends," is what Granny Crackers calls them.

"Can you believe it? His own private nurse and teacher. I imagine no other poor, hurt, foster child can beat Phoenix in blessings."

I'd never heard her refer to us as foster kids before, but it's who we are. Lately she's used the label *foster kids* quite a bit while talking to the hospital social workers and applying for welfare assistance.

"Thank God for Obamacare," she told Dixie. Granny Crackers also plans to sue the police. "Money for Phoenix's future," she said. "The least they can do is put the boy through college."

Ava is still living at The Healing House. She takes the bus every day to visit her son. Granny Crackers welcomes her in, but they don't talk much. Ava spends her day posing as a good mom, caring for Phoenix, cleaning our house, and cooking him lunch. She leaves by five o'clock to return to the shelter by six for group counseling. If she misses a meeting she'll be kicked out of The

Healing House. The same thing would happen if she were to return high, drunk, or late.

While Phoenix was in the hospital, Granny Crackers needed Mo and me. The three of us alternated hospital runs and took turns sitting in The Barrel. For seven days after the shooting we lived like a family of wolves, sticking together, not worried about life outside our pack. Cruelly, the day I chose to leave the den and return to school was O.G.T testing day.

Every student in Ohio must pass the standardized Ohio Graduation Test to graduate. I'm not quite sure who decided an entire high school career should be determined by one test taken on a random day, but it's an unfair reality.

Honestly, I wasn't even aware it was testing day. My anxiety was anticipating the reactions to the shooting. What would be said? The current headline reads Brown Teen Shot, His White Sister Spared. Regret and anguish had moved into my frontal lobe.

Mrs. Honeywood saw me walking to my locker and pulled me aside. "Oh, Savannah, it's testing day. Baby, you should probably go home."

"Are you telling me to skip school?"

"No, not skip. It's just . . . I don't think it's the right time to take a test."

At her truth my simmering stress boiled over. I sounded defensive, like I was questioning her motive. "Are you worried my low test scores will affect the school's rating?"

"No, Savannah, sweetheart, I'm worried about you. How it will affect you."

I know that Mrs. Honeywood was being genuine and caring, and I should have responded with respect and gratitude. But the truth is, her tenderness caused me to unravel. Sewn together with scar tissue, I ripped out my stitching, piece by piece, and left the fabric of my life on the floor at her feet. "You know, Mrs. Honeywood, you're probably right. My intelligence should not be tested today, seeing that I'm walking around in a fog. But here's the sad truth: there are no good days. I guess last month I would have tested better, when I stayed up half the night watching a house go up in flames. Perhaps three months ago, when my mother was in the psych ward, or the day she overdosed. What if I had taken the test the beginning of my freshman year? Hmm . . . let's see, that's when my Mimi died. Before that? Well, that was the year I spent watching cancer kill her."

Mrs. Honeywood blanched.

"You see, Mrs. Honeywood, it's really hard to pick a good day for my I.Q. to be fairly tested, so if you don't mind, can I borrow a number-two pencil? I left mine at home."

She held up a pencil with trembling fingers, and I plucked it from her hands as casually as picking a flower. As I turned away it wasn't me crying, and it felt good to feel strong.

After school I walked to Mateo's. The thought of going home gave me an uneasy feeling in my stomach. I'm tired of seeing Phoenix wounded and stretched out in a La-Z-Boy, and Ava, a basketball hidden under a stretched shirt. She's an uncomfortable presence in our snug home. She attempts to make amends by baking humble pot pies and wiping a dust rag of humility across the furniture.

I'm mortified that my mother is seven months pregnant. Everybody knows she's a drug addict. A baby is like putting sprinkles on a shit cake. In her own strange way, Ava had tried to protect us from this reality by disappearing. For the first time I can remember, she was truly trying to be clean, sober, nurturing, and attentive. While she focused on recovery and redemption, I struggled to forgive her.

Mateo stepped out of his dark house into the autumn sun. His squinting, smiling eyes and flirty grin instantly warmed my heart.

"How did you do on the test?" I asked, walking up the porch steps.

"Who knows? I think I did okay in math and probably failed the English section. You?"

"Just the opposite. I'll walk with you to The Sol Shack."

"Nah, the baby's sick. My aunt had to go in to work, so I called off." Since his father's deportation, Mateo's mother has been despondent. Mateo has to act like a man.

"Aww, poor thing." Lucia is a sparkle, an adorable and ornery three-year-old with big black eyes. The thought of her suffering with sickness increased my sadness.

"Yeah, she's finally napping."

I could see the other kids through the screen door. Four fat heads lined up on the couch, Mateo's brothers, niece, and nephew. They stared like zombies at a large flat screen, watching colorful trolls dance and sing. Mateo's mom was slumped in a chair staring into space. She's a changed woman, no longer the happy homemaker pushing forth her welcome and love with traditional recipes and spicy salsa.

Mateo spoke to her through the screen. "*Mamá, estaré en el patio trasero. Llámame si necesitas algo.*"

Her head absently nodded.

"Let's go around back," he said to me.

The tent was still up. His aunt had absently abandoned her annual routine of packing away the nylon fort at the end of summer. We crawled inside the hideout. The sun shone on the golden fabric. We lay on our backs, staring at silhouettes of tree branches and the shadows of fallen leaves. My sorrows and his woes fluttered inside the tent like mosquitos. Our conversation flowed like two champions in a game of pity chess.

"My life sucks. Check."

"My mamá is drowning in depression."

"My mom is pregnant. Check."

"My dad was deported."

"My little brother was shot. Checkmate."

Mateo rolled onto his side and combed his hand through my hair. He stroked my face with his fingers from forehead to chin, a touch so soft and sweet it made me tingle.

Our kissing started soft, his hand slowly skimming over my hollows and curves, and turned into the blind leading the blind as we read each other's body like braille. Our fingers danced across flesh like smooth pages of a book, a mound of soft tissue, a pulsating dot, a hard dash, our breaths heavy. I thought about peeling off my tight leggings as we lay touching. Perhaps I'd invite something else in.

I wanted badly to push out all the hurt, replace my internal ache with an external discomfort. I'd heard of girls having their cherries popped, the blood and tearing pain. I was tempted. I gave no sign of it to Mateo, though. I wasn't going to offer what he did not ask for. I let him take the lead. I was his silent dance partner, mimicking his moves and keeping time with his steps.

I allowed his hungry kisses to feed my starving soul. Lying on top of me, he pushed his hips into my bones. I spread my legs wider, allowing him to fall between. Our flesh was separated by layers of material. Nonetheless, I could feel every bit of him through his sweatpants as he ground against me. Slipping into a daydream, I envisioned us doing it. In my fantasy our two bodies had become one. I embraced his lust and weight as we arched into each other. Our breaths quickened. Both of us were guilty, commiserating thrusts, longing for pleasure. I felt his body shudder against my shiver. My toes curled. His kissing slackened with panting breath. I continued my smooches until he rolled away with a look of embarrassment.

"I have to go in, check on Lucia, cook dinner."

"I know." I smiled. "I'll see ya tomorrow."

I walked home toward the pink glow of a setting sun thinking about our magical moment. I could honestly say nothing had happened during our innocent exploration of body and soul, even though something did.

Mateo and I had shared a heartbeat and something enormous. And the best part? I'm still a virgin.

Chapter Thirty-Two

*W*hen I came home from school, Phoenix and Ava were sitting together at the kitchen table. Phoenix is doing much better. He's no longer stuck in a reclining chair unable to move. He now rotates his resting places, moving from the living room to the kitchen to the front porch, proof that his body is slowly healing.

Today Phoenix and Ava had built a Lego city that stretched from one end of the table to the other. Phoenix had long since grown beyond the toy phase. He was a Lego architect. The shelves in his bedroom hold Lego masterpieces, crazy constructed automobiles and rocket ships. It was evident by the red, blue, and yellow blocks erected into buildings that Ava and Phoenix had spent the day playing. The sight was both heartwarming and strange.

Moments of normalcy and love are painful reminders that life could have been much different. The glimpse of a drug-free mother is as painful as our reality. I wanted to ask her why she allowed drugs not only to wreck her life, but also trample all over her children, including the little baby growing inside of her.

I walked by mother and son inspecting their elaborate city as I passed. I refused to act impressed and headed out the back door where Granny Crackers was sitting in the doorway of The Barrel. She seemed agitated. I assumed the Lego city had bothered her as well, hit a nerve, and left her questioning and pissed, as it had done me. But that wasn't it.

Before we had a chance to talk, Mo arrived in the little red Mazda.

Granny Crackers stood. "Bring me the keys, Montana Rose. We need to talk."

Mo let out a long sigh, as if he had been holding his breath, anticipating a confrontation.

"Your principal called. He asked how things were going at home and when were you coming back to school. That's a pretty odd question, seeing that you've been leaving the house every day to go to school for over a week now." For a brief moment the space between Granny Crackers and Mo was filled with a tense and uneasy silence.

"I'm not going back," Mo numbly replied. "I'm sorry I lied."

"Where've you been?"

"Nowhere in particular, just driving around. Ya know, getting lost, trying to find myself." Mo shuffled his feet.

"As of tomorrow you're gonna find your ass in that school building."

"No, I'm not!" Mo's stance reeked of obstinance, his feet firmly planted, head held high, chin out. "I won't go back. And you can't make me."

None of us have ever challenged Granny Crackers. Mo's tenacity caused her to stumble. Granny Crackers sat in her chair, like a boxer returning to her corner.

I fought the impulse to run to her side, massage her shoulders, and give her a pep talk. I wanted to urge her on, tell her, "You got this. You can win this fight. Don't back down to that little version of you. Sure, you feel pinned to the ropes by his youth and self-will, but you outmatch Mo with your internal strength and wisdom."

"Is it the bullies?" Granny Cracker asked.

"It doesn't matter," Mo said, laying the car keys in her hand. "I'll finish my senior year online."

Montana's last punch, thrown softly, knocked the wind out of Rosie. She got up and went into the house.

"What gives?" I asked Montana as the screen door shut.

"Don't you start, Savannah. You're supposed to have my back."

"How in the hell can I have your back if you won't talk to me, if you push me away and keep secrets? Tell me what's wrong. Tell me what happened."

Mo walked away, wandered into The Barrel, and sat on an exercise bike. He started pedaling. I could tell he wanted to run away from my questions. He was going nowhere. I stood in front of the stationary bike waiting for him to stop.

"It's really just this one asshole," Mo began. "He gets the others started. Most guys backed off after Granny Crackers and Jason visited the school. They stopped using me for a punching bag. But this dick just keeps coming. I've tried everything to get him to leave me alone, different tactics on different days. I've cussed him out, embarrassed him, ignored him, laughed it off. I thought if I could just keep my distance, then I'd be okay. It worked some, until the day he caught me alone."

"What did he do? Beat you up?"

"Nah, the homophobe sexually assaulted me."

"What?"

"Yeah, MF-er pinned me up against the wall with his body, pushed himself into me. He whispered in my ear. He grabbed my crotch. And he licked the side of my face."

"Gross! He licked your face?"

"Fuck, yeah."

"What did he say in your ear?"

"Feels like pussy to me." Mo looked down, played with the bracelets on his wrist.

"When did that happen?"

"Same day Phoenix was shot."

"Jesus, Montana, you've got to tell someone."

"I just did. I told you."

"You need to tell Granny Crackers and the principal, get his ass expelled."

"What makes you think he would get expelled? I have no marks; he didn't hit me. I'm not hurt. Besides, there were no witnesses. It's just his word against mine."

"That's bullshit, Mo. You can't let that asshole chase you from school, take your dreams away."

"I'm not giving up my dreams."

"You were so excited about auto mechanics."

"Maybe so, but it's not my dream. I'd just rather work on cars than study math, but it's not my future."

"Oh." I was running out of arguments. I had wanted the vocational program to be a positive for Mo. I thought he'd finally found his happy place, when really he was just settling. "What about your talk on equality and the MeToo movement, and the courage of women who speak out?"

"Look, Savannah, I know you want me to be bold, tell the school, fire everybody up. But I just want to leave. Some assault stories are like that, people who just want to move on without announcing it to the world. That's what I'm gonna do. It may not be the heroic ending you're looking for, but this is my experience. I own it, not you."

Fighting with Mo is tiresome, and I was worn out, nearly defeated. I thought I had one shot left. "That's fine, Montana. But remember your promise to Granny Crackers, that you would never take another beating in silence."

"You think that's what I did?" Mo screamed, his face red with anger. "I thought you knew me better than that. Truth be told,

Savannah Jo, I kicked his nuts up into his throat and left him lying on the floor holding his balls in his hands and choking on spit. I'm pretty sure that prissy little bitch will never touch me again. I'm still not going back."

Mo stormed into the house and shut himself in our bedroom, shutting me out. I should have known Mo would fight back. How stupid of me to suggest he had done nothing. I hung out in The Barrel. When I could no longer stand the loneliness, I went inside, crawled into Phoenix's bedroom closet, and played with the kittens.

Chapter Thirty-Three

I can't help but notice that the fires in Paris Village have stopped. It's been more than a month since an abandoned structure has been eliminated by flames and eyesores turned to ashes. I wonder if the homeless have also noticed and have gone back to squatting. It's just a matter of time until the empty houses fill up with junkies and geeks. It's sad what happens inside those homes, dirty needles strewn about; people sleeping on floors, shitting in buckets, and turning tricks. I empathize with the arsonist, whoever he or she is, wanting to burn them down.

I suppose the mayor also understands, because Paris Village has been selected for gentrification. The city has promised to dump a bunch of money into my hood. The plan includes renovations and construction, facelifts to storefronts and businesses. Dilapidated buildings will be torn down and replaced by luxury condominiums fit for classy urbanites. Old, empty homes will be bought and restored. New homes will be built.

The idea of transforming Paris Village has residents both excited and scared. Some are afraid of rent increases that will come with higher-valued properties. These people believe that gentrification is a way to displace the poor. It's a scheme by developers and politicians to move out the low income and minorities and move in the artists and gays. I'm neutral, because our family is all that; my tribe is poor, white and brown, gay and straight, a clan of bohemians and artists. I guess either way we belong in Paris Village.

I never thought I'd settle into this harsh landscape, but I guess I have. I suppose the key to living in any environment is finding your people. Since the shooting I've learned that the majority of people in Paris Village are good. Underneath most of my neighbors' offbeat personalities and urban wear, live beautiful hearts. The proof of kindness in the hood glitters in the gifts and cards left on our porch, the meals brought to our door, and prayers that sprinkled down on us like confetti.

The kittens are growing as Phoenix heals. They're orange long-haired balls of fluff resembling the season they were born in. Playful and cute, they climb in and out of their box, pounce on each other, hide behind furniture, and bug the hell out of their mama. That was until Ambrose took Tupelo.

Granny Crackers hasn't mentioned finding homes for the babies, which surprises me. I never thought she would allow one kitten, let alone three. Granny Crackers is a dog person. She always jokes, "Want a box of shit in your house? Get a cat."

Now we have multiples. It would be easy to find homes for the kitties. Everybody wants one, simply because they come with a heartbreaking rescue story. I think she's letting Phoenix decide. After all, he almost lost his life saving those cats. If Phoenix chooses to let a kitten go, Twyla and Dixie have first dibs.

Ambrose is delighted to have Tupelo. A pet is good for him. He has so much love to give. Ambrose is a nurturing man. He cultivates kindness with gifts of fruits and flowers. He rolled a wheelbarrow full of pumpkins, turnips, squash, and gourds to our house. Ava was overjoyed. That evening was beggars' night, and she received the harvest as one might receive a Christmas present. We spent a Saturday afternoon masquerading as a happy family. We carved and painted our veggies and decorated with the autumn crop. I was quickly reminded that my mother is an artist. Ava's pumpkins could win a contest. She turned the big orange globes into a family of faces, painted gourds into goblins, made jack o' lanterns from turnips, and carved the butternut squash into ghosts. We helped.

"What the hell?" said Granny Crackers looking at the spooky vegetables. "I was gonna cook some of those."

"My bad," said Ava sheepishly.

From our stockpile of medical gauze Ava hung billowy, creepy drapes across the front porch. She wrapped Phoenix like a mummy. He sat in the center of our ghoulish entryway in a chair covered with spiderwebs, a large bowl of chocolate bars on his lap. On the porch steps sat our carved creations. The front walk was lit by candles. The best part of Halloween was that Phoenix was happy.

It seems like forever since I've seen him smile. Ever since the shooting, Phoenix's face could be read like a palm. For days his contorted expression was a graphic reflection of pain. As time moved forward, his hard grimace subsided into a sporadic wince, which eventually became a pout. His body's recovery has been visible. Physically he is healing. His mental health is harder to assess, prognosis undetermined. I know he's still having bad dreams. I've heard him cry in his sleep. My other clue? I'm still having vivid flashbacks. Phoenix's despondency indicates that his thoughts are worse than mine. Ava alleviates some of his mental anguish. A mother's love is like medicine; even a bad mom can kiss away the pain of boo-boos.

Ava had done it again, wooed us with her flair. She is an artisan mother, bewitching with her craft. Her laughter is like decoupage, covering our scars with thin layers of colorful, clinging paper.

Family fun is an illusion. Our mother's charm, pasted alongside missed milestones and pieces of broken hearts, turns normal moments into beautiful mosaics. It's as if she thinks that by painting with light she can cover up all the darkness. But one day of artful parenting and finesse doesn't change the last ten years of abandonment. The reality that comes with child neglect is that the good days sting as much as the bad, because you spend the whole time waiting for the paintbrush to fall.

While we decorated the front porch, apple crisp baked in the oven. "Savannah Jo, will you take this to Ambrose and tell him thank you?" Ava said, handing me the warm pie. "I need to hurry back to The Healing House."

I took the tart apples and my sour mood to Ambrose's house. I walked among ninjas, witches, princesses, and super heroes running up and down the walks with plastic buckets and bags full of treats. Ambrose was sitting outside, a big metal bowl of Tootsie Pops between his feet.

"Mmm-mm," he hummed, when I handed him the pastry.

"Ava made it. It's a thank you for the pumpkins and everything."

"Well, isn't that nice?" Ambrose stood. "You tell your mama I appreciate her." He ambled into his house and placed the pie on the table.

"Appreciate her?" I hollered through the screen door. His choice of words irritated my sensitive skin. "She's the one who needs to be appreciative, Ambrose, not you." Two little witches ran up the front porch. I put lollipops in their plastic cauldrons.

Ambrose returned and looked at me with disappointed eyes.

Fully aware that I was cloaked in bitterness, I overshadowed her gift of sweet apple with my dark attitude. "What?" I asked defensively as he shook his head. "It's true. So she made you a dessert. She made it from apples you gave her, nothing special about that. She's just paying what she owes. Truth is, it's gonna take Ava a lifetime to pay off her enormous debt with pennies of generosity."

"Aren't you being a little hard on your mama?" Ambrose sat again in his chair.

"Nope," I said, flipping my hair.

"Savannah Jo, you're too young to be so jaded."

"Jaded, or worse, that's what happens to the offspring of Ava Dale."

Another bunch of beggars ran up the front steps. Ambrose quietly handed each child a Tootsie Pop. As soon as they ran off, he turned to me. "Savannah Jo," he said as he scratched the whiskers on his chin. "Let's pretend that you haven't eaten ice cream in years, and I show up and give you a dish of your favorite flavor. Would you be mad at me? Refuse to eat it?"

I knew what Ambrose was trying to say, but a missed dessert and a mother's love were not equivalent. "That's not the same."

"Sure it is. They're both about the nows and the moments. You see, your problem is that you're pining over days that have already been thrown away. You're picking through the past like you pick through dumpsters, expecting Ava to refurbish mistakes in the same manner she restores furniture. It can't be done. She can't change what has already happened. You gonna have to accept that."

"How?" I asked, dropping a Tootsie Pop into a princess's sack.

"By focusing on all that you have and not obsessing over all that you've missed."

I sat on the front stoop while Ambrose lectured. I could have ignored him or walked away like most reprimanded teenagers, but I'm accustomed to uncomfortable moments. I listened to his painful words of wisdom, the whistle of the autumn wind, the laughter of children. I masked my sadness with a smile, watching kids in costumes run through the front yard.

"Sweetheart," he said softly. "I know you've been through a lot. And you feel like life has handed you nothing but heartache, feelin' like you ain't never been loved. Baby, that's not true. I know your mama and your granny, and I knew your Mimi, and you have been loved and are loved as much as any child.

"Lord, your Mimi," Ambrose went on. "She had so much love, and every bit of it she threw on you kids. That woman believed y'all spun the stars. I imagine her dying must feel like somebody turned out the lights. When you're mourning a loss so deep, it's hard to see the love around you. But Savannah Jorja Dale, you are loved."

"That's not it," I said pushing away his honest logic. "I'm angry because she's a pregnant drug addict."

"Savannah." He sighed. "Your mama has been sick for a long time. Disease in a family affects everyone. But she's in recovery now, using every bit of her strength and energy to heal. Ava doesn't deny her mistakes. She lives every day facing her regrets. She sees the shame reflected on the faces of her family. She feels remorse in every baby kick. I know you're not impressed, Savannah Jo, but when you think about it, you should be.

"Imagine the courage it takes to board the bus every day and come to your house, knowing you will feel judged and scorned. It's a strong mother's love that keeps her coming. Her heartfelt apologies are poured into every mundane task."

I wiped the tears from my chin and said nothing. Another cluster of trick-or-treaters showed up, and Ambrose and I took turns dropping suckers into sacks. I unwrapped a Tootsie Pop and put it into my mouth. I needed a sweet distraction.

Ambrose patted my back. "Sweetheart," he said. "Redemption is a sacred act. Forgiveness is the most difficult and greatest gift you can ever give, because it's a gift to both the receiver and the giver."

Ambrose rose to let Tupelo out. The cat immediately wandered over and curled up on my lap. I stroked its yellow fur like it was a therapy pet. Once my nerves were calm and my eyes were dry, I handed Tupelo to Ambrose and walked home beside a family of Oz characters.

Chapter Thirty-Four

$\mathcal{P}$hoenix returned to school. His welcome was both celebratory and emotional, like a wounded soldier coming home from war. Mr. Phillips, the principal, informed Granny Crackers that he was organizing a "clap in" for Phoenix's return. That morning Mo drove Phoenix to school, per Granny Crackers's instructions, tricking Phoenix by saying, "A bus ride will be too bumpy." Mo made sure to arrive ten minutes late, adequate time for all the teachers and students to line both sides of the long hallway. The reception was videotaped and shared on social media. As soon as Phoenix stepped through the doors, the clapping started. Phoenix proceeded toward his locker through a gauntlet of applauding teachers and cheering students. In the video he's overwhelmed, fighting back tears, walking a path of hollers, hugs, and high fives.

The supportive response to our family drama has changed my perception. I used to think that Paris Middle School and Paris High were ghetto institutions that didn't give a damn about the kids. I was wrong. Mr. Phillips visited Phoenix in the hospital and called Granny Crackers every week. Teachers sent gifts and letters, and entire classes made get-well cards. Phoenix meets with the school psychologist for counseling, and the school is providing him with extra tutoring to catch up on his work. He has an entire building supporting him. I'm okay with that, because I have Gypsy Honeywood. She lets me escape to her class anytime I feel sad. She makes excuses for me, protects me from trouble, and prescribes art like it's medicine. Mrs. Honeywood is helping me build a portfolio. She is the first person ever to talk to me about college. She tells me I'm gifted. She says I can get into art school. She believes in me, and I need her help, because nobody in my family has ever been to college.

Besides encouraging my dreams, Mrs. Honeywood alleviates my white guilt, in the same manner as Ambrose's church. She has been my counsel, both priest and lawyer. I feel comfortable in her presence. I let down my guard and confess my sins, seeking salvation or innocence. I'd committed the same crime as Phoenix, breaking and entering to kidnap cats, yet my engagement posed no threat to the same police officer who felt an urgency to shoot my brother. Perhaps I'm not viewed as dangerous because of my sex. Women, although proven to be tougher than men, are feared less. But mostly I know that speculation comes down to the color of skin.

"I'm sorry people are prejudiced," I told her while working on my oil painting canvas that I've titled *Discrimination*.

"Racism is not your fault, Savannah. On the contrary, you are part of the arch, bridging the gap of injustice. If everybody saw the world as you do, it would be a better place."

"There's nothing special about me, Mrs. Honeywood."

"Oh, Savannah, you're so wrong. Baby, your photos, poems, and paintings are precious perceptions. Your vision reaches beyond the surface. You see through skin and money and into the depths and layers of humankind. You peer with your eyes and search with your soul." She smiled at me.

I looked down. It's hard to feel worthy of such praise.

While Phoenix and I are in school, Mo stays home and self-teaches. Online schooling comes with the headache of Internet crashes, lengthy assignments, confusing instructions, and missed emails.

Granny Crackers provides no encouragement or help and tries to use psychology to fix Mo's technical issues. "If you need help learning, Montana, you can go back to school."

Ava would love to be of assistance. Now that Phoenix is back to a normal routine, she is lost. She arrives every day desperately needing a purpose. Granny Crackers spends her days in The Barrel, and Mo holes up in our bedroom. Both of them dismiss her usefulness. Ava ignores the snubs and shuns, although I know they must hurt, and busies herself baking goodies and cleaning our house.

Most of Ava's attention is thrown onto Phoenix. She redecorated his bedroom while he was at school. Rummaging through old cans of paint, she poured various colors together to create shades of blue and green that she brushed onto Phoenix's sky-colored walls. She turned flat drywall into fluid by adding shadows, waves, swirls, and ripples. She found an old hammock in The Barrel and stretched it across the bedroom wall, nailing it from corner to corner so that it hung like a fisherman's net. In its ropes she placed the gifts that had been left on our porch. The netting cradled teddy bears of every size; stuffed butterflies; and plush fish, sharks, and dolphins.

"I think you're nesting," said Granny Crackers, staring at what looked like a nursery room wall in a man-child's bedroom.

Ava shrugged her shoulders. On a large square of cork board, she tacked up swimming ribbons and medals. She dusted Phoenix's shelf and dresser and lined up his trophies.

Phoenix loved the transformation. To him the stuffed animals were rewards honoring his strength and bravery. The plush gifts made him feel proud and loved, and Ava, like a braggy sports mom, had displayed them all.

Clean and sober Ava is a different mom, an altogether new person. She's been humbled by circumstance. Once a wild and dazzling flame, her light has dimmed to a burnished glow. I don't know if she's happy. I do know she's present, showing up faithfully. Although she seems fine now, I worry about what will happen when the baby comes and then leaves. It's easy to see that she loves her unborn son. Her affection is evident in the way she caresses her baby bump and talks to her stomach. Perhaps this baby saved her.

Ava hit bottom when she died in front of her children, was revived by her granny, awoke in the hospital, and was told she was four months pregnant.

"Your mama has been moved to the psych ward," Granny Crackers had told us.

"Why?"

"She had an episode in the ER." Ava had flipped out and torn up the little cubicle she was in. She sent the bed rolling into the hallway, flipped the metal tray, and kicked over the trash can. She had to be restrained.

"What the fuck?" said Mo. "Why's she so mad? You just saved her life."

"Well, maybe that's reason enough." Granny Crackers went to bed.

Mo, Phoenix, and I stayed up half the night talking about our mother and how much we hated her. The next day we started visiting.

I had seen my mother's attempts at recovery before. Ava showed up at Mimi's house one sunny afternoon dope sick and desperate. She shut herself in a bedroom, vomited in a bucket, and rolled around on the bed for days, sweaty and chilled.

"Your mom has the flu," Mimi told us. Sick for a week, that flu nearly killed her. When she finally emerged from the room, she was weak, shaky, apologetic, and loving. She spent the following days dipping in and out of depression. Eventually, like watching turtles race, she crossed a line and seemed better, and then came Mimi's diagnosis of end-stage cancer. The news was so excruciating that it sent Ava straight back to painkillers and left the rest of us numb. Months before Mimi died, healthy Ava had perished. In her place stood a junkie, who then vanished.

In The Healing House, rehab looks different than a cold turkey withdrawal. It's not just Ava that needs detoxed. For the first four months of development, Junior was being baked in a black tar oven marinated in Oxy juice. Both mother and baby need to be weaned. Methadone does the trick. The Healing House not only provides Ava with shelter and counseling, but also medication. It includes advocacy in the adoption process.

Although I fight it, I feel sorry for my mother. She reminds me of a winter tree, beautiful, bare branches, shedding children like leaves.

A poem written by Savannah Jorja:

THE WINTER TREE

The winter tree, warmth forsaken,
Stands naked
For all the world to see,

Judge and begrudge,
And although they try,
They cannot deny her beauty.

SUSIE NEWMAN

In ice she dazzles.
Her branches are bare, not fragile,
Strong enough to withstand the storms of time.

Dreaming happy days of sunshine,
She grieves
Lost leaves

But knows seasons change
And a life rearranged
Does not define or deflower

Her power.

Chapter Thirty-Five

O nce again Mo has changed pronouns, no longer a he or she, now identifying as a they or them, also known as a non-binary person. After Mo's long voyage to Neverland in search of self and living as a sad, lost boy, they have finally found themselves. Although using gender-neutral pronouns sounds confusing, it makes the most sense. Mo has never felt completely male or female. Like most monumental decisions, non-binary was reached by canceling out the other two choices.

Montana lived for nearly sixteen years as female. What hurt her worse than never fitting in was that she always stood out. In a park full of cute gray squirrels, she was an albino. In a desperate longing for acceptance, Montana became Mo and lived as male for a year and a half. Changing from Montana to Mo was like buying a new pair of shoes that you love. At first they look good and feel just right, but after walking around in them, you get painful blisters. By becoming non-binary, Montana is undefinable, which is accurate, because Mo's essence is far too unique to be categorized. Personally I don't care if Mo is a she or he or a they or a them. Montana is happy.

Their new label came with a new hairstyle. Ava cut and styled Montana's hair. While Phoenix and I were at school, the two played beauty salon. Ava gave Mo a fohawk, or faux mohawk.

She tapered and shaved the sides, spiked the longer strands on top, and dyed the tips pink. Honestly, it's adorable, and I'm super jealous for reasons on many levels.

When you think about it, haircuts and shampoos are personal things. I never thought Montana would soften to the feel of our mother's touch. I can barely remember a time when Montana wasn't treating Ava with hostility. Now they're getting along. I give full credit to the baby not yet here, already a successful mediator. The appearance of a pregnancy belly and Ava's subtle, persistent and quiet actions mellow the harsh truths and dilute our bitter attitudes.

Montana has widened boundaries. They left the confines of our room and sits at the kitchen table doing schoolwork. Ava sits next to them, working on a scrapbook for Phoenix. Ava has collected every note, letter, and card sent to Phoenix. She has a pile of newspaper clippings and copies of poems and song lyrics where Phoenix's name is a beat. The memorabilia commemorates all the love and support that flowed through his life during this river of time.

Granny Crackers likes the harmony. A hermit in a crowded house, she hums to the tune of coexistence.

Mo's search for identity has been a crisis for everyone. Watching somebody find themselves is like being a spectator to a helpless game of hide and seek, constantly wanting to scream out, "You're cold, very, very cold. Oh, no, wait! You're getting warmer." Currently Mo is smokin' hot, beautifully handsome, with a peaceful glow and new hairstyle. Mo's contentedness, Phoenix's healing, and Ava's sobriety have allowed Granny Crackers to decompress. Once pumped full of pressure, tight and tense, she is exhaling.

Our family has relaxed into some picture of normalcy, if it's at all normal to have a pregnant mom who is giving up your sibling. Ava had made the choice of adoption back when she thought there was no other option. Hatching a plan from the 1950s, she'd intended to stay hidden until after his birth and then come home skinny and pretend she didn't have a baby living somewhere in our city. It made perfect martyr sense until a tragedy sent her running home. Like a fool I had assumed that since her secret was out and everybody seemed relatively happy, she would look at other alternatives. I didn't mean to start an ugly Jerry Springer fight with my mother in front of our friends.

Jason and Kaleem, fresh green neighbors in early summer and golden friends by autumn, have become a part of our household. Even with Phoenix on the mend and back in school, we are still in need of their rescue. Mo's online government class is much more difficult than anticipated, and having a history teacher next door has been a huge help. While Jason teaches Mo, Ava leans on Kaleem. She is full of "what to expect when expecting" angst. You'd think this was her first child. The anxiety accompanies the self-blame of carrying a fetus addicted to drugs.

"Can we keep him?" I blurted, shocking the room.

Jason's and Mo's heads shot up from a textbook. Kaleem nearly dropped the hand weight he and Phoenix were using for physical therapy. Granny Crackers peered from around her newspaper.

"No," my mother stated flatly.

I was taken aback by her short, firm response. Her mouth was drawn across her face in a straight line. "Shut up," her eyes glared.

Like a lemon being squeezed, my optimism dripped onto the floor as I realized I had no say. Feeling powerless, I bargained. "Why not? Granny Crackers already has guardianship over us, just add one more."

"Granny Crackers is eighty."

"But Mo will be eighteen soon. I'll be sixteen. Mo and I could raise him with Granny Crackers's help. We can do it. Once you prove to everybody you can stay clean, you can get custody."

Mo nodded in agreement.

"You two are not stopping your education to raise a baby."

"But Mo's homeschooling."

"Savannah, please stop," my mother begged.

My innocent bargaining had conjured up an awkwardness so thick it felt like a presence in the room, making everyone uncomfortable. I believe Jason and Kaleem wanted to run from our home, but were frozen in place.

"What? It'll work. Children's Services are supposed to keep families together."

"Savannah, stop!" Ava commanded me. "Don't you know this is killing me?" Her voice cracked with frustration. "I've played out every scenario. It won't work."

"But what about us? He's our baby too. Don't we get a say?"

"No. No, you do not."

"But that's not fair!"

"Savannah, please!" my mother begged. "Just let me do something good. Please, for once in my life, I want to do what's right."

I looked to Mo and Phoenix for backup, but they both avoided my gaze. So did Granny Crackers. Somehow during our exchange I had sprouted the wings of a villain and Ava a superhero's cape, and all because she's now virtuous enough to know that she's not good enough . . . we're not good enough. Because of her we are a dysfunctional family not fit to raise a baby.

"I hate you!" I sneered, spearing her with anger. "You ruin every life you touch." My stomach dropped out of me. I wanted to swallow the bullets I had just spit, but it was too late. She'd been hit.

Ava stood wounded. Plump tears flowed from her green eyes and landed on her fat belly. She looked pathetic standing in a shadow of sadness, her pretty face illuminated by a pregnancy glow.

I scanned the room and saw the gaping mouths of shocked faces. I had been mean. I flew out the door not knowing where I was heading and landed on Ambrose's front porch. He let me in. I curled up on his sofa. He helped me straighten the blanket of yarn while I covered myself with the afghan from the back of his couch. Tupelo jumped into my lap. Ambrose filled the tea kettle. After the sound of a loud whistle, he brought me a steamy cup of Constant Comment.

I curled my hands around the chipped blue teacup, inhaled the black tea and orange rinds, and exhaled pain and exhaustion, a rivulet of citrus drops running down my face. "If there is a God, he hates my family," I flatly stated.

"Savannah Jo." Ambrose sat down beside me. "You shouldn't say such things."

"Why? It's true." I didn't know how bad I hurt until our issues fell from my mouth like stones. "God took Mimi from us. He got Mo's sex wrong, made Ava a drug addict, shot Phoenix, and planted a baby in Ava that we have to give away." Speaking my truths was like a rockslide of sorrows; my spirit tumbled downhill, and I felt smashed. Sometimes sadness lives so deep inside your soul that you just endure it, like a splinter in your heel that hurts only when you step a certain way. My confession was a misstep, and the pain was excruciating.

"Oh, sweetheart." Ambrose's eyes and voice filled with pity. "Or perhaps God spared Phoenix, ended Mimi's suffering and called her home, and this baby is a gift."

"A gift to whom?" I sobbed.

"Well, who knows how many there'll be?" He took my hand. "I'd say the first person to receive is Ava, his birth mom. This baby saved her life, led her into treatment, and when you think about it, it was a gift that brought Ava back into your life and in Phoenix's, Mo's, and Granny Crackers's, at the exact moment when you needed her and when her body and mind were the healthiest they've been in years." Ambrose spoke softly and slowly, his voice like warm milk and honey. "And this baby is a gift to his adopted parents, whoever they might be. A couple or person who has dreamed and prayed for a child to love and who will complete their family."

I wiped my nose on my shirt sleeve.

Ambrose got up and fetched me a box of tissues.

"That's just it. He should complete *our* family," I argued. "We should keep him. After all, he came to save us, right?"

"And he did . . ."

We sat for a moment in silence. I wiped snot and tears from my face.

Ambrose contemplated. "Savannah Jo," he began, "life is like the weather, unpredictable, with chances of rain, and sunny days interrupted by thunderstorms and blizzards. But even with the uncontrollable weather, a person has choices. You can grab an umbrella, wear thick socks and snow boots, put on a hat or jacket, or lather up with sunscreen. Now some people don't consider their choices and make bad ones. Those people will stand outside in a snowstorm without a coat and blame their being cold on the weather. Your mama has been one of them. Ava's lived unsheltered for a long time, letting the wind blow her from here to there. The woman has been caught in rain, slapped by the wind, frostbitten, and sunburned, and finally she's taken a situation and made a conscience choice, a choice bigger than herself. Ava is actually thinking, and more than that, she's thinking of someone else first. She's putting another's life before her own, and honey that's big."

I knew Ambrose was right, but that didn't make it hurt any less, and once again, I was just a kid with no control. I pulled the afghan over my head, wanting to disappear, and cried into the couch cushions.

"Savannah Jo," he said gingerly, pulling the yarn from my face, "I know you want to keep this baby, but honey, sometimes to truly love someone you have to break your own heart."

After I cried for another hour, Ambrose walked me home, because it was dark outside.

Granny Crackers was sitting in the recliner waiting for my arrival. "Oh, baby," she said, looking at me, my face red and puffy, my eyes nearly swollen shut from crying. "You're gonna have to let him go."

"I know." I crumpled to the floor near her feet, my head landing in her lap.

"Shh," she whispered. Her gnarled fingers combed through my hair.

It must have been pure emotional exhaustion that caused me to close my eyes and fall asleep. I woke in the wee hours, my body aching from its awkward position and the feel of the hard floor. Granny Crackers was leaned back in her chair softly snoring, her fingers still in my hair.

A poem written by Savannah Jorja:

LOSING BABY

I weep for the oak that's a tiny acorn,
Loving you before you're born.

Hush, little baby, don't you cry.
Mama is a blackbird baked in a pie.

We have no voices,
You and I,

SUSIE NEWMAN

Painted into existence by raven feathers,
A moody blue me and a baby tethered

To an umbilical discord.
Bleeding hearts pour

On a sweet little fellow
Nursing a bottle of yellow.

No happy hour
On a day that's lemon sour.

Me, mourning a sunflower
That's still just a seed.

Chapter Thirty-Six

*L*ife's not fair. The worst thing that could happen has happened. I'm devastated, beyond repair. My sweet Mateo has moved. My best friend has gone far away, and although we FaceTime, the distance between us hurts like a death. I've cried myself to sleep every night for more than a week, big horrible heaving sighs, and wake up to swollen eyes. I don't want to go to school. I look a mess and feel friendless. Granny Crackers says I'm being dramatic. I'm not. There should be a limit on sadness. Sorrow follows me like a stalker who won't leave me the fuck alone.

"Pull yourself together, Savannah Jo," Granny Crackers said, opening up my bedroom door to find me stretched across my mattress like a wounded soldier, sobbing into a heart-shaped pillow, while Mo helplessly sat on the edge of my bed rubbing my back.

"I can't," I howled. "My heart's broken."

"Hearts mend, child. You'll live."

"You're so mean."

"Savannah Jo, I'm sorry Mateo moved. I know it hurts. It'll get better. You're a beautiful girl. You're gonna have lots of boyfriends in your time."

"Oh, my god!" I wailed. "How can you say such things?"

"Good luck, Montana," Granny Crackers said before shutting our door and walking away.

"Granny Crackers doesn't mean to be cold," Mo defended. "She's just experienced in love and loss. And she doesn't want you to be so sad. She's worried. You've been hysterical for more than a week."

It's true. I have cried every day since Mateo told me he was moving. Ten days ago, on a day when the weather was decent, Mateo called and asked me to go on a walk. Since then the days have turned cold and gray, matching my mood. Mateo and I strolled through the park hand in hand, the wind in our hair, the sun on our shoulders. We crunched through fallen leaves, climbed on the jungle gym, sat on the swings, and with nobody else around, we crawled into a play tunnel, lay nose to nose, and spent an hour just kissing.

"Savannah, I need to talk to you," Mateo said as I nibbled on his ear.

"What's so important that we stop kissing?" I giggled.

"We're moving."

At first I just thought he meant across town. "Oh, well . . . it's okay," I said. "We'll both be getting our license soon. We'll just have to work harder at seeing each other."

"Nah, Savannah." His eyes filled with tears. "We're moving to Texas."

I crawled out of the tunnel on pained knees, suddenly aware of the hard plastic and unforgiving earth. Mateo followed. We sat on a cement picnic table, the ground beneath littered with shards of glass. Mateo tiptoed over the fragile subject, trying not to break my heart, while safeguarding his own.

"Aunt Camila can't handle it anymore," he explained. "It's too much, trying to support and watch her own kids and my mom's kids too. She needs help. We're going to go live with my *abuela*."

"Maybe you can stay," I begged. "Tell your mom and Camila you want to finish school. You have a job. Maybe we can find you a place. I bet Ambrose would consider taking you in or Solomon."

"No, Savannah, I can't do that to my mama. My family has been ripped apart enough." Mateo ran his fingers through his thick black hair. "I wish you knew my parents before ICE took my papa. My *padre* would love you. He's a jokester, always trying to be funny, and my mama used to laugh all the time. She was always cleaning and cooking, a real homebody. She would spend all day preparing giant meals, invite over family and friends. Every day in our house was a fiesta, my papa blaring his Latin music, dancing and clowning around.

"When immigration enforcement arrested my *padre*, my family broke in two. When they deported him, they shattered the piece that was my mama. She isn't the same. We have to stay together. My *madre* needs me now more than ever. My sister and brothers need me. They can't lose another person. Camila needs me too. She needs help."

Mateo squeezed my hands, and I tried to be strong for him. I know what it's like to helplessly have your life orchestrated by family sorrow.

"It's more than money," Mateo confessed. "It's more than my mama's depression. It's Santiago. We need to move him away. If my *padre* were still home, Santiago would have never strayed. My *abuela* has a big house to fit us all. She can watch the little ones and console my mama. Maybe my mom will get better if she's around more *familia*. And we will be closer to the border, closer to papa."

I wasn't surprised when he mentioned Santiago. Mateo's cousin has been messing with the wrong people. I had heard Santiago was running drugs, stealing, and breaking into cars and homes. His best friend, Darius, became a gangbanger and pulled him along. Now they're both living the thug life. Two weeks ago Darius's house was shot up. Its siding is riddled with bullet holes. Nobody was hurt. Camila is not taking any chances.

"We ain't staying here, waiting for you to get your little ass shot or one of us killed," Camila screamed at her seventeen-year-old son. I believe the shooting must have scared Santiago too, because he didn't argue.

Mateo and I walked home, our path of gloom lit by the orange glow of a full harvest moon.

The next day I went to his house and helped them pack. Moving is a lot of work, and Camila was in a hurry. Mateo got boxes from the Sol Shack, and even though we tried to be organized, I'm sure unpacking is going to feel like a jumbled and confusing treasure hunt. Mateo's mom got out of bed to help, pulled forth by the thought of her own mama. While Mateo and I folded clothes into containers, packed away books and toys, and took photographs off the walls, his mama cooked. We had Taco Tuesday and had it again on Wednesday, Thursday, and Friday, with tamales, enchiladas, and rice and beans. I love dinner at Mateo's house. On Saturday night we scarfed down pizza after a day spent loading boxes and furniture into a U-Haul. On Sunday morning I stood on the wet grass in the rain and watched them drive away.

The days spent helping Mateo pack had been as special as we could make them. It helped being surrounded by little ones. Mateo's young siblings, nieces, and nephews love me. They beg for my attention like a fan wanting an autograph, and I enjoy the spotlight. Small children are a pleasant preoccupation while doing an unpleasant task. Their antics, giggles, and play were welcome distractions, and Mateo and I laughed more than we cried.

During the times when Aunt Camila shooed the children up to baths and bed and Mateo and I were given a break from packing, we would sneak off into the tent to cuddle. Stolen moments of fleeting kisses soon became heated make-out sessions, our passion stirred by a helpless feeling of desire and loss. Hot feverish touches, friction, and lust sparked a flame, and we came as close as you can get to having sex without actually having it. Our forbidden game of show and touch turned into truth or dare, and curiosity outmatched fear. Our hands and mouths wandered in and out of each other's clothes like explorers craving adventure, starving for satisfaction, willfully holding back. We rolled around on top of sleeping bags under a golden canopy, casting sensual shadow puppets onto the yellow nylon. The tent was the very last thing we took down and packed away. Watching the Hernandez family caravan drive away made me feel empty, like all my joy was haphazardly tossed into a box with knickknacks and trinkets and was heading to Texas. It's a sadness I cannot shake. Melancholy sits on my shoulder like a parrot, and I just want to fly to Del Rio.

On day nine, when everybody was tired of my crying, Ava came searching and found me in The Barrel, crumpled in a recliner. We hadn't talked much since our fight. I had spent two weeks splashing in teardrops with Mateo and no time reconciling with her choice. But this much I know: no matter what I've said to hurt my mother, she forgives me. Ava recovers from fights quickly and prefers not to talk about it. She is a perfectly imperfect and completely flawed but forgiving soul. When you spend your life making mistakes, you learn to let things go. Between Ava and family there have been a million terrible things said and done that have magically disappeared. As far as my mom is concerned, when the arguing stops, the fight is over. Perhaps that's the way it has to be. If we hauled around our mistakes and grudges like rocks in a backpack, we would quickly weigh ourselves down and not have the strength to move. If Ava has taught me one thing, it's how to pardon a fool.

"Hello, Sunshine," she said, slowly lowering herself into a canvas chair. Cradled in the seat, her bottom sank toward the ground and her pregnant belly nearly touched her chin. "You doing okay?"

"No," I responded honestly.

"It sucks. I'm sorry your best friend is gone."

"He was more than a friend. I love him."

"Of course you do."

I had expected her to brush away my expressions of love as a silly crush, but instead she took me seriously.

"And there is nothing in the world sweeter than first-love kisses."

"You mean I'll never feel the same way again?"

"Nah, baby, I just mean everybody else will taste different."

"I'm so sad. Why does it have to hurt so bad?"

"The first cut is the deepest," she sang. Ava is the type of person who can find a song lyric for every situation. When I didn't smile, she changed tactics. "You know what you do with a broken heart?" she asked.

"No. What?"

"You make art." Ava got up and snooped in plastic bins, poking around shelves. "Ahh, this should do." She pulled forth a cardboard box of varicolored dinner plates.

"What am I supposed to do with those?"

"Break 'em." She carried the box to the driveway and then came back for a large tarp.

I followed her outside.

Ava spread the plastic out like a drop cloth and then handed me a plate. "Drop it," she said. "Toss it to the ground as hard as you can. Come on."

I breathed a heavy sigh. The thought of breaking a box of plates that could easily be sold caused me anxiety. I knew Granny Crackers would make me pay for the broken goods, charging me verbally and then demanding money. "I don't want to get in trouble," I confessed.

"You're already troubled, baby. Besides, I'm trying to teach you how to pick up broken pieces and make something beautiful."

Her logic made sense, and she was the first person who tried to help me feel better. I held the plate high above my head and slammed it to the ground, breaking it into three pieces. Ava quickly handed me another plate, and I repeated the same action. The fractured ceramic bounced, and the second plate shattered. The release of energy brought me bruised comfort and confirmation, like punching a wall when you're angry. I threw plate after plate until I was standing almost ankle deep in broken dishes.

Ava picked up the small broken pieces and placed them in an empty bucket. The bigger pieces, she handed to me and told me to break them with a hammer. Doing it felt good too. We filled the entire bucket with jagged pieces of colorful ceramics. My hands were bleeding, nicked with a thousand tiny scratches. While I rubbed my knuckles, Ava used the shop vac to clean the tarp. I was still unsure what was happening and worried once again about a box of broken dishes.

Ava came out of The Barrel carrying a light end table on her belly. "You're going to mosaic this table," she said, putting it on the ground in front of me. "You glue the pieces on first, and then you grout. The fun parts are creating a pattern and breaking the glass."

Obediently I began placing the symbolic, broken pieces into a creative design. Just like she predicted, it wasn't long until I became engrossed in trying to create something artsy from trash. A feeling of connection ensued between the shattered plates and me.

I swirled the rough chunks of red, orange, bright yellow, maize, and dark gold into a colorful sun and outlined it in sharp bits of blues, greens, and purple. Losing myself in color and imagination was a nice reprieve from sad thoughts and loneliness, and I slowly understood why Ava painted at three o'clock in the morning.

As I collaged jagged edges side by side like an unscripted puzzle, Ava sat beside me, a Nestea balanced on her belly. "Can I ask you something, Savannah?" she said softly.

"Hmmmmm." I responded, focused on my design.

"Did you and Mateo do it?"

Her question stunned me. How rude of her to pry into my personal life! I wanted to tell her it was none of her damn business, but saying that would just make me look guilty, so I told her the truth. "No," I said, gluing down a piece of my broken heart, "but we came very close."

"Ahh," she said as she rubbed the side of her stomach. "Coming close is even better than having sex. I'm sorry he's gone, baby."

"It is? Better?" I was no longer angry.

"Oh, yeah," said Ava, smiling as if she were happily floating on a lake of memories. "Making out is where it's at. After you start having sex, it loses its sensation."

I rolled my eyes, choosing not to believe her. She was just trying to talk me into staying a virgin, but she didn't have to, because I can't imagine giving my virginity to anyone but Mateo, and he's gone. I continued sorting through smashed plates while Ava dug through the corners of her mind, reflecting on past hookups.

"Do you remember the day Mimi took us zip-lining?"

"Of course I do." I thought she was trying to change the subject. It was Mimi's fifty-fifth birthday. Ava was sober; Mimi was in remission.

"Double nickels," Mimi had said. "Calls for something fun."

We drove out of the city and into the hills. Mimi smiled from ear to ear, not telling us where she was heading, throwing us a surprise on her own birthday. She was giving like that. When she pulled into the zip-lining tours, the car erupted in cheers.

"Not just the day," Ava said. "Do you remember the way you felt, the emotions? Anticipation, suspense, and excitement, the glorious, pure pleasure and breathtaking climb up the hills. The arousal and nervousness felt right before you zipped through the trees, and then the freeing exhilaration of flying through the woods. Do you remember?"

"Yes." I remembered. It was my favorite memory.

"Well, that feeling, that's the hot and heavy making out before sex."

"Then what does sex feel like?"

"Sex is nice too. I'm just saying, the next time you go zip-lining, it won't be nearly as thrilling." Ava grinned.

We took a moment to reflect on her teachings and remember zip-lining with Mimi.

I broke the silence. "I'm sorry. I didn't mean what I said the other day. I know you're thinking of the baby. Trying to do the right thing. It's just—"

"Shh, Savannah," my mother whispered. "No apologies."

After hours of intricate work and roughing up my hands, gluing, grouting, scraping, and wiping, the mosaic table was beautiful, and Granny Crackers let me keep it.

Chapter Thirty-Seven

ason and Kaleem invited us to Sunday lunch at their house. Kaleem wanted to cook us an authentic Arabic meal. They're always doing nice things for us. I assumed their invite was just another neighborly gesture.

The interior design of Jason and Kaleem's home is like *Queer Eye* decorates a small-scale Islamic palace. Persian rugs lay under plush furniture in shades of rich burgundy and jade, and large hanging bubble lights illuminate the rooms in gold. Their home is aesthetic, with clean lines, open space, books, art, and a prayer mat. Our house is eclectic chaos with messy tables, stacked corners, and cluttered shelves. Instead of feeling welcome and at peace, it made me want to go home and clean.

In addition to the meal being exotic and the kitchen smelling of spice, the entire dining experience was foreign. My family eats supper straight out of the skillet. Mac and cheese goes from pan to plate, and then you find a place to sit down. It could be the kitchen table, but we're just as likely to eat in the living room or our bedrooms. The only rule is to return your plate to the sink when you're finished. Granny Crackers throws a shit storm if we leave dirty dishes lying around. A messy house and a nasty house are totally different things.

Jason and Kaleem's dining room was lit by golden wall sconces and the soft glow of yellow candles. The table was set with silver plates, sage linens, and goblets brimming with ice water. Large serving dishes of chicken shawarma and couscous sat beside a basket of warm pita.

We sat around a formal dining room table filling our mouths, stomachs, and souls. In between bites we talked about culture, food, language, politics, and religion. I decided right then that one day I was going to live in a beautiful house where friends would gather for stimulating conversation and a gourmet meal. It wasn't until the orange cake and spiced hot tea were served that the baby was mentioned, and we realized Jason and Kaleem had a motive.

"Ava." Jason cleared his throat. "Kaleem and I would like to adopt the baby."

My mother coughed on her tea and blew crumbs across the table. "Excuse me?"

We all stared at the two men in disbelief. Kaleem wore a sheepish smile.

Jason, controlled a second earlier, stumbled over his words and thoughts. "We, we, we know this feels sudden and awkward, and um . . . we don't mean to be offensive, not at all. I completely understand if you're taken aback. It's just we've always known we wanted a family. We've talked about adoption or fostering kids. We've even considered finding a surrogate to carry our own children. Then we moved here. And there you were with these beautiful kids, and we didn't mean to get so involved in your life; it just happened, and it filled a void. Now you're going to have another baby, and you're looking for parents, and all we're asking is that you look our way. This just feels like it's meant to be. Like the universe has slammed us together. Don't you see it?"

"Oh God." Ava exhaled. "Jason, Kaleem?"

My mother was caught off guard. When asked to see the

miracle in her misery, it was too much. She was up on her feet, her hands flailing along with her mind. "We gotta go, kids, come on, everybody; get your coats."

"Ava, don't leave. We're sorry."

"We gotta go. I need to think. We'll talk later." Ava was out the door before the rest of us had even gotten up from the table. We were all a bit stunned and moving slow.

"I'm sorry if we upset you," Kaleem mumbled. His bright face had fallen.

Granny Crackers patted his arm. "It'll be fine." In her hand she held a piece of china, on it a large piece of orange cake. "I'll return the plate," she said, heading toward the door.

Inside our house we watched my mom walk in circles around the coffee table, into the kitchen, out of the kitchen, down the hallway, back to the living room, around the coffee table. Mo, Phoenix, and I sat lined up on the couch with chihuahuas on our laps. Granny Crackers sat in a chair eating cake.

"What do I do?" Ava asked on her third lap.

"Let's think this through," Granny Crackers said, licking her fork. "Mmm, this is good cake."

"I don't know if I can have him right next door." Ava sighed. "I want an open adoption, but that's too close. And will it be good for you guys?" She nodded at us.

At that moment life felt surreal. What do you say to your mother when she asks you if she should give the baby to neighbors, like we're trying to find a home for a puppy?

"I'm okay with it." Phoenix was the first to interject. "I like the thought of having my baby brother right next door."

Ava smiled at Phoenix. His positive innocence obviously warmed her heart.

Leave it to Mo to throw a skeptical chill in the air. "Perfect,

Phoenix, but have you thought about how this baby might change your relationship with Jason and Kaleem? They won't need a fake son if she gives them a real one." It was typical Mo; when dealing with stress, lash out and hurt the person next to you.

"I'm sure Jason and Kaleem are not like that," said Ava, raising her eyebrow to Mo and consoling Phoenix, but a raised eyebrow wasn't going to stop Montana.

"I'm just saying things could get weird." Mo continued. "Our little brother living next door, and we have no say in his life. And what if they move, or we ever have a fight? Maybe they won't want us too close. Could change our relationship completely."

"Yeah, it could," Ava admitted. "But I can't worry about my feelings, just his . . . and yours. Either way, I'm giving the baby up for adoption, so the real question is whether Jason and Kaleem are the right parents." Ava was settling down, getting a hold of her thoughts and feelings. She was still reeling with emotion, but at least she was trying to think rationally.

"Will they tell him he belongs to us?" Phoenix asked.

"Yes, It's called an open adoption. Whoever gets him, he'll know about us."

"Do you think he'll be mad we didn't keep him?"

"I don't know, son, but he won't be mad at you. This is all my fault." Ava wiped a tear from her cheek. Her suffering was visible; the truth revealed itself. Giving away her baby was hard, and even though it broke her heart, she was strong enough to push through the pain, ignore sorrow, and do what was best for the baby. I wish I would have realized her self-sacrifice three weeks earlier, before I said she ruined every life she touches.

I felt incredibly sad for my mother at that moment, watching her agonize over a choice that I thought was obvious. What I mean is, if you're already going through the adoption process, which she is, meeting families and talking to lawyers, then wouldn't it be a blessing to have the perfect couple next door apply for the job? In a selfish sense, I was thinking Jason and Kaleem's offer had been a godsend. If we couldn't have the baby, let him live beside us. In my mind I compared the baby to the serenity garden. It will be nice and hurt a little to have something beautiful that doesn't belong to you right next door, but at least we'd get to visit. Having him live with another family wasn't going to hurt any less, he'd just be farther away.

"I think Jason and Kaleem will make really good daddies," I said.

"They will make really good daddies someday." Ava sighed. "It's just they blindsided me . . . and it would be a lot to handle . . . my boy . . . who's not my boy . . . but close enough to touch."

I was having a hard time understanding my mother's dilemma. Did she really think that seeing him every day would be harder than not seeing him? I've learned that just because people are out of sight doesn't mean they're out of mind, a painful lesson hammered into my head by the fist of God. The ultimate teaching being Mimi's death, and then Mateo's move. As far as I was concerned, if the baby was going to take up residence in our hearts, he might as well live close by. I think Phoenix agreed with me, and Mo was on the fence, but then again, Mo lives on the fence.

"Your mom's decision is not that easy, kids," Granny Crackers quipped. "Sure, Jason and Kaleem are nurturing, but they're gay."

"Sooo?" snapped Montana. "What the hell does that have to do with it?"

"Well," said Granny Crackers, "it can't be easy for a child to be raised in a gay home. And if there is a nice heterosexual couple wanting the baby, why would she choose Jason and Kaleem?"

"That's bullshit!" Mo knocked the chihuahua from their lap. "Jason and Kaleem would parent just as good as any straight couple, and probably better than most."

"Mo, calm down," said Ava. "Them being gay has nothing to do with my decision."

"It doesn't?" Granny Crackers straightened herself in her chair. "Oh . . . I see, you're worried because Kaleem's a Muslim."

"No!" Ava shouted. "Jesus! Old woman, just stop talking."

Granny Crackers flashed me a slight smile and a little wink. Oh, my god, the woman was a genius. She was baiting them, playing devil's advocate, and using reverse psychology to change their minds.

"Well, now, Ava, you say those things don't matter, but have you thought about it?" Granny continued. "You'd be putting your son in a gay home with one brown dad and one white dad, a Muslim and a Christian, during a time when our country is divided. We all witnessed discrimination and bigotry nearly kill Phoenix. Do you really want to put this baby in a home where he could possibly be a victim of racism and hate, especially when there is a socially acceptable and loving couple who wants him?"

"There's nothing wrong with living in a brown and white home," Phoenix defended. "Look at us."

"And who cares if they're gay?" Mo stood up. "They're smart, they're kind, they're funny, and they're compassionate too. For Christ sakes, Granny Crackers, one's a teacher and the other's a nurse. How do you get more nurturing than that?"

Ava stifled her tears. She scrunched up her nose and made a juicy smile, as if choking on a lemon drop. "The kids are right. I could look the entire world over to choose the perfect father for my son, and it would end being a toss-up between those two. Maybe God knew what he was doing when he placed them together and dumped them next to your house. For the life of me, I never understood why they moved here. Now it makes sense."

Granny Cracker's manipulation had worked. Mo was on the defense, and Ava was talking with some clarity.

"This pregnancy is bigger than me; that I know. This child is meant to be here. For some unknown reasons, I've been requested by the universe to be his surrogate. Maybe to get clean for my three other kids. Who really knows why miracles happen?" Ava sat down and rubbed her stomach.

We allowed the room to fill with silence until she was ready to speak again. It was obvious she had a lot to say. Her feelings had been sealed inside the locked closet of her mind for the past five months. Freed, her thoughts wandered. The offer from Jason and Kaleem had ripped the tape from her mouth, and words came clumsily tumbling out. She got up and began pacing again.

"Honestly," she began, "knowing that I was meant to carry this baby for someone else releases any uncertainty I have. The hardest part is knowing who the right family is. I've met several couples, but haven't made any promises. I don't know why. They're all nice people. It just needs to feel . . . you know . . . right." She left the room mid-thought, went to pee, and returned before we had a chance to gossip.

"Suppose," she said, "Jason and Kaleem are meant to be his fathers. Maybe it's part of a predestined journey and I'm a piece of a bigger plan. And I need to get over myself." A bulb had been turned on, and Ava's mind was flooding with light. She had been living in a melancholy daydream and kept her feelings under the covers. Ava never talked about herself to us, and we never asked how she was doing. Every once in a while she bashfully exposed a flash of guilt, a glint of shame. Now she was talking freely and unabashed about giving her baby up for adoption. It felt almost healthy.

"I'm gonna do it," she said with her chin down and her arms circling her stomach, cradling her son. "I'm going to tell them yes. Not today. Today I just need to sit with it. I'll tell them to-morrow." Her finality led her mind to wander through a to-do list. "I need to talk to my social worker. If she has a problem with it, I'll remind her that I'm still the baby's mother, and I get my say. They'll have to be interviewed, meet with lawyers and social workers; there's a lot to do." Her decision, and Granny Crackers's argument, had given her a new perspective, and perhaps for the first time, some hope.

"Really, guys, when you think about it, families like the one Jason and Kaleem will make are needed. How else will change happen if there's not uniquely different people happily and boldly living life out loud? Jason and Kaleem are more right than wrong." Ava's brain clouds had finally cleared, and her mind was shining with a new vision. For the first time in forever, she was speaking with confidence. "I want Jason and Kaleem to have this child. This is their son, not mine."

By the time my mother had concluded, we all wanted Jason and Kaleem to have the baby.

Granny Crackers, secretly pleased with her accomplished mission, kicked her recliner back. Putting her feet up, she closed her eyes. "If you think so, Ava, it's all right with me."

Chapter Thirty-Eight

*I*t snowed three inches last night. White drifts cover piles of brown leaves and antler branches, heavy with snow, bend to the ground. The city will ignore the narrow one-way avenues of Paris Village and clear only the main roadways, making our streets the perfect place for children to play and vehicles to get stuck. Bad-mannered ghetto kids pop up from behind parked cars lining the street and throw snow bombs, not only at each other, but also at unsuspecting and harmless strangers. One snowball tossed at a misjudged target could get you an ass beating or an exhilarated sprint, being chased by an angry victim. It's risky play to punk someone in the hood. I'm a pretty safe bet, because I appear nonthreatening, so I was hit with two snowballs while walking home from the bus stop. If that wasn't bad enough, I had to walk around a construction vehicle and out into the slushy street to get down the sidewalk, brown sludge soaking through my canvas sneakers.

Winter hasn't stopped the renovation of Paris Village. Gentrification has begun. The homes that burned by arson have been flattened, their lots cleared for new construction. The old Buckeye Brick building is being developed into condos. That massive warehouse once employed more than half the town, including Granny Crackers's parents and two of her husbands. It shut down in the early 1990s. By summer 2019, the industrial space will be converted into modern apartments with brick walls and exposed pipes, trendy and posh.

My wet feet led me into the door of The Sol Shack. I sat in our booth, mine and Mateo's, and tried to FaceTime my best friend, but I got no answer. Solomon brought me a bowl of jambalaya. Remnants of snow balls dripped from my hair to bead the screen of my phone.

"This will warm you up," he said.

"Solomon, I don't have money today. I just needed a drink of water and a warm seat."

"No need for money." He smiled. "Taste the jambalaya. I just made it. It's good, hey?"

"Yes, Solomon, it's very good." The spice warmed my insides, although my loneliness seeped to the bone with an ache like frostbite.

I have no friends. Without Mateo here, life sucks. I don't fit into any social groups. I don't play sports or an instrument. I'm not into clubs or theater. I don't party and smoke pot, and I hate gaming. My phone doesn't buzz every two minutes like everybody else's. I'm not part of any group texts. I'm not even bullied, getting attention by being picked on. In fact, I think everybody likes me. They say hi, tell me my outfit's cute, ask me if I know what the homework assignment is. That's the extent of our pleasantries. Besides that we view each other's lives on social media. They like my selfies. My comment box is full of the fire icon, meaning I'm hot. I like their posts of shopping mall trips and parties and wonder why I'm never asked to go. When it comes to social invites, I'm off the radar.

I'm lonely. Mateo's absence feels like a death. It seems my closest and longest friend is Grief. Since Mimi's death more than a year ago, Grief has been my companion. For a few months I replaced Grief with a boyfriend. The passion I felt for Mateo sent Grief packing like a jilted lover, and I was glad to see him go. But now Grief is back, connecting to my heart stronger than ever. At one time, I shared Grief with Mo and Phoenix. We had our own little mourning club, and Grief was the leader. Now I date Grief alone. Both Phoenix and Mo are doing better. I am thankful, but I'm also lonely. As I eat my jambalaya, I think about my family.

Phoenix is back in the pool. Jason takes him to the YMCA three nights a week. It's more than physical therapy; it's been excellent for his mental health. For a while I thought I'd never see Phoenix smile again. His life had been interrupted by weeks of pain and fear, and his days marked by anguish. Phoenix's wounds heal with time. Unfortunately it seems that as his body grows strong, his mind remains wounded, and as his physical pain subsides, his fears increase.

Cops terrify Phoenix. He reacts like a rabbit in gunfire whenever he hears a siren. With the exception of school, and now the Y, he doesn't go beyond the front porch. He's afraid to wear hoodies, let alone be outside after dark. Despite weeks of counseling he still has nightmares.

Swimming has been the therapy he needs. Phoenix looks forward to pool days with Jason, and although I feel jealous and wish someone would take me swimming, I also wish Jason would take him more, so he can replace his frightened hours with splashing in the water and floating on his back.

Granny Crackers says it's not right to live scared, but she's careful not to push, knowing that Phoenix's fear is justified and his precautions may save his life. It shouldn't be so dangerous to raise a brown boy to become a strong black man and keep him safe. Although it's Phoenix's story and not mine, racial discrimination causes this white girl to feel helpless.

It doesn't help that the officer who shot Phoenix kept his job. The internal investigation ruled the shooting justifiable considering the extenuating circumstances. The police in our area are anxious. The streets of Paris Village are paved with turmoil. The fires increased everyone's anxiety. The investigators rationalized that it was reasonable to consider Phoenix, an unarmed thirteen-year-old, a threat. He was snooping around a vacant property. He didn't respond to verbal commands. His hands were stuck in his jacket and his voice was gone, which made him suspicious. Truth is, shooting Phoenix was warranted simply because he's a brown male. If I'd walked out of the house before Phoenix, had been the one to surprise the cops, that weapon wouldn't have been fired. That's what I live knowing.

People are still pissed, but time has passed, and Phoenix is recovering. He is fortunate to be alive. Other injustices all over the world have taken the spotlight. Phoenix is a just a pebble in a steady stream of racism.

The swimming pool is Phoenix's happy place. The small bullet-hole scar in the center of his chest fans out in the shape of a butterfly, a permanent symbol, tattooed by fate.

Seeing Phoenix smile again feels as miraculous as seeing him survive a gunshot to the chest. Just as magical is the sound of Mo's laughter. Montana Rose, who has been lost in the dark blue, finally surfaces.

Montana has a girlfriend, Emma. They met on Tinder, a dating app. On it you swipe left to reject and right if you're interested. Tinder is usually used for hookups, a.k.a. sex, but at times two people looking for a meaningful relationship find each other on Tinder.

Emma is blond and pretty, a lipstick lesbian who wears miniskirts and heavy makeup and smells like flowers. Although I'm happy for Mo, I feel pushed aside. Emma comes over nearly every day. The two hang out in our bedroom, kissing and touching each other's boobs. It makes me feel lonely and miss Mateo.

I like Emma. She is sweet and funny, but it's rude for them to take over our bedroom and make me feel like a third wheel. I had said something to Ava, thinking she would understand. "Why does Emma get to hang out in my bedroom with Mo? Granny Crackers never let Mateo in our room."

"It's different."

"Bullshit. They're in there having sex. It's not different. And not fair. And I have no place to go."

"First off," said Ava, "Granny Crackers may not realize what they're doing. People see what they want to see. And second, Emma can't get Mo pregnant, and vice versa. The biggest fear for anyone raising a teenage girl is a pregnancy." She rubbed her baby bump..

"That's sexist," I shouted. "You mean you think it's okay for Montana to make out in our bedroom, because they're gay, so Mo gets to explore sexuality, and I have to hide my kisses?"

"Montana is two years older than you."

"So in two years I can have sex in my bedroom?" I smirked.

"I didn't say that."

"So you admit you're a sexist."

"Savannah." Ava sighed. "Can't you just let Montana have some—"

"Have some what?" I interrupted.

"Joy. Let Mo have some joy."

Ginny, the old waitress, interrupted my thoughts, refilling my water glass and taking away my empty bowl.

"You okay?" she asked.

"Yeah, I'm good." I lied.

The truth was I was sitting alone on a Friday after school

feeling sorry for myself. My cold feet were warming, and a free bowl of jambalaya had filled my stomach, but I still had a hole in my heart and nowhere to go. I knew Phoenix was at the pool with Jason and Montana was in our bedroom having joy with Emma. I texted a love letter to Mateo. I pulled my journal from my backpack and sketched broken hearts and wilted flowers. I then wrote a poem.

A poem written by Savannah Jorja:

DATING GRIEF

I am sitting in a booth
Of red vinyl
Pressed up against my lover,
His arm heavy on my shoulder,
His breath in my ear,
Whispering despair.
Outside the window
A cold wind blows.
Icicles hang from gutters,
Sparkling white crystal turned to mush.
My lover's veins flow with slush.
The virgin snow
Has been trampled,
Mud prints on my heart.
One fork scrapes one plate
On a date
With Grief.
The thief
Who stole my joy.

When I could no longer stand spending time with myself, I

rose and walked home. It's a good thing I left when I did. I was in the house only five minutes when the doorbell rang.

"Savannah dear," the visitor said when I opened the door. The chihuahuas barked obnoxiously from the back of the couch.

"Mrs. Honeywood?"

"Oh, sweetheart, I'm so sorry for the intrusion. I hope I'm not a bother. I just couldn't wait until Monday. I had to tell you tonight and in person."

"You're not a bother."

Granny Crackers took her beer and dogs into the kitchen.

"Please come in." I opened the door wider and welcomed the elegant and stylish woman into our tacky living room. Our house is not dirty, just overwhelmed with redneck treasures. Gypsy Honeywood's big brown eyes scanned the wall of Elvis plates, glanced at the shelves jammed with Precious Moments, and rested on a curio cabinet full of antique dolls, their cracked porcelain faces and beady eyes the stuff of hauntings.

"What's the news?" I asked, turning down the volume on the big screen TV.

"Well," Mrs. Honeywood said, taking a breath, "it's very exciting, Savannah. I submitted your photos to a young artist contest, and sweetie, you won."

"What?" I had no idea that she'd submitted my photos, and I wasn't sure if I should feel happy or angry.

"Yes! You won. Your photos are going to be on display in a downtown art museum, Gallery Four Fifty-one. Oh, Savannah, you should be so proud. It's such an honor. And awesome for your college applications. Out of all the young artists in all the schools, so many applicants, you won! Imagine, a sophomore at Paris High. I love it." Mrs. Honeywood was talking a mile a minute, and I was trying to take it all in. "Your photos will hang on the wall for the entire month of December. There is even a reception night planned. It's a meet-the-artist and wine tasting for adults. Lots of people come. Colleges of art will see your work two years before you even graduate. This is big, Savannah, big!"

I stood speechless and stunned, not knowing what to say. I'd heard throughout life that a person could be saved by one teacher. Was that what I was experiencing?

"Congratulations, Savannah Jo," Granny Crackers said, seizing the room. "I'm so proud of you, Sunshine." She kissed my cheek. "Mo, get out here! Your sister won a contest! Thank you, Mrs. Honeywood." Granny Crackers grabbed hold of Gypsy's hands with trembling fingers. "Thank you, thank you, thank you," my grandmother cried, happy tears gleaming in her eyes.

Chapter Thirty-Nine

Some things just shouldn't go together: shorts with a turtleneck, relish on ice cream, and babies in bars. Poor taste has never stopped Dixie. She and Twyla threw a baby shower for Jason and Kaleem at Bob's Bar. The bar doesn't open until four o'clock on Sundays, so they talked Bob into letting them use the place to throw the party at noon. They decorated the inside of the dark dive in pastels: baby blue, soft pink, and butter yellow. The old wooden tables, scarred with initials, disappeared beneath plastic tablecloths. Balloons clung to a rain-stained ceiling, and paper streamers draped over everything. The pool table was full of gift bags and tissue paper. The bar was lined with sweaty crock pots, bags of chips, and one large white sheet cake with blue piping declaring "It's a Boy." The place was technically closed; however, Dixie sold beer on tap and collected tips. The guests were mostly families who shared the community garden. Although it seemed a tacky party for a refined and sophisticated couple like Jason and Kaleem, they were over the moon, their mood contagious, spreading happiness. Ava, quiet and reserved, got only a mild case, but she was there, totally present.

I thought about the things Ambrose said on Halloween night about Ava's courage, showing up, knowing she'd be judged and how redemption is a sacred act. Ambrose was wrong about one thing. He said Ava couldn't refurbish days like old furniture, but honestly, she can. It doesn't take any effort for an ordinary person to be happy during happy times, but it takes an extraordinary person to stand in front of critics, spin kindness from regret and tears, and turn wasted days into magical moments.

The weekend before the party, Ava scrounged around the house looking for the perfect gifts. Granny Crackers, the hoarder, has an abundance of baby stuff. She finds things on Craigslist and free stuff on websites and on the curb. She makes a good profit off nursery items. Besides The Barrel, there's a stockpile of items in the shed and basement.

"Help me, Savannah," my mother said, noticing my sad mood and loneliness. Mo was off sucking face with Emma, and Phoenix was at the pool.

Ava and I rummaged through headboards and bed frames until Ava spotted the perfect Jenny Lind crib, its spindle posts leaning up against the basement wall.

"Bingo!" she shouted. Basement treasures are the bomb. We climbed around stacks of boxes, moved obstacles, unearthed the railings, counted bolts and screws, and laid out the disassembled crib like archaeologists digging up dinosaur bones.

"And it's all here." she said.

Carrying it upstairs piece by piece was another set of challenges. Our basement is a labyrinth, a maze created from crates of stuff and bins of nonsense. I opened the flap of a heavy box as I pushed it out of my way.

"Damn! She must've knocked off a hair salon in the eighties," Ava said, staring down at the case of Aqua Net. Two more cases nestled beside it.

"Hairspray?"

"Boxes probably fell off a forklift just as Rosie was walking by. Don't underestimate your Granny Crackers, Savannah Jo. She'll sell all them cans to someone. The woman is a damn redneck entrepreneur."

I helped my mother put the crib together in The Barrel. We wore layers of clothing and were warmed by a space heater. Frosty breaths escaped our muted lips while we constructed the bed in silence. It wasn't hard to do, and I didn't need a lot of direction. I just followed Ava's lead, helped support the rails, and handed her the things she pointed to. Once assembled, the aged crib looked timeless. Its twisted cherrywood spindles appeared handcrafted and made me feel nostalgic. I liked the dark wood and vintage style. Ava wanted color.

We painted the baby bed the color of lemon zest, bright and cheerful. With me on one side of the crib, Ava on the other, we coated the wooden bars in optimism. Ava quietly hummed a compilation of cradle songs as she worked, one tune moving into the next: "Brahms's Lullaby"; "Twinkle, Twinkle, Little Star"; "Hush Little Baby"; "Rock-a-Bye Baby."

I'm worried about my mom. I think this adoption is harder on her than we know, and I wonder if she'll slip right back into drugs after giving her baby away.

After Granny Crackers saw the happy-looking bed, she ran out and bought a new crib mattress and tangerine sheets.

The next day Ava and I prowled through harvested dressers until we found the perfect chest of drawers. We trash pick dressers all the time. One whole wall of The Barrel is lined with bureaus. Seems like we're constantly hauling one from the side of the road. They come in handy. We store stuff in them until it sells.

Ava removed the drawers and began painting the chest to match the crib. I helped. Instead of humming lullabies, we listened to Ava's playlist, the deep, jazzy soulful voice of Amy Winehouse: "They tried to make me go to rehab, but I said, 'No, no, no.'" Ava sang and danced, splashing paint the color of sunshine inside the frozen garage. I was cold and tired, exhausted by the prior day's work. The bright yellow must give my pregnant mom some of her energy, because she worked like a fat, happy bumblebee flitting around in a snowstorm. Ava defies all logic. I'm just glad she flipped her melancholy mood to joyful acceptance.

When it came time to paint the drawers, she taught me how to blend colors.

"Just a little white," she said as I added linen to zest and created daffodil. Ava painted the bottom drawer. "Okay, Savannah, add a bit more." She'd paint a drawer, and then I'd swirl in more white, lightening the hue, so that the drawers varied in shade from bright to light. The next drawer was the tint of a baby chick, and the third drawer the same flavor as a pineapple core. The top drawer was the color of straw. By the time the paint had dried, Ava decided we should fill the drawers.

Granny Crackers loves baby clothes, her best-sellers. Folks sell off their stuff all the time, trying to get rid of things they no longer need. Granny Crackers pays better than consignment shops or The Kidney Foundation. She'll buy a bag of used baby clothes for five dollars and then sell each piece separately.

Ava and I picked through the stacks of clean, folded, color-coordinated infant wear in The Barrel and found some great stuff. We searched through trash bags and bins of unsorted clothing. We set aside the nicest onesies and sleepers. We made a pile of receiving blankets, and Ava found a little yellow bunting.

"Let's throw them in the washer."

"We're not allowed to use the washing machine," I told Ava.

"Don't be silly. Of course we can." Ava gathered half the pile and left the rest for me. I followed her with apprehension, my arms full. I wasn't being silly. Granny Crackers had specifically forbid Mo, Phoenix, and me from doing laundry, accusing us of overloading the washer.

"You kids are going to break my machine, stuffing two loads in it. I'll wash and dry clothes from now on."

We didn't defend ourselves, because we had one less chore. Granny Crackers is big on assigned chores. A free gas-station calendar swings from a nail on the kitchen wall and lets Mo, Phoenix, and I know who is assigned to wash dishes, clean the bathroom, dust, and vacuum. Granny Crackers is in charge of laundry duty. She collects our baskets of dirty things and hands them back to us cleaned. We fold our clothes and put them away.

Beside the washer sat several trash bags that were tied shut. They looked light, as if they were full of air, or baby socks and bibs.

"I wonder what's in here." Ava untied one of them. The entire bag was full of dryer lint.

"That's weird," I said, looking at the other bags piled under the stairs. "She's collecting dryer lint?"

"Holy shit!" gasped Ava. "She did it with dryer lint and Aqua Net."

"Did what?"

"Nothing." Ava was visibly jolted. I watched my mother struggle, a shaky mess, trying to quickly tie the bag shut, her mood suddenly nervous. Her forehead broke into sweat, and her hands trembled.

The realization hit me in the face like a wave. "She did it, didn't she? Set the houses on fire?"

We locked eyes, a shocked stare, two cartoon characters, our heartbeats thumping from our chest.

"Oh, my god. She's insane, isn't she? I mean really, really crazy." Ava stood speechless.

My mind turned, slowly at first, and then picked up momentum like a washing machine stuck on spin cycle. "She started the fires, first the drug house." I stared at my mother and breathed a deep breath. "She got rid of that problem, and then started on the others." She had burned down possessed houses as if she intended exorcisms: the rape house, the rats. My mind ran through a maze of destruction, desperately trying to find a way out. "Oh my god . . . the houses . . . kittens. Save the kittens . . . Phoenix . . . Phoenix shot." I panted words like clues, a complex riddle that led from my mother's overdose to dryer lint and then to a chest wound.

"Shh, shh, shh." Ava pressed two fingers to my lips. "Savannah, you've got to calm down. Pull yourself together."

I was connecting dots and drawing lines of madness, following a trail of breadcrumbs straight to hell. "It's her fault," I cried, feeling broken. "No, no, no, it's your fault!" I shifted blame, pointing my finger. "You caused this. She went crazy trying to save your life."

"She's not crazy, Savannah."

"Yes she is."

"No, baby, you don't have to be crazy to do crazy things," she said, straightening herself up. "Besides, you don't even know if she did it. I don't either. We're guilty of jumping to conclusions." Ava was backpedaling, working hard at erasing speculations. "We're worse than rogue cops, ready to prosecute our own grandmother based on circumstantial evidence. You can't possibly believe an eighty-year-old woman is guilty of arson because she has cases of hairspray and bags of dryer lint." Ava grabbed my hands. She smoothed my hair, anything to deescalate my emotions. "You know, if we make assumptions, so will others, so you can't ever speak of this again. You understand, right? You can't even tell Montana."

I nodded.

My mother breathed a sigh of relief. "Focus on this," she said. "The fires have stopped, gentrification has started, and sweetheart . . . I promise, I'm clean. I'm going to have this baby for Jason and

Kaleem, and I'll place him in a house of love and be there for you, Phoenix, and Mo." She held up her hand. "I solemnly swear." My mother leaned in and placed a Judas kiss on my wet cheek.

I knew at that moment that I had learned one of my biggest life lessons, that good people sometimes snap. And a broken person can be fixed.

Jason and Kaleem were overjoyed by the happy-colored baby furniture. They sheltered Ava in a tearful group hug, a huddle of hope that lasted a full minute.

Chapter Forty

Once I found out I won the young artist contest, I had to go through my whole portfolio to see what else I was going to exhibit. The task was harder than expected. Mrs. Honeywood helped me. We needed to develop a theme so the art would flow together. My teacher encouraged me to share some poems. She said that my emotional photographs and my written words were meant to hang side by side.

"Savannah, your photographs are poetry. And your poems are touching visuals. The two media make you a unique artist." Mrs. Honeywood refers to me as a photo-poet.

"A photo-poet is very rare," she said.

Gallery Four Fifty-one asked me to write a bio, a short description of my work and myself to be used for promotion.

"I don't know what to write," I complained. "They're just edited cell-phone photos and thoughts on paper."

"Don't worry about the bio," Mrs. Honeywood said. "I want to write it."

"That works for me." It was a relief to have something scraped off my plate.

The Meet the Artist & Wine Tasting Event had me living like a neurotic. A big round glow of anticipation hung over my head for weeks and followed me around like the moon. I felt anxious and worried. The two emotions washed over me like a tide, pulling in and out, scraping my heart in the sand. My private diary would be hanging on a gallery wall for everybody to see, my soul exposed for critics. I felt naked.

I was nervous wondering what my tribe of family and friends would think of my art. Many of my pics are images of my hood, scenes of urban strife, Paris Village captured through an unflinching lens. I can't help myself. I like to take photographs of the stuff that touches me, good and bad, the things I find beautiful and sad, that make me smile and hurt. I photograph dark moments streaming with light in my search for God. I hope that my pictures of humanity are raw and soulful portraits that move people in the same way people move me.

On the eve of the exhibition, Granny Crackers took me shopping. We bought a maxi dress the color of rich honey. The next day I took ten dollars of babysitting money and my bag of shell-colored beads and walked to Shania's house.

"Will you braid my hair?" I asked, holding out the bill. From a kitchen chair I watched MTV's *Sixteen and Pregnant* while she twisted my hair into a style that made me a goddess. I spent the rest of the day viewing makeup tutorials on YouTube. I kicked Mo and Emma out of our room so I could get ready in private. When I emerged an hour later, dressed and glittered, they sucked air.

Mo jumped up and spun me around. "Girrl, you look like a golden queen."

"I know." I beamed. It was the first time in forever that I'd felt pretty.

"Wassup, Mrs. Bad and Boujee?" Phoenix said.

I stuck my bottom in the air, did a Beyoncé twerk, and everybody roared.

While we were cutting up in the kitchen, a knock on the front door echoed through the house. It was Ambrose, who was driving

Granny Crackers and me. I had to be there early. Mo would trail behind and bring Phoenix, Emma, and Ava.

"You a G," said Phoenix, as Ambrose swaggered into the kitchen wearing a three-piece plum-colored suit and wingtip shoes. Giving us a wink, he tipped his felt hat and did a little shuffle.

"Oh, my gosh! You look so good!"

I giggled.

"How about me?" Granny Crackers said.

We turned toward her.

"Oh, Rooosie." Ambrose produced a baritone growl, a smooth, deep Barry White imitation.

Granny Crackers blushed. Mo and I cocked our heads at each other, remembering how Ava said Granny Crackers and Ambrose "did it." It's weird to know your great grandmother has a booty call and awkward to see that she still enjoys it.

She had unbraided and brushed out her pigtails. It hung down her back in silver waves. Her bib overalls had been replaced with a classic black pantsuit, and instead of moccasins she had real shoes on her feet, shiny red flats. I could hardly believe the transformation before me in both of them, and all for my own art show. I loved that the occasion called for swagger. I was excited to see everybody was putting on the Ritz.

Gallery Four Fifty-one is a thirteen-room red-brick house in the historic part of downtown. The museum is eclectic and unique, luring art lovers from all over. Each of its large rooms is themed: contemporary, pop, abstract, avant-garde. Behind the house is a sculpture garden. If you can't make it to Gallery Four Fifty-one, you can take a 3D virtual tour and buy art online. The gallery prides itself on hosting weekly events, showcasing both local and famous artists. The reality that my photographs and poems hang on its highbrow walls makes me pinch myself.

Mrs. Honeywood rushed to me as soon as we walked in the door. She was as excited as me, maybe more. "Savannah, your exhibit is stunning."

"Really?"

"Absolutely!"

The front room is by far the largest space in the gallery. There it hung, my work, right on stark white walls. High-top tables were scattered throughout the open space. Caterers dressed in black held silver trays of finger sandwiches, cheese cubes, and chocolate-covered strawberries. An elegant bar stood in the corner. On an ornate credenza by the front door was a stack of programs that introduced the young artist contest and featured me. I read the words that Mrs. Honeywood wrote.

Savannah Jorja Dale's poems and photographs acknowledge the world is not a perfect place, but it is beautiful. This young artist accepts that everyday moments are full of experiences both lovely and sad. In her compilation of light, language, sound, and space, life is seen as a series of adventures, good and bad. She writes poetry of perceptions and deep thoughts that are wise beyond her years, penned with the innocence and wonder of a child.

Miss Dale uses the presence of light and juxtapositions to break and mend the heart of her audience simultaneously. Her images of sunlight flooding a hospital room or a burning house against a copper sky with rising sun are equally fragile and fierce. This composition awakens compassion and stirs emotions.

The artist documented her world with a Samsung Galaxy S using the basic editing tools for contrast, saturation, and temperature and the Vignette app to apply filters. Savannah Jorja Dale is a sophomore at Paris High.

I was overcome by her praise. Life felt surreal. On the other side of the program was a self-portrait and a poem. In the summer, I had set my camera on a timer and taken my picture in

Ambrose's garden. I had edited the photo, added a vibrant filter, and bathed myself in light.

A poem written by Savannah Jorja:

SUNFLOWER

When I was young
I was a sunflower.
I held the taste of honey on my lips.
I cried dew drops.
I smelled of nothing.
I fell in love with light.

When I was young
I kept my face pointed toward the sky.
I could hear the twinkling chatter of stars.
I knew the secrets of the moon.
I was best friends with the sun
And bumblebees
When I was young.

Wearing a golden dress and in the spotlight, I drifted about in a dreamlike state. My photographs and poems were fastened to the affluent walls of an upscale gallery. The day before, my search for God had been private and sacred. Now it was being critiqued and celebrated. I felt a bit queasy. It was more than butterflies. My emotions were fizzy, like bubbles in sparkling wine. I watched the door, waiting for my siblings to enter.

Slowly the gallery filled. Handsome people in tailored clothes walked around with glasses half full of fermented fruit the color of smashed grapes. Many stopped to talk to me. Some I knew, most I didn't.

I heard Dixie's bright laughter before I saw her. She sparkled in rhinestone studs on crushed velvet. Twyla meandered through the gallery in a crimson coat tightly clutching her cabernet, her face flushed with warmth. At one point she blew me a kiss.

Artsy-fartsy people walked about, crowding the space. Everybody seemed moved by my work. In between casual conversations and sips of wine they stared, silent and intent, at my photographs. Their soft sighs of wonder and applause fluttered around the room. Like flower-fed hummingbirds, they flittered in front of my poems and sipped of their essence.

I stood planted in one spot. My bohemian beads flipped from side to side as I scanned the gallery. I ran my hands over the yellow silk encasing the real me. Mo was right. I was a golden princess, and I had made it to the ball. My emotions coupled up and spun around me, dancing the tango. I felt happy and pretty, sensitive and tender, good and vulnerable, as if I were sunbathing topless. I was melting in a comforting glow.

My family arrived without me even noticing. They were eating, drinking, and mingling. I found Phoenix first, devouring a pillar of cucumber sandwiches stacked on a small plate. Beside him stood Mo and Emma dressed in color-coordinated outfits of pale pink and fuchsia, drinking ginger ale from champagne flutes. My siblings were having fun.

I spotted Jason and Kaleem in comfortable conversation with Mrs. Honeywood and the curator. At the bar stood Granny Crackers, Ambrose, and Dixie, and across the room, twelve feet and yet a million miles away, was my mother.

Ava was camouflaged by her surroundings. The artist became the observer. No one was more engrossed in my images than she was. She swam in my poems and occupied each photograph as if she'd been pulled into a diorama, walked the pavement, and sat on the furniture. Truth be told, Ava is ten times more talented than I am.

I approached cautiously, only because she appeared to be immersed in prayer. When I placed my hand on her shoulder she looked at me, her green eyes pooled with tears afraid to fall. I know the feeling, concerned that once you start, you won't be able to stop.

"They're so beautiful," she said.

"Really?"

"Oh, Savannah Jorja, my sweet peach, really, I have never seen anything lovelier. Baby, you've captured miracles, sightings of God, like Bigfoot." Finally someone saw the full picture.

"Thank you," I said.

She leaned in, grabbed my beaded head in her hands, and softly kissed my forehead. Standing face to face, she pressed her full lips to my skin. Our magical moment burst, though, and splashed around our feet. Startled, I jerked. She stared down at her wet dress.

She gasped. "Oh, my god."

We stood stunned.

Granny Crackers looked our way, examined the scene. "Leave it to Ava to spill her drink in an art gallery."

"Rosie, I think her water broke," Dixie corrected

"Ahh shit!" muttered Granny Crackers.

Jason and Kaleem rushed to Ava's side. Mrs. Honeywood and the curator left in search of towels and a mop.

"I'll bring the car around," Jason said. He rushed out of the warm gallery and into the wintery wind, leaving his coat behind. Kaleem helped Ava bundle up.

"I'm sorry, Savannah," Ava said on her way out the door.

Granny Crackers and Ambrose followed behind. Mo and Phoenix left to take Emma home. I stayed at the Meet the Artist event until it was over, smiling and shaking hands. Dixie and Twyla were happy to wait with me. They ate canapés and sipped wine, but for me the spell was broken. All I could think about was my mother and a helpless baby boy ready to enter this cruel world, perhaps sickly, his life already greatly affected by the choices of others.

"What a magical night," Mrs. Honeywood said as she laid her hand upon my shoulder. "Your own art exhibit and a new sibling." Her words felt like a splash of ice water on my warm face.

"Oh, no," I responded. "The baby isn't ours to keep."

"Oh?" A feeling of awkwardness fell between us like a stage curtain. The light in her smile dimmed into a look of unease.

"My mom is a surrogate for Jason and Kaleem," I explained. It was improv, or just a little white lie, one I stole from Ava, because the truth was too painful to admit.

"Oh, my, how wonderful." Mrs. Honeywood beamed.

"Yeah, it's great," I said, acting happy.

"Tell Rosie to give me a call," Dixie said when Twyla pulled up in front of the hospital.

"I will." I got out of the car.

"Your show was wonderful," Twyla sang. "You're so talented."

"Thank you." I stepped in heels on freshly fallen snow, hoping not to fall. I pushed through a revolving door into a vast lobby and wandered down corridor after corridor until I found a sign that said Labor and Delivery. When the elevator opened, Granny Crackers and Ambrose stepped out.

"Did she have the baby?"

"Nah, we're gonna go find some decent coffee. Montana and Phoenix are on the fourth floor."

"Okay," I said, pushing the button. I felt like an audience member late to a show, relieved I hadn't missed anything. I joined my siblings. We amused ourselves and rushed time by watching TikTok videos. Jason and Kaleem were at Ava's side. They were two comforting coaches to push her along, and the baby had two anxious daddies ready to welcome him. Sometimes your world blows up, and instead of falling apart, pieces come down and rearrange themselves, settling into a new place.

Her fourth child arrived quickly, no meds or epidural needed. She endured natural childbirth, bravely pushed through the pain, exposed her raw soul, tore off a piece of bloody heart, ripped goodness in two, and selflessly handed it over to the gentlemen at her side.

After the baby's birth, Jason and Kaleem followed him to the NICU, and we went to see our mother.

Ava is good at hiding her thoughts and faking emotions. We laughed and joked in her room, waiting until the men came back with news.

"I've never seen someone run so fast looking for a mop," Ambrose said of the curator. The high-strung and flamboyant man had slid through the museum holding a wet floor sign.

"Lord, he had wings on his shoes." Granny Crackers chuckled.

Jason and Kaleem stepped into the room.

"How is he?" Ava hastily queried.

"He's going to be fine, Ava. You've done well." Relief quickly flooded my mother's face. She exhaled tension and inhaled ease. "What's his name?" she asked.

The men smiled and in unison sang, "Dallas Amir Rasheed-Fletcher."

"Dallas?" Ava beamed. "I love it."

We followed Jason and Kaleem out the door, abandoning our mother, hoping to see the baby. Having a NICU infant is a different experience from having a healthy baby. We waited one by one to meet our brother. As I stood in line I realized I had left my phone on Ava's bedside table. I flew from the celebratory procession and stopped short before sailing into her room. Granny Crackers sat on the edge of Ava's bed. My mother lay crumpled on her pillow. I hid behind the door and eavesdropped like a sinner, invading privacy and stealing secrets.

"Shh, now, child." Granny Crackers wiped Ava's tears. "You've done a good thing."

"My mother would hate me." Ava sobbed.

"Hush, now. Your mother could never hate you."

"I hate me," Ava confessed.

"Well, I don't. I respect you."

"Respect?" Ava tried to push Granny Crackers off her misused verb.

Granny Crackers stood her ground. "Yes, you did a strong thing. Ignored excruciating pain, your chronic ache of regrets and sorrow. Mourning can cause terrible afflictions. Your addiction to numbing agents made me believe you wanted to join your mother."

"I did."

"Well, then, it must have been hard changing direction. Abandoning your desired destination to death to grow an unexpected life. You were given the precious seed of hope to nurture and grow, and you expected to give it away just as soon as it bloomed. And you did. I can respect that. Dallas belongs to Jason and Kaleem. They'll make good daddies. You have three other kids that need you. I need you."

"You don't need anyone."

"You're wrong, Ava. We all need someone."

The two women hugged, and I walked away without my cell phone.

Dallas is a tiny baby, barely six pounds, and seventeen inches long. Born with NAS, he lived in the NICU for the first week of his life. Neonatal Abstinence Syndrome is treatable and happens to unborn infants exposed to methadone and opioids. Things would have been a lot worse if Ava hadn't followed medicated, assisted treatment. The hospital observed him for respiratory issues and digestive problems. He's a bit of a jittery baby, startled by sound and touch, but life for him will get better.

On the night Dallas was born, Mimi came to me in a dream. I was standing in the snow, a blanket wrapped around my shoulders.

"You look cold, baby," she said, handing me a Golden Delicious, its vibrant color brighter than any apple I'd ever seen. "This will warm you up."

"Where did you get it?"

"For you, Savannah, I scooped it from a sunbeam, molded it in my hands." She placed the toasty ball in my palm.

I stood astonished, snowflakes in my hair, cupping the warm, glowing apple.

"Go on." She laughed "Take a bite."

I sank my teeth into the juiciest piece of fruit I had ever bitten. It was delicious, equally sweet and sour. I was warmed to my toes swallowing the sweet taste of comfort. Nostalgia settled on my taste buds, making me excited. "I've tasted this before, Mimi. I know I have. What is it?"

"Happiness." Mimi giggled. "Child, you're eating happiness."

I took another bite and laughed. Bright yellow juice dripped down my chin like paint.

Epilogue: December 1, 2028

When I received a handmade invitation from Dallas inviting me to his tenth birthday party, I knew I had to go home. Dallas had drawn a cartoon row of superheroes on white paper. A bubble above Black Panther read "Come to my party." The caption above Batman gave the time, and Superman, the place. It was a cute piece of art that had been copied and mailed to a select few. I felt privileged, which was exactly the point. Most ten-year-olds would call or text or have their parents do it. Not Dallas. With two old-fashioned fathers, he's stuck with handmade cards and snail mail. The thought made me smile, longing for home.

I don't mind the travel from Chicago to Ohio. It's only a six-hour drive or a one-hour flight, and I make the journey several times a year. With Mrs. Honeywood's help and encouragement, I got into art school. I received a scholarship to the Art Institute of Chicago and earned my Bachelor's Degree in photojournalism. After college I stayed in the "Windy City." To pay my bills, I work for a small publication, but my real gig is cinematography. Making independent documentary films is my passion, my heart and soul. In my films I aim to uncover emotions, flesh and bones, reveal real moments, and show life in a way it hasn't been shown. With my camera lens I can go as deep into the world as I wish.

I guess I've always been on this path. Since my frantic search for God at fifteen until now, at twenty-five, I've aspired to make images of humanity that shine a light, spark a nerve, speak the truth, and lift us up. Maybe one day one of my movies will be recognized at a film festival and I will make it big. For now I make enough money to pay for a studio apartment I share with Toby, my bulldog, and I can honestly say I'm content. Being content is better than being happy, because it's a steady relationship. Happiness and sadness come and go like a fickle boyfriend.

It's crazy to think that ten years ago I was on a desperate search for happiness. The hunt took me to another state, around the city, and through four years of college. I searched for bliss in textbooks, lectures, and lovers. I tracked joy in experiences, best friends, failed relationships, and lost jobs, only to learn the lesson that Granny Crackers tried to teach me so long ago: "Happiness lives inside of you."

Holding onto the personal invitation, I called Montana, knowing Mo and Sarah would have received the same artwork and we should book our flights together. During my junior year of college, Mo moved to Chicago and joined me. We shared an apartment. I went to school. Mo got a job.

Montana left Ohio a lost soul. In Chicago they found themselves and their soul mate. Mo's wife, Sarah, is a force to be reckoned with. She's strong, smart, and innovative, a woman who has known since childhood that one day she would own her own business. At twenty-one, instead of hanging out in bars and nightclubs, Sarah was socializing at start-up business groups and networking at seminars for developing entrepreneurs. A fearless dreamer, driven and determined, Sarah had the gumption and grit to be a business owner. What she lacked was a vision and a hobby. Without a recreational passion, Sarah didn't know what type of business she wanted to own. Her head was filled with a million ideas: a shirt shop, yogurt stand, cafe/bar, or vegan bakery. Then she met Mo.

Montana brought the skills and life lessons learned in Paris Village to Chicago. An unconventional misfit, Mo was working dead-end jobs at night and hustling during the day. Like a mechanic that buys and sells used cars, Mo trafficked in bicycles. Montana constantly picked up discarded and used bikes, restored them in our little two-bedroom apartment, and then resold them online. Mo's tiny bedroom looked like a garage, and they kept their clothes in baskets and slept on the couch. I tried not to get upset. I began staying with friends, or rather boyfriends, but that's a longer story filled with mistakes and heartbreak. One day Mo sold a bike to Sarah, and I decided to stop looking for love in men and start loving myself. In that instant all three of our lives changed.

Currently I am comfortably single and Montana and Sarah are happily married. Together they own a bicycle shop. "Let's Cruise" builds, sells, and repairs custom-made bikes. Sarah and Montana appear to be custom made for each other. They're a yin and yang couple, complex and opposite forces, trading off roles like sides of the bed. When one is bright, the other is dark. When one is soft, the other is hard. You never know who will be the positive and who will be negative or who will be masculine and who will be feminine. What you do understand is that their relationship is a balance and that their interconnection is deep.

Montana and Sarah were married on the beach. For their honeymoon they biked across France, staying in hostel after hostel. Now they organize biking adventures and map out long rides, fifty to a hundred miles a day, for a growing group of biking enthusiasts. In the four years that Sarah and Mo have been together, they have pedaled through seven of our fifty states, parts of Canada, and pieces of Europe, with a bucket list to bike in all fifty states and see as much of the world as they possibly can.

"Wow, ten years old," Montana said, answering the phone. "Sarah is already online looking for cheap flights."

"I was counting on it." I laughed.

"It will be good to see everyone."

"Yeah, I'm totally in need of a family reunion." Thinking of Dallas made me happy. It seems like only yesterday that he was a sweet jittery baby with sensory overload. Now he's a handsome, healthy, silly fourth grader, a caramel-colored child with tight curls and black eyes who plays baseball and likes art.

Jason and Kaleem no longer live in Paris Village. They bought a four-bedroom house with a two-car garage in a neighborhood with high property taxes and good schools. The two refined and cultured gentlemen have morphed into a pair of helicopter parents with an itinerary of activities filling their calendar and juice boxes filling their fridge. Dallas is spoiled, but not rotten. He's sweet to his little sister, Delilah, and idolizes his big brother Phoenix. Jason and Kaleem adopted Delilah at birth from the biological mother who was a victim—sad, sixteen, and pregnant by her stepfather. Delilah is five years old, a redheaded spitfire. She's precocious, charming, and a bit of a wild child.

I like to think I had some influence on Phoenix and that after I left for college, he realized he could be successful too. Phoenix received a swimming scholarship to The Ohio State University. He graduated last spring with a Bachelor's Degree in athletic training. His career path was inspired by his two faithful mentors. Phoenix is a healthcare provider for student athletes.

Jason and Kaleem huddled over Phoenix like godparents. They guided him through PTSD, bouts of depression, and anxiety. Jason and Kaleem steered Phoenix away from the dark, out of anger, and into the light. Because of their direction, he arrived in a good place. Phoenix and I talk several times a week. We are tighter than most brothers and sisters. Where Mo and I are close in proximity, Phoenix and I are close at heart. Our bond is special, our relationship sutured together by a speeding bullet and a shared heartbeat. His blood on my hands proved more relevant than having the same mother's blood flow through our veins.

Phoenix and a couple of friends live in one of Granny Crackers's rental properties. She gives them a break on rent, but free rides are not her style. At ninety years old, Granny Crackers is still a hard-ass. She walks slowly, but her mind is sharp. She's kept her faculties, sense of humor, lioness spirit, and independence. Too bad Rosie's best friends weren't blessed with her longevity.

In 2020 a pandemic blazed across the face of the earth. A coronavirus waged war on humanity. Fear of catching the virus caused people to hide in their homes. Businesses shut down—stores, restaurants, shops, and schools. The economy plummeted, hospitals overflowed, the morgues were backed up, and the world lost many lives. Dixie was one of them. She died on June 20, 2020. Her Pall Mall cigarettes didn't get her, but COVID-19 did. Sadly, due to the plague, we couldn't even have a proper funeral. Instead Twyla organized what she called a "zoom no-gloom service," and we shared our stories with each other online. Quarantined in our own personal spaces, dissimilar living rooms in different homes, we sat in front of our computers, a Pabst Blue Ribbon in everyone's hand, sharing Dixie tales, hysterical anecdotes of a widely crazy and amazingly fun woman. I laughed more that afternoon than I laughed all of 2020. There will never be another person like Dixie Dawn, making my world forever a bit sadder, but blessed to have known her at all.

Just days after Dixie's zoom no-gloom service, her kids, one by one, invaded her house and possessions like masked bandits, pushing Twyla aside. Each one of them disregarded the fact that Twyla had been her grandmother's companion for the previous three years. I felt sorry for Twyla at the time. Death makes people greedy, and she was too sad to fight over keepsakes. But karma can be a good and virtuous friend. Several years ago, Twyla met and married an old millionaire who swept her away to his mansion in Miami.

The same year Dixie died, a black man named George Floyd was cruelly murdered by a white cop during an arrest. Housebound citizens watched the brutal and heart-wrenching footage and took to the streets. Every city throughout the nation was filled with protesters demanding police reform.

The constant media coverage dredged up my family's memories of Phoenix being shot. Dreadful images flooded our minds and pulled us under water. We were drowning in fear and hostility. Ambrose was Granny Crackers's lifeboat, sailing her through Dixie's death. As quarantine buddies stranded on an island, they kept each other afloat through the storms of a pandemic, a tidal wave of racial unrest, and economic collapse. Three years later, on a cold November day in 2023, Ambrose died, and Granny Crackers dove headfirst back into the lake of grief. She wasn't the only one swimming in heartache. I too was treading in a river of sorrow.

For me, mourning Ambrose was like losing a grandfather, favorite teacher, minister, counselor, and faithful friend all at the same time. For Granny Crackers it was more than that. Ambrose's death coincided with my "looking for love in all the wrong places" phase. I took my broken heart out on dates. Granny Crackers shut herself in. As I drifted in and out of sheets with lovers, she was sinking in blankets of sadness. If it hadn't been for Ava, loneliness would have joined Granny Crackers to Ambrose and Dixie.

The only bad thing about living a long life is all the people you lose along that journey. Yes, Granny Crackers has lived a long and adventurous life. Some would call her lucky. But she's also had to bury a daughter, siblings, husbands, lovers, and friends. I imagine a soul could get worn out from so many goodbyes. Ava saved Granny Crackers. I saved myself.

With gentrification in full swing, Paris Village was changing. Where once it was just a squatters' neighborhood with dilapidated houses and high crime, it is now an art district with brightly colored murals painted on the bricks of trendy shops, galleries, cafes, restaurants, and night clubs. After Ambrose's death, Ava persuaded Granny Crackers to rent a business space. The Barrel moved from Granny Crackers's garage to the corner of Main Street and Bardot Avenue. It's a charming and eclectic storefront guarded by its three resident cats, Clover, Wildflower, and Buckwheat. Their mother, Tupelo lives with Granny Crackers.

The Barrel sells a mix of antiques, painted furniture, art, vintage treasures, and home decor. The garage now serves as a workshop where Ava restores antiques and turns unwanted junk into treasures. At ninety years old, Granny Crackers works every day, or rather hangs out in an antique shop haggling prices and shooting the shit. Ava runs the place. Ava works ten-hour days and keeps The Barrel open seven days a week. When she's not in the shop, she's crafting, creating, refurbishing, and finding merchandise to sell. Ava stays busy. She either loves what she's doing or doesn't trust herself enough for free time. As far as a social life goes, there's Jerry, a fifty-year-old antique dealer and new-age hippie who is completely infatuated with my mother. Ava likes Jerry too, but she keeps him at arm's length. Just like Mimi and Granny Crackers, Ava is fiercely independent. I come from generations of women who like their space. I have found I am one of them. Every once in a while Jerry is able to persuade Ava to go with him to yoga or The Spiritual Temple or on a nature hike or spend the night in his bed, but not on Sundays. On Sundays, The Barrel closes early and Ava has dinner with Dallas, Delilah, Jason, and Kaleem.

Just like Paris Village, Ava has been remade. Eleven years ago my mother resembled a vacant house, a haunted structure with broken windows and messy rooms. Now she's a daffodil-colored cottage with happy window-box eyes. Her beady opioid pupils are now bright, beautiful poppies. Her new teeth give her a perfect, white picket-fence smile. At forty-five she's living her best life. Her art and creative flare are finally being recognized. She even has a following, women who love her whimsical style and buy her old refurbished furniture and art pieces to put in their new houses. Mimi would be proud.

Time takes you on a peculiar journey, twisting and turning you around a million minutes and seasons, weaving your yesterdays and tomorrows into a tapestry of days, and every single second is part of an eternity. Ten years back is a long time ago, and it's just yesterday. I remember being fifteen, trying to crush sadness in a tent with Mateo. Sweet honeyed memories of that golden canopy will live with me forever. I once read in an old book "You'd have to ask birds and children what strawberries and cherries really taste like." I believe the same is true for teenagers and kisses. Perhaps, because children are sensitive souls, unarmed and vulnerable, easily tenderized by pounding days, they feel everything more deeply.

At fifteen I challenged my tears and fears and fought sensitivity like a boxer. After Mimi died I tried to build resilience as if it were a muscle. I became obsessed with pain and suffering, which led me on a mad and desperate search for God. I found him in a million glimpses of light, streaming through darkness.

Maybe I wasn't just a sad and masochistic teen putting myself through tolerance tests and it's good I skipped hand in hand with discomfort. Distress and I were BFFs. Walking barefoot on jagged rocks didn't toughen my skin. I still feel everything. The only difference it made is in knowing that I can survive sorrows and heartache.

Ten years ago my pain was visible, and not just mine but, Mo's, Phoenix's, and Ava's . What my young eyes didn't see, but is obvious now, is the hurt that Granny Crackers must have felt. At seventy-nine she buried her daughter, waved goodbye to her son who took to the road, and began raising great-grandchildren for a granddaughter who was strung out on drugs.

Back when I was trying to calculate how much pain one person can endure, Granny Crackers met her sum. I'm certain that for a millisecond of time my grandmother went crazy, and houses were set ablaze. A few years after the fires stopped, I came across a handwritten list in a roll-top desk. On the folded sheet of yellow paper were numbered streets and addresses. Numbers one through four were crossed out. Curiosity and a gut feeling led me on a walk to new homes that had replaced burned ones. After Phoenix was shot, the arson stopped, saving a dozen or so houses written on a legal pad. Phoenix's injury, gentrification, and a sober Ava was enough water to extinguish Granny Crackers's fury. Her feelings of guilt are deeply hidden within the smoke and mirrors. Granny Crackers's temporary madness is a secret that Ava and I share.

We all have an ember of madness that lives inside us. Given sufficient oxygen, it becomes a torch. Carrying a torch is dangerous, but it can save you in your darkest hour. My life has taught me that people break, become unhinged, fall completely apart, and then recover. After all, without mud, there would be no lotus flower.

Losing Mimi was like being submerged in murky river water. I thought I'd never stop grieving, and honestly, I haven't, but laughing gets easier. They say time heals all wounds. What they really mean is that it leaves a scar. Mimi is always with me, and she lives in the deepest crack of my broken heart. Everybody with any age carries around a battered heart. We have all felt our share of pain. I used to think it was just the poor unfortunate souls of my neighborhood who dealt with the ache of loss, but I've learned pain doesn't discriminate. It inflicts everybody. I imagine hearts look like broken vases glued back together. I guess the longer you live, the more people you lose, the more hits the heart takes, like worn-out knees or a bad shoulder.

Older people replace hips all the time with no problems. Ten years ago I wanted to do the same with my heart—put in a fresh beating ticker, pumping with careless wonder. Now I realize a new heart would mean I would hand over the old, along with all of its patches, bruises, nicks, and stitches, the shrapnel that hit me when Phoenix was shot, the deep wound of losing Mimi, the bruises my mother left. I could never do that. I need the ache of Mimi to keep her close. I hold onto this battered heart like clutching a family Bible, its names, birthdates, and death dates written in permanent ink. Hearts ravaged by sacred moments are seared with beautiful scars. Perhaps that's how it's meant to be, and my life is as divine as anyone's.

CPSIA information can be obtained
at www.ICGtesting.com
Printed in the USA
BVHW040055301022
650515BV00003B/21